The Swamps of Jersey

By

Michael Stephen Daigle

ACKNOWLEDGMENTS

The book is dedicated to my family, Terry, Max and Emily, who finally figured out what I was doing hunched over the computer all that time. And to our old dog Jaxon, who couldn't care less what I was doing as long as he got walked.

My deep gratitude and thanks to Diane Havens and Devorah Fox for their support and encouragement, and for their thoughtful reading and illuminating comments on the manuscript; and to Susan Toth whose carefully copyediting saved me. And thanks to Alice Marks who read the work and took the time to offer a clear perspective.

A special thanks to Virginia Justard, my lifelong friend, in whose home in Andover, Maine Frank Nagler first came to life.

TABLE OF CONTENTS

CHAPTER 1

The ringing phone grabbed Detective Frank Nagler from the fitful sleep he had found crammed into an office chair like a discarded suit jacket. It was three a.m.

The phone rang again, buzzing like a swarm of flies. He rolled dizzily sideways, slammed his feet to the floor and sat in the chair, feeling his back clench. Crap, that hurt. The phone rang again. And again. He rubbed his eyes with the palms of his hands and waited for one more ring, then picked up the receiver. "You're kidding," he replied wearily to the dispatcher's request. "What's next, locusts? Yeah, never mind. Thanks. Just what we need after all this. Be there soon."

He wrapped himself in his long black raincoat that had become his shield against the wet and raging world, and leaned into the outer door as the hurricane winds slapped him awake.

He had not seen the sky for days, felt the heat of the sun, wore dry shoes or walked outside without that raincoat since the storm blew in and sealed the hills above the city with a dense smothering grayness, a swirling menace of thunder clouds and shrieking winds that pounded the city with an apocalyptic rain that sent the Baptist preachers howling to the hills about sin and damnation. It emptied the grocery store shelves of everything but a few cans of cream of mushroom soup, and locked the residents in the top floors of their homes as the river crashed its banks, flooded streets and rearranged the city landscape like a madman with an earth mover.

The placid, blue August sky had been replaced by rain that came and stayed. Rain with menace, rain that pulsed around corners dark with dislodged pieces of the earth as it ripped away every weak thing it could; rain that claimed, rain soulless and dark as evil; that challenged knowledge; rain that took possession.

The ancients knew what to do with rain like this, he thought wickedly, squinting into the horizontal blast of water.

Conjure an honest man with a ship and spin a parable about the wages of sin. Nagler laughed sourly. *And then get out of town.*

Nagler plowed his car through the treacherous bumper-deep water that filled the downtown streets. Random spotlights, swinging

1

loosely from dangling wires on damaged poles or hanging off ripped roof tops banged with the hollow, doomed echo of cathedral bells at the end of times and flashed a shifting and sinister light on flooded parking lots or intersections rippling with dark water. Store after store was dark, some with boards covering glass windows; others had jagged shards of glass that gleamed menacingly in the fractured light, hanging in dented window frames.

****

The storm had knocked out power to the city, and as the streets void of humans filled with the rising river, the mayor declared an emergency. The usual drive from downtown Ironton to the Old Iron Bog took ten minutes, a straight shot up Rockaway Avenue. But at turn after turn, Nagler found new roadblocks, orange-and-white barriers with flashing yellow lights manned by some poor cop in a gleaming, black slicker with orange stripes and water streaming off his wide-brimmed hat, waving a flash light.

Nagler rolled down the car's window and flinched as he caught a face full of rain.

"What's open? Gotta get to the north side. Got an emergency call from dispatch." He blinked to keep the water out of his eyes.

"The only bridge open is Sussex, but Rockaway's flooded, so you'll have to head up Washington to the high school and circle around," the cop yelled back. "Caught some of the radio chatter. What's up?"

"Got it," Nagler yelled back as he rolled up the window and wiped the water off his face, failing to answer the cop's question.

****

Half an hour later Nagler edged his old Ford down Mount Pleasant, squinting through the wet, smeary windshield into the flashing safety lights as he looked for a place to park. He found one that was too narrow but jammed the car in edgewise anyway, braking hard when at the fringe of his headlights he saw a jagged black space where the embankment had washed away.

"Oh, damn." *Great, all I need now is to drive off the road.*

2

He shouldered the car door open and the scene exploded into sound: Yakking radios, a dozen vehicles left running, grinding fire trucks, winches, distant shouting voices. But the sound that mattered most to Nagler was that of his right shoe being sucked into the liquid soil. "Aw, shit. Damn it." *Dress shoes. What was I thinking? This is the fine quality of decisions we make when we don't sleep.*

Ironton was sprawled at the bottom of a narrow bowl-like valley, with streets climbing the hills like fingers hanging on for dear life. For the better part of a week as the last waves of an August tropical storm stalled over the state, the bowl filled and overflowed.

Nagler, like the rest of the police department, had been on extra duty to deal with the storm emergency. The weariness of sleepless nights, more than the dampness, dripped through his skin to his bones and joints and he walked with a heaviness that made him think that if he stopped moving he would end up standing in one place for hours, unable to lift a foot or bend a knee.

He tugged his foot from its watery hole, almost losing his shoe, and winced at the discomfort of wet socks and wet shoes and general unpleasantness of what he was about to examine.

Floods and disaster. And now this. He looked back at his car, the tires inches from the torn edge of the roadway. He pulled his long coat tighter, his dry foot slapping at the wet pavement and his wet foot clumping along like an oversized clown shoe - Slap, clump. Slap, clump. Slap, clump - until he reached the soft opposite path, where both shoes sank in.

The days of rain left city families with waterlogged mattresses floating in their living rooms, powerless refrigerators filled with rotting, soggy food, natural gas bubbling through black water from a broken main and the family photos on the hallway walls bled white, the faces, the scenery, the goofy hats washed away. City officials had debris-filled streets caked with mud and blocks of holy wreckage, rivers where streets used to be, holes where there used to be walls and a city that looked like someone had tossed it in the air and let it fall again in a creative chaos that only disaster brings.

And Detective Frank Nagler had the headless, handless body of a young woman in the Old Iron Bog.

He paused at the edge of the road that led into the bog just as a

3

bank of lights hoisted above a fire truck blasted to life. Before him was a shadowy scene of twisted trees and shrubs, dark paths to nowhere and ghostly forms shifting in and out of the dim lights.

Nagler took a deep breath and plunged in. "Where's the victim?" he asked a crime scene tech, who nodded in a general direction of a small clearing off the single-lane road that was the main entrance into the bog.

"It'd be easier if she had a head, huh, detective?"

Nagler squinted down at the rescue squad kid waiting as a medical technician zipped up a black body bag that contained the torso of a young woman.

"And maybe hands," the kid added brightly. "Man, I don't envy you," he said as he turned to carry the bag toward the ambulance. Nagler just nodded. *Why are you so excited? It's the middle of the night in a raging storm and you're hauling a corpse. And that's good for you? You're lucky I'm exhausted.*

"Open the bag," Nagler grumbled. "Unzip it."

The kid fumbled at the zipper but finally opened the side of the bag halfway. "All the way." And the kid complied.

She was young, Nagler thought, too young to be here. Why did that surprise him? *What were you expecting?* Someone had hacked off her head and hands, just like the kid said. She was thin and looking at her hips, underdeveloped and still growing. Maybe late teens, early twenties. There were no needle tracks he could see. "Thanks," Nagler said, and stepped aside as the kid re-zipped the bag, and the kid and another fire fighter lifted it and walked up the muddy slope in the rain. "Jesus," he said. "Just a kid."

He pulled his collar tighter, shoved his hands into the coat's deep pockets and scanned the old bog, cast gray, dark and suspicious in the heavy rain. Tall reeds and cattails, grabbed by the swirling, growling wind, dipped and rose, twisted and flattened and filled the area with soft missiles as the plants were shredded. The air slammed him like wet fist. *The world's in a rage. And it all landed on your pretty head.* He shrugged. *Wherever it might be.*

****

4

Police Supervisor Chris Foley reached Nagler's side and shoved a cup of coffee into his hand. Nagler nodded, but wondered what Foley was doing there. He let the silent query pass. The man had coffee.

"What do we know?" Nagler asked.

Foley was a straight shooter, a razor cut, white shirt kind of cop. He examined crime scenes as if they were math problems and left no remainders. But he never saw the magic the math produced, Nagler knew, never imaged that in a crime sometimes one and one equaled three. Crimes for Chris Foley were a formula, a step-one, step-two affair. Sometimes the formula worked; sometimes it didn't.

Foley read from his notes, which were wrapped inside a plastic bag. *The man is prepared, I'll give him that.*

"The body was found by a couple of high school kids out here drinking beer and fornicating. They were underage. We will speak with their parents. I mean, in the middle of this storm, they come out here, and? Anyway... About one hundred hours. Let's see. They said they fell asleep, woke up when they heard a vehicle drive in, started throwing on their clothes since they said they assumed it was the authorities... Hum... vehicle stopped in the distance... heard some voices, at least two."

He turned a page. "Door slammed, vehicle drove away." He stopped reading. "The kids said they sat in their vehicle for a while. They figured it was no big deal. Someone dumping trash, happens out here all the time, they said. But they decided they had better leave. They said they saw the body as they drove out, stopped their vehicle, walked around a little bit and then left when they discovered it had no head. The boy said he slipped as he scrambled back to his vehicle and planted his hands in the mud, but in this rain, it's not going to matter."

"Speak to their parents, Chris?" Nagler said. "Jesus, they're just kids out here screwing. This ain't Sunday school." Nagler scanned the damp, muddy scene, and for the first time became aware of the sharp aroma of oily rot that boiled out of the soft, churned up soil and stuck to his clothes like bad dreams. Then he smiled. Not all the dreams were bad. "I suppose you would have turned me in, too."

Foley paused a moment, looked at Nagler, and then again at his notes. "What?"

Nagler turned away so Foley would not see his grin.

5

It's early in the morning. Cut him some slack. Car drove in? In this mess? The road was fairly solid, despite the rain, so maybe it was possible.

"Where'd you park, Chris?" Nagler wondered why he had not been told Foley would be there.

"Off Mount Pleasant to the right. There's a little wide spot, like a turnaround," Foley said. "Why?"

"Just wondering how a car got in here in with all this muck. Maybe four-wheel-drive, a small truck or something with high clearance."

"The kid was driving a big, high-wheeled pick-up with wide off-road tires, probably his dad's," Foley said. "I mean I'm driving my city emergency management SUV. High clearance, all-wheel-drive. Something like that would get in here." Foley laughed. "I wish it was painted a different color. It's bright yellow, for crying out loud."

"A little too conspicuous, Chris?"

Nagler had always known Foley was a good investigator. Started at the local department and worked his way through the ranks and was appointed to a regional task force a couple of years ago. They had worked cases together in the past. But he was as stiff as a two-by-four and as narrow minded as a telescope viewed through the wrong end. Didn't make him a bad guy, just a pain in the ass, especially at three in the morning standing in the rain in a damn swamp.

The coffee landed in Nagler's stomach with a crash and was jamming its way to his brain, pushing back the sleepless, dull ache. Nagler shook his head to force himself to stay awake and felt a surge of alertness as a couple of cylinders began to fire.

Foley gave Nagler the once over. "Little casual this morning, aren't we, detective?"

Was that a joke? I'm wearing pants, right? Never could tell with Foley. Nagler ran a hand through his hair and scratched the stubble on his chin.

"Dressed in the dark, maybe two days ago. Little hard to match my socks and tie when I can't see them. Been out in the streets for the better part of the last week. Besides, I wanted to look my best for you. You have power?"

Foley shrugged. "No. I just have my week's wardrobe set up in the closet... Never mind, Frank."

"Yeah, sure." Nagler pursed his lips and shrugged. Then he asked, "What are you doing here, Chris? Aren't you in charge of the city's emergency response to the storm?"

Foley turned slowly. "Yes, I am, but we haven't had a decapitated body in some time. Thought you might need the help. I am, after all, a police supervisor. I'm headed to the emergency office after I leave here."

Can't be soon enough. Nagler slugged back some coffee rather than say anything. "So where'd they find her?" *Guess I better find out what he knows.*

"Over here."

Foley led Nagler along a narrow sandy road overgrown with small trees, cattails and waist-high grass to reach a clearing. Nagler noticed there was a sustained groove in the road, possibly a sideways tire track and a truck wide path where the grass had been knocked over, possibly by the kid's truck.

Foley stepped carefully around the mud and debris so his tasseled loafers would not get ruined, but caught his jacket sleeve on a small tree branch and spent more than a minute examining the cloth. "Sorry, Frank. I just got it back from the dry cleaners."

Whatever. Nagler pushed through the dripping overgrowth. *Rain, mud, no sleep, no coffee and now Foley. No more slack. That was quick. Jesus.*

This was The Old Iron Bog, an old swamp that for generations going back to the iron mining days three hundred years ago had been a dumping ground for waste rock, slag, bad iron parts, bent rails, then in modern times, trash, cars, and everything society needed to hide.

The roads had been cut by the miners to gain access to the swamp, and improved, if that was the word, by the towns that dumped garbage here for years before it was outlawed.

The place seemed undisturbed by a week's rain, as if the hole at the bottom of the bog was deeper than anyone could guess. Nagler recalled a story about the construction of the interstate highway. Engineers were battering a steel piling into a hole on the edge of the bog when the piling broke through the roof of an old mine shaft and disappeared into the void. The engineers stared at one another, pushed back their yellow hard hats, scratched their heads, consulted their maps, and stared into the hole.

In the heavy rain, with muddy filth coating everything he touched and the dank, smell of pollution and rot thick enough to taste, Nagler decided the old bog had no romance or redeeming quality; it was just a big hole in the ground. *This swamp will swallow us all.*

They were going to build a shopping mall there, Nagler thought. A peeling, battered billboard hung for a year or so along Mount Pleasant. Wonder what happened to it.

Yellow tape marked off several hundred feet of road and swamp. Foley's voice brought Nagler back from the fatigue-driven dreamy state. "The car stopped about here" – Foley walked about ten feet away. "They took the body out of the car, and dropped it. Seems they might have tried to wipe out their footprints because there appeared to be some drag marks in the mud."

"How many people do you guess?"

Foley shrugged. "At least two. The kids said they heard voices, more than one. One thing I don't like?" Foley said with a question in his voice. "They could have pushed her into the water. Why not? Look at this place. There's five feet of thick weeds and brush on either side of the road here. She would have sunk out of sight - the water is absolutely pitch black - maybe got hooked on some roots and never came back up. Even if she did, you'd never see her."

"You're saying they were just sloppy?" Nagler asked. "Or they wanted us to find her?"

Foley just waved his hand in the air as he turned to walk away.

"What about tire tracks?" Nagler asked. "Still looking for good ones. Rain's making it harder," Foley said before walking away.

Then Foley stopped, turned and looked at Nagler with hard eyes and a crystal stare. Nagler wanted to be impressed with the determination, but with water dripping off Foley's hair and down his nose, all Nagler wanted to do was laugh; he stared down at the muddy ground so he wouldn't smile. "What, Chris?" Crap, I'm tired.

"We've been here before, you know, Frank. Charlie Adams."

That name. Nagler placed a hand over his face and wiped away the water while he closed his eyes and felt the darkness return. *That's when you learned to be cold. We're not going there. Not now. Not again.*

"This isn't Charlie Adams, Chris," Nagler said harshly. "He's still in jail and not getting out anytime soon. I was at his last parole hearing about three months ago. It was denied, again. Why did you think of Adams?"

"But he loved dumping bodies here," Foley said.

"He loved dumping bodies all over. That was twenty years ago, Chris. He had no copycats and the killing stopped when we caught him. A lot has changed in this city in that time. Let's not head in that direction unless the evidence leads us that way."

"You're right, Frank."

Charlie Adams, the city's last serial killer. There had been a feel to that case from the beginning and this one with one butchered girl doesn't yet feel like that. "But if we find another body, I'll reconsider."

About a dozen police, rescue and fire vehicles lined Mount Pleasant with one set of wheels in the road and the other in the muddy ditch. Cops in hip waders crashed in and out of the brush and weeds, and a fire boat was being backed into the swamp. They had not yet found any clothes, or her head and hands, and the body had no jewelry. It was just the body. Naked. Butchered. Forgotten. *That's why it's not Charlie Adams.* Nagler slowly felt his way through the slippery paths of the dark bog, heading back to Mount Pleasant. *Adams brought bodies here, sure, but made finding them easy. He liked the fame, the publicity, liked knowing we knew it was him and thinking that he was one step ahead of us. This is not the same. But for the life of me, at three a.m. and on one cup of coffee, I don't know what the hell this is.* "Damn it," Nagler muttered as his foot slipped off the path into a watery hole.

Nagler stopped to regain his balance, lifted his head and gazed over the old bog. The rain had let up, and in the earliest light of dawn, the black canopy began to shift to a lighter gray. Maybe, finally, it would stop raining. The muted rumble of rush hour traffic on the interstate about a half-mile away started to filter into the swamp to fill in what until that moment had been an oddly quiet place. The sounds, even the chatter of the police radios, had been sucked into the deep endlessness of the swamp. The overgrowth absorbed all the noise just like it sucked nourishment from the water. But the roar of daily life on the highway would soon overpower the dense swamp. By mid-morning once the trucks started rolling down from the quarry, ten at once, each carrying forty tons of rock, the water would begin a tremble that would shimmer on the surface until well after dark.

It's a hell of a place to die. He felt his weight slide into his tired legs and he turned around and grabbed a small tree for balance.

Nagler slowly walked the site for a few more minutes, talking off and on to a fire captain, one of the county investigators, or just observing, trying to imprint the scene on his very tired brain.

The sand coated his already soaked shoes and had squeezed inside his socks so it felt he was walking on wet sandpaper; he knew he'd find a ragged blister on his heel.

The rubberneckers lined Mount Pleasant, crawling by in dark vehicles, faces white in the glare of passing headlights, watching the lights flash on the police cars. With the power out, and most streets blocked by fallen trees and floods, there weren't many other routes out of town. A local cop with a flashlight waved them on and they passed, one by one, a solemn parade as they took in what they could see and imagined the rest.

Nagler rubbed his forehead, stopped and looked up and down the street into the confusion of cars and lights. Where the hell did I park? He wondered. He squeezed his eyes shut and let the kaleidoscope of swirls and circles fade to black. Then he turned to face the swamp and remembered he had come in from the left, then walked that way.

Add another thing to the list. He began to mentally schedule who he had to see and how quickly they might have any information: the crime scene techs, the medical examiner, re-interview the kids who called it in. Another session with Foley. It was odd he came to the scene. He was the leader of the city's emergency response office and had a whole city trying to get its head above water. Nagler laughed. *I must be really tired if that line is funny.*

Not like I don't have anything else to do.

For the last three weeks he had been receiving packages with invoices and letters on City of Ironton letterhead. The letters said the material was a link to a big cover-up of theft in city hall. But what he had received so far was so disjointed it was hard to see that. After the first few letters he wondered who was trying to pull a fast one - he asked himself more than once, *who did I piss off* - or use all that paper to make a little, tiny point about government waste. There were two or three media-savvy gadflies who had filed several complaints to state agencies about access to public records and other things, and maybe these records were from one of them. But why send it to him, Nagler had asked himself. The invoices had information that had been blacked out, none of the dates were in any sequence, and even if one or two of the invoices seemed to be leading from one account to another, the last pieces were missing. *God, it's like some stupid Russian novel.* Sometimes he wanted to dump it on someone else, let them wade through the pile of paper, but then he would flip through a couple more pages and think: What if it was real? Nagler had asked the chief about it and was told to just keep collecting the letters, just in case it began to make more sense.

He sighed and turned to walk back to his car; fine mist began to fall again. "Just send the last chapter."

"To what?"

"Shit, did I say that out loud?" Nagler asked.

"Yeah, you did. Said 'just send the last chapter,' out loud. Didn't think anyone was listening, did ya?"

It was Jimmy Dawson. "And now you're gonna have to tell me the rest."

"Don't you ever sleep?" Nagler shook Dawson's hand and actually wondered what had taken him so long to get there.

"I'm Ichabod Crane. I hear the headless horseman is out tonight."

Dawson was a reporter for the local paper. He was cynical, hard-nosed, fairly nasty at times, but always got it right. He knew the rules of the game and Nagler knew he could lay out a story on background and no one would ever know the source.

"Yeah," Nagler said. "Some young woman. Headless, handless. Good chance she was dumped here after being killed elsewhere. A car, no description, was seen in the neighborhood. No clothes, no ID." He shrugged. "Right now, no clue."

Dawson finished writing and waited for more description.

"How do you do that?" Nagler asked.

"What?" Dawson asked.

"Read your hand writing. Especially while taking notes in the dark."

"Write extra big. Trick I learn when I was a movie reviewer."

Nagler and Dawson had been meeting like that for years. There was a respect between them, a knowledge that comes from being in the same places under the same circumstances too many times.

"You have power?" Nagler asked. It was the question of the day.

Dawson laughed. "Been almost living at the office. My road was flooded and half the trees are down. Office complex has a generator. There's a couple of us there."

"Sounds chummy."

"You in later?" Dawson asked.

"After ten."

"I'll call you," Dawson said as he walked away.

Then he stopped.

"Hear from Lauren Fox?"

Are you kidding? Nagler stared at the reporter as he walked away.

"Hey, Dawson. Don't you want an answer?" Dawson stopped walking and half-turned back toward Nagler, spreading his hands and bowing, as if to say, "Well…"

Nagler stared a moment. Too much to say about it. "No," he finally said.

After he watched Dawson walk down Mount Pleasant, Nagler wandered back to his car, stopping every few steps to shake mud off his shoes and to imagine the street several hours earlier without the police vehicles, fire trucks and a slow parade of cars, when an unknown vehicle drove slowly and carefully through the darkness, the driver probably stopping more than once looking for a dumping spot, then moving on until the side road was found. Did someone get out and shine a flashlight down that road into the darkness? Did the driver have companions with whom they discussed their options? How many people were in that car?

He knew this street well as a dark, slightly spooky section of Ironton. Little had been built along the road, mostly because of the bog which spread for acres in each direction. Even if the electric power had been on, there were only a couple street lights and those were hundreds of feet apart. Everything here moved in shadows.

Nagler looked up and down the street again. A gray dawn was rising, and Nagler shut his eyes against the light to hold the image of the blackness and a single vehicle slowly moving through a murky night. With the power on there might have been enough light to make this little side road visible, but in the blackness of a heavily clouded sky, air still damp with mist or slight rain, it seemed a long shot. The kids who reported the body to the police said they had been here dozens of times – man that kid was getting a lot of action – so for them finding the top of that side road in the dark was easy. But a stranger?

That knowledge made the case more local, more personal.

When he got to his car Nagler was surprised to see how close he had come to driving into the gully. "Damn," he said, "That was lucky."

What wasn't lucky was how close his car was to the vehicles on either side. While he was at the crime scene, the compact sedan that had been parked to his left had been replaced by an extended body pick-up with an emergency light rack on its cab, whose owner it seemed took delight in parking as close as he could to Nagler's car. One of us, Nagler thought wickedly as he started his car and slipped the transmission into reverse, ain't going to like this. The car rolled for second or two and he felt the satisfying thump as the bumpers touched. He rolled forward, then back, and again felt the slight collision. Three or four such efforts allowed him to get the front wheels correctly angled and pull the Ford into street while the alarm in the truck sounded, a whoop-whoop echoing off the dark silence of the Old Iron Bog.

The effort to extract his car from the tight space allowed Nagler to avoid the name that was trying to edge its way into his head.

Lauren Fox. Damn you, Dawson.

He turned up the volume on his police radio and let the irritating squawking overwhelm the silence in the car. He slammed the car door as he stopped by his home to get dry socks and shoes.

Not now.

CHAPTER 2

They had seen heavy rain before, they said. The weathermen were always wrong, even with their satellite photos and computer projections. The storms always turned east, bounced off North Carolina and ran toward New England.

Instead this one arrived like a freight train, a wall of water doing a hundred miles an hour; horizontal, slashing rain that crashed through windows, smashed into walls, driving wind and water that wrenched homes from their foundations, tossed cars into trees and yanked down power poles like matchsticks; for good measure, if anyone thought they were safe, the rain forced itself through tiny cracks to pool on the basement floor, to drip under the windows, to violate like a silent thief the very notion of safety.

Rain measured not in inches, but feet; not in days, but years, centuries. A storm measured in thousands of feet per second. Rain that washed away memories and histories, awakened in moistened ground the seeds of despair and bitterness that lay dormant under a veneer of calm.

The roadside ditches filled. The creeks and streams boiled up and overflowed, and in the hills above the city they joined forces and crashed past the rocks, dragging saturated hillsides along for the ride; water filled depressions in the woods and in backyards under the swing sets in the crushing fall toward the river.

The churning brown water, fearsome in its wanton fall, smeared cellar windows and car doors and red flower boxes filled with marigolds as the flood rose and splashed against locked front doors, seeping under the carpet while frantic homeowners ran sump pumps in their basements two at a time.

In the downtown, in the bottom of the bowl, the residents stood on rooftops, huddled in third floor attics as their world was swallowed and the sounds of doom battered the walls around them. They searched the sky for light and their souls for words of comfort and salvation. If the walls gave out, they each wondered whose hand would reach out for theirs.

The river took it all, swelling beyond its banks to slam into homes and bridges and roads, scouring stones and soil from foundations, ripping the mere constructs of society away like so much wishful thinking. It roared with a life of its own, its voice growing deeper as the water gained depth and weight while above, the wind shrieked as it ripped at roofs and porches and tossed away all the insubstantial things in its path. When the water slammed into corners, it formed dark, deep whirlpools that sucked below the surface all that it grabbed, all it had claimed.

The footballs and basketballs came first, bouncing atop the current along with a few aluminum chairs as if a backyard game had been interrupted. A chunk of plastic fence surfed along, curving and dipping as the water rose, the full grape arbor from Mrs. Girardi's garden dipped in and out of view taking with it the Christmas wine she gave as gifts to her family, followed by an acre of Sam Johnson's newspapers that had been blasted out of his shed when the door caved in and the editions of all the days of his life became flotsam; then in its last turn, the flood lifted the Salvatores' wood frame greenhouse from its cinder-block foundation and carried it along, suspended like a parade float until it was thrown into a telephone pole where it splintered and left the plastic sheeting fluttered loudly in the stream.

When the flood finally crashed into the middle school and swirled and pooled into a menacing lagoon at the bottom of Berry Street, the city looked like Venice the day after hell broke loose and someone held a rummage sale.

It left behind silence, an oh-my-God-can-you-believe-it-silence that comes from souls empty of grief and fear. They stared at trees and poles tangled and wrecked, at cars upended, at roofless, windowless homes and asked themselves, where are my neighbors? "Are you okay?" they asked each other, the voices soft and shaky, words in a vacuum; they shook hands, held one another, touched. Retouched.

After the storm cleared Nagler was put in charge of a crew assigned to examine each home and building on several blocks on the east side of Ironton. Everything, including the investigation into the death of the woman in the bog, was put on hold, on an order from the mayor, who said finding possible flood victims, buildings in danger of collapse, broken water mains or sewer lines and natural gas leaks took precedence for at least twenty-four hours. So along with an ambulance squad, two firefighters, a code officer and utility company workers, they knocked on doors, stepped over broken porches and fences, noted where trees had smashed through roofs, counted broken windows and logged the number of dogs running in the streets and hungry cats inside the broken homes. East Ironton was one of those "traditional low-lying flood zones" the newspapers always wrote about, a mile-square of flat streets bounded on the north by steep hills and undercut by a brook whose watershed had been rearranged by two hundred years of construction. The city in recent years had tried to force it into large underground channels, but the brook persisted in finding its own way, and after spring rains was often found flowing through cellars and popping up in backyards in small geysers.

None of that mattered with this storm: the streets had been awash with six feet of water for three days after storm drains backed up and the debris collected in intersections had become dams; small boats were used to evacuate residents.

Nagler stood in the kitchen of a Riley Avenue home and noted the damage. The first floor doors and windows had been smashed open and the living room furniture had been arranged in a manner that would give a Feng shui master a migraine. Kitchen chairs were piled in the corner trapped by an overturned table and the small appliances rested in the sink. The still air stung his nostrils with the deep, moist scent of rot. A wavy brown line on two walls showed the high-water mark. The slight, slow tick-tick-tick of the battery-driven kitchen clock was the only sound as the tail of the red-and-black cat figure marked the passage of the seconds.

Nearly half the homes had been damaged. On the sidewalk Nagler compared lists with Dan Walker, a fire fighter who had canvassed the opposite side of Riley.

"We were here during the height of the storm, Frank," Walker said. "Some of these people wouldn't leave. Especially the older ones, whose families built these houses. It's everything they own. What a damn shame. One old lady slapped me when I tried to lead her out, but I told her if she didn't come now the next time I saw her, she'd be dead."

"What house was that?" Nagler asked.

Walker nodded his head toward an intersection half a block away. "The red one on the corner. It had an old field stone cellar foundation that washed away and the wall on that side of the house opened up, which let in a lot of water. The center stairwell washed out and brought down part of the second floor. If she didn't drown, she would have been crushed."

Nagler shook his hand. "Good work, Dan."

Walker said thanks and turned to examine Berry at the next intersection.

The storm hid all that destruction, Nagler thought. There was so much water in the air it distorted any view of the landscape hidden behind the swirling, gray mass, rotating, stinging, shape-shifting so often it produced vertigo. We knew it was bad; now we know how bad.

Some homes in East Ironton that were not flooded were struck by trees or tree limbs, some by power poles toppled like Lincoln logs, one after the other, broken and strung together by the nest of wires. Roofs, porches, patios, sheds, cars, fences, satellite dishes, propane tanks, all damaged, crushed, tossed; histories and lives rearranged in one crashing, wet instant.

In the darkness of the torrent, Nagler imaged what was happening beyond the scope of his vision, beyond the range of his hearing. In the full warmth of daylight, it was worse that he imagined.

"Hey, Frank, we got a problem." It was Dan Walker running toward him. "It's Sam Rothwell. He's up in the attic of his house pointing a rifle at the guys in the street. He says he'll shoot if they try to enter the house."

Nagler shook his head. "Damn it. That old fart."

Sam Rothwell's house was half a block away and Nagler could see three or four of his crew ducking behind cars in the street. Nagler was surprised the house was still standing. Half the porch posts were torn away and the porch roof was threatening to pull down the front wall. Windows had been blown out and the chimney was missing.

Nagler sighed. He'd been at this house what seemed like a hundred times in his career. If it wasn't Sam Rothwell threatening to shoot up the neighborhood, it had been his father, Max, who had to protect his still where he brewed high-octane grain whiskey. Sam just needed to protect his right to drink.

Nagler scanned the upper floors for a peek at Sam.

"What the hell are you doing, Sam," he yelled. He motioned for the other in the street to move away. "Sam? You up there? How much you been drinking?"

Nagler flinched when the barrel of Rothwell's rifle emerged through the window. "If you shoot at me, Sam, I'm gonna be really pissed," he yelled.

The rifle was withdrawn, and a hand reached through the window and took down a piece of ragged plywood. Then Sam Rothwell's head emerged. "Hi, Frank. How ya been?"

"Been better. You might have noticed a storm rolled through town recently, sort of busted everything up, including your house. You need to let us help you get out before the front of the building falls off."

"Thought something was going on," Rothwell yelled back. "They shut my power off a month ago, so I've been sort of living up here. Had some bread and bologna, but it's gone. Just got half a case of bourbon. The place was rockin', I tell you. Shit was bouncin' off the roof and walls and I heard glass breakin' and then a tree landed on some house out back..."

"Look, Sam. I'm gonna call a ladder truck and we'll get you out of there," Nagler said.

"No you ain't," Rothwell said as he stepped back and jammed his rifle back into the window. "There was already someone here from the government that said they would take my house and throw me out on the street."

Nagler knew that the city had issues with Sam paying his taxes and keeping the property up to standards, especially years ago after they found the still, but as far as he was aware, no one had been out doing formal assessments of damaged property. Hell, it had just stopped raining, so crews were out doing what his was doing, some basic inventory of the damage.

"Sam, when was the last time you had something to eat?" Nagler yelled up.

The rifle in the window wiggled up and down. "Why, you delivering pizza? I'll take pepperoni and sausage."

The ladder truck that had been called to the scene turned the corner at Berry Street and slowly and carefully rolled past the fallen poles and trees. When it was two houses away, Sam Rothwell fired a shot that shattered an attic window across the street.

"Fuck you, Sam," Nagler yelled. "You do that again and I'll shoot you myself. Now empty that rifle and toss it out here."

After a minute or two, the rifle was dropped out of the attic window, followed by a handful of shells. Rothwell tore of the rest of the plywood out of the window and stuck his head out. "I'm sorry, Frank. I've been drinking all week and haven't eaten in two days. I'm fucked," he said and started to crawl through the window.

"Sam, don't!" Nagler yelled. "You can't see it, but half your porch is in your neighbor's yard."

Rothwell jerked back and looked down. "When'd that happen?"

Later, when Rothwell had been removed from the attic, placed in the back of a rescue vehicle and fed coffee and sandwiches, Nagler asked him how he was doing.

"You gonna arrest me for shootin' that house?" Rothwell asked.

Nagler shook his head. "No. Accident."

"What am I gonna do now, Frank?"

"City can put you up in a shelter for a few days. A place to sleep, shower, regular meals." Nagler looked over at Rothwell. "No booze. Where's your sister live?"

Rothwell stared straight ahead. "Morristown. Ain't seen her in a while."

A silence settled in. Rothwell drank his coffee and ate quietly. To Nagler he seemed like a man finally knocked flat on his back. Even when he was wrong Sam Rothwell was a spit-in-your-face defiant son-of-bitch, like his father, like a lot of Ironton's families who knew the good times and the bad, felt the success of the mills and the pain of their closing, but still walked on, cared for their children, schools and churches. Rothwell's lined face held eyes that jittered and withdrew; his hands clutched the coffee cup like it would be his last.

"Can I ask you something, Sam?" Nagler said.

Rothwell shrugged.

"When did that city guy threaten to throw you out of your home?"

Rothwell focused his eyes on the ground. "Day or two after the storm hit, I think. There were people all over the street getting people to leave."

Nagler nodded. A mandatory evacuation for East Ironton had

been ordered. "So maybe this guy was just trying to get you to safety?"

"No," Rothwell said. "It was different. It was a threat. 'We're gonna take your house and sell it to someone else.' The house wasn't damaged and the street wasn't flooded. It was something else. I know I owe taxes, but I've been through that before and I know how that goes, and this wasn't that. This was, 'Leave, we're takin' your house.' I don't how to fight that. Family's been in this town for a couple hundred years. Family names are on the war memorial. Like all the neighbors. Seems wrong someone could steal that out from under us. That's when I got the gun out. Damned if they were gonna steal my house."

"I'll bet," Nagler said. "Your father would have done the same thing."

Rothwell smiled and looked off.

"He took a shot at me, too," Nagler said. "Told him if he ever did that again I'd take an ax to his still."

"No, you didn't."

Nagler smiled. "Something like that. Tell me, you sure that guy was from the city and not just some scam artist?"

"I'm sure," Rothwell said. "Was driving a city car."

CHAPTER 3

The Pakistani girl behind the counter at Dunkin Donuts asked, "Onion bagel?" Nagler smiled wearily and nodded. "And a small regular," he added. His daily routine.

The doughnut shop somehow had power, one of only two downtown businesses to open back up after the storm. "How'd you guys get power?" Nagler asked. The girl just smiled back shyly and shrugged broadly. Then, in a moment of silence, Nagler heard the metallic whine of a generator. *Good for them.*

He took a seat at a window table and listened through the glass as the NJ Transit engine blasted its horn at the Warren Street crossing.

He could picture the three-block line of traffic the street closure usually caused. Hundreds of commuters rushed to find a parking space and walked briskly to the platform with their backpacks, computer cases and umbrellas. Was that the first train since the end of the storm, Nagler wondered. Might be. Service had been stopped while trees were removed from the tracks and power was restored along the line.

Nagler finished his bagel and took his coffee with him as he walked back into the shattered downtown.

That was just wrong, he thought, sadly. The streets were empty, as hollow as a ghost. A few power company crews swung through in the air in buckets attached to small cranes as they reattached wires and transformers; squads of three or four men with buzzing chain saws labored over fallen trees.

The storm scoured the street clean: No fat buses waddled from stop to stop and no commuters dodged the Hispanic day workers on the busy sidewalks. The commuter parking lots were half filled and stores were closed, some with plywood instead of windows. Instead of pigeons cooing and nodding along the roof tops, the upper floors of about half the buildings were missing windows that had been blown out with shingles dangling over the sides of the roofs; Nagler imagined the water damage. Here and there a tree limb was still tangled in power lines that had grabbed it as it toppled or was blown along.

Riverside was where the storm left its true mark. The row of huddled brick factories along the river had been vacant for years. Rotted plywood filled window frames, rusted metal roofs rattled like loose bones as the wind pried open the entries into the buildings, and ripped off the cheap signs that said "FOR SALE OR RENT. 250,000 sf. WILL SUBDIVIDE" and sailed them away to be dropped in the commuter parking lot or in pieces in the river where they acted like dams or stacked against yet another empty building that no one wanted to buy. The river shoved aside the doors, caved in the plywood in the first floor windows, spilled into the buildings and rushed through, smashing whatever was left inside against the chain-link fence that surrounded the property until it collapsed.

The city was settled three hundred years ago along the narrow river that flowed through its long slender valley, its rippling progression only broken where the iron makers forced it through a narrow channel to feed a holding pond that provided power for the mill that had given economic life to the region.

Starting with nails and farm plows, the complex, which grew to a behemoth of forges, foundries and stamping mills for more than a mile along the river, made cannon balls and weapons of war, rails for the tricky canal portages; then rails for the railroad that replaced the canals, iron for wheels for wagons and carriages, then frames for automobiles that replaced the carriages and trains; then tubes for tunnels under mighty rivers. The city rose and fell on crests and troughs of economic fortune until at last the iron mines were replaced by suburbs and the great mills fell to vacant brick hulks inhabited by rats and birds and the homeless.

By the time Nagler had been born, the glorious iron days were a faded memory; some shops hung on like ghosts. The triumphant centerpiece, the great Union Iron Mill that was once a giant humming, burning heart in the center of the city, was torn down and replaced by an urban renewal parking lot. We watched, Nagler recalled. Watched from outside the chain link fence as the machines chewed into the sides and walls of the mill, bit off pieces and ground them up, bite by bite, tearing down the past and leaving an uncertain future in its place. For weeks after the demolition, people clung to the fence and stared; the river, still channeled into the millrace, ran brown with dust and debris for months.

When he was a child, Nagler and his friends would creep along the back side of the old stove-works and put their cheeks to the stone

22

wall. The heat from the internal fires flowed through the walls, and their ears would burn. Their fingers would throb with the pulse of the machines pounding and rolling within. Nagler remembered how he absorbed the sensations till his body trembled with the awe of creation, the inexplicable sense of being and the knowledge that within the great hulk, there was life.

But now even the parking lot was gone. The torrent rolled up the rusted chain link fence like a ribbon and wrapped it around the one power pole left standing, and grabbed the bricks, dirt and cement left over from the millrace and piled the debris in the middle of Warren Street. Two small cars had been tossed through the walls of the nearby convenience store as the flood ripped by, leaving the ground decorated with loaves of soggy bread, flattened boxes of cereal and piles of plastic soda bottles, strips of newspapers and cans of baked beans, like a picnic gone bad.

But it was the silence that got to Nagler. Hadn't been that quiet in the downtown since a blizzard a decade ago. The city had been shut down for several days until the National Guard blasted its way into town with heavy equipment. It was going to be quiet here for some time to come. A city needed shoppers to make a town center noisy, teen-agers and loud music; cabs and large trucks blocking the intersections and drivers honking their horns and yelling at each other in Spanish or Chinese while they shook their fists at one another while some Irish cop yelled back and pointed to get them back in their cars and move along.

Ironton was never silent; it rattled with the power of life being created daily as the shops opened, the trains grumbled by, and within its narrow canyons of brick and stone buildings, thousands of footsteps tapped, slapped, pounced and jumped along the city's sidewalks, the sound of a thousand nails being cut from bar iron replaced by the tapping of modern life, of commerce produced not by sweat but by thought, discussion and often, guile.

It had been years, Nagler knew, since the red, white and blue bunting trimmed the old Richman department store on parade days, been years since the streets had been lined by crowds eight and ten deep, since the squads of police, firefighters and soldiers filled the street curb to curb.

Nagler laughed sourly. He was standing in the middle of the busiest intersection in the city at the height of rush hour and knew he had a better chance to get hit by pigeon shit than a vehicle.

Nagler nodded grimly to those few residents who with their police escorts stepped carefully along sidewalks filled with trash, limbs and beyond the orange and white barriers, covered with snaking black power lines. A father of four had been killed when he tried to lift one of those lines from his car roof.

Danny Lopez stepped out of his liquor store and dropped the over-full trash can on the curb. He greeted Nagler and the men shook hands.

"How bad?" Nagler asked.

"Bad enough," Lopez said. He was a short, dark man with colorful tattoos up and down both arms. Nagler remembered him as a kid, always in trouble, on the edge of falling into the gang world. But time in the Army cured him of all that. He bought the liquor store a decade ago, one of the first Hispanic shop owners in Ironton.

"My cellar was filled with water so all the beer and whiskey bottles fell to the floor when the cardboard just melted in the water," Lopez said. "I got piles of beer bottles all over the floor. I should just let customers bring their own boxes and fill them up." He laughed, but it was a sour laugh. "One thing after another. When are they going to do something about that stupid river? This is what, three big floods in fifteen years? I see other places. They get flood walls and someone digs out the river channel. Who do we have to talk to, who do we have to pay off to get anything done? Who's gonna fix it? Ain't gonna be this mayor."

Nagler just shook his head. Sometimes it was just best to let it all flow by. "I'll bring a box back for some of that beer," he said as he walked away.

"Yeah," Lopez said. "You do that."

"Hey, Danny. Anyone from the city been around to talk to you about the damage, looking at the building?"

"No, why?"

Nagler shrugged. "Just been hearing things. Mess like this brings out the crooks. Be careful what you say to anyone."

Danny Lopez nodded. "You know me, Frank. I don't trust nobody. Not even you."

24

"Thanks, Dan. Appreciate the support."

****

The city had been declared a disaster area, and Nagler could already see city crews in white hard hats leaning over the torn cliff on the river's north bank, pointing cameras into every damaged spot, silently measuring with long yellow tapes, the yards of streets that erupted when the river backed into the storm drains and then into the streets, and the pounds of embankment that were now a half-mile down river, piled like a battery against the frame of fallen trees.

The last time the city had been this quiet, the last of the old mill buildings had just been flattened. Jimmy Dawson wrote that the silence was the sound of forgetting. Even Nagler had to agree he was right.

Nagler stopped near the central bridge and watched as a man suspended by ropes dangled over the side of the rail and poked at the stones of the arch with a long metal pole. When they fell, they dropped into the black river with a metallic splash that echoed off the solid stone underside. That seemed to be what the politicians and shady business leaders had done to Ironton. Tore it down brick by brick, deal by deal. Sold the dream, then sold another one when that one failed; scrubbed them all clean like newborns and hid the rotten center. How often had they announced their new plans? A new shopping center! Dozens of shops, thousands of shoppers, right here in Ironton. New housing. Affordable, convenient, near the new shops, leave the car at home! A new town civic center, a new fire station. A new school.

A new lie, polished up, wrapped in shiny paper and dragged out every time. When Nagler was starting out in the department, the mayor was Howard Newton. He was a flashy guy with a wide smile. Drove a big Chrysler and always had a few sharpies at his heels. To a cop in his early twenties, Newton seemed larger than life. Newton couldn't walk down the street without being stopped to shake hands, greet store owners or chat with the cop on the beat. Maybe his memory was bad, but when Newton was mayor things were moving in that town. He always seemed to be cutting a ribbon to open a new business somewhere. Newton was also a grandstander, a deal maker. He was always taking on the state legislature over some perceived slight in the most public way possible, and whether they liked it or not, state officials rewarded Newton with a better cut of state aid for Ironton or money for some highway or bridge or railroad project. Nagler recalled that no one really wanted to know the details of those deals, but at least Newton seemed like he cared. Howie Newton loved the sound of his own voice: He was big and loud and carried the city on his back for more than a decade; just what the city needed then. So it seemed. In truth, the underground chatter about Newton, that he was running a big scam, was probably true. No matter. At the time the city just seemed to be better off – yet even then – it was rotten at the core.

So now we do this. Nagler scanned the soaking ruins of downtown, the broken streets and watched as the city's residents held each other, wiped away tears, pushed back their hats and scratched their heads.

The river raged on under the bridge, grumbling on like time itself. Nagler wondered if all that water could wash the city clean of all the lies, deals and smiling faces that had turned the once-great city into a collection of empty mills, ragged streets and broken homes. Maybe so much of it would wash away this time there wouldn't be any other choice but to start over.

Nagler looked over at the wreckage of the old parking and laughed sourly; he wondered if the damage would have been so bad if they had let Lauren Fox work on that old parking lot and turn some of that asphalt to a grassy bank along the river, a more natural river bank.

"It would start here," she explained to him one day, and stepped off about ten paces from the wrecked chain-link fence that leaned over the churning river. "We'd rip up a section of this wall and river bank maybe thirty yards wide and it'd run for, I don't know, a few hundred feet, maybe a few blocks, maybe more, all the way to Union Street, and we'd get rid of all of this cement and dust and dirt. Put in grass, some small shade trees and when the rest of the area is rebuilt, a lot less dirt and junk would run into the water and help clean up the river."

She turned into the sun and smiled broadly. Her face was narrow but her smile gave it an exotic look; she shaded her eyes and stared at Nagler intently.

She began to walk slowly toward him, deliberately swaying her hips widely in exaggerated, slow steps at a pace that he couldn't decide was supposed to be seductive or comic.

"If we installed some tables and seats, it would give people a place to have lunch, or after the sun dropped behind Baker Hill and it began to get shady and cooler, maybe people who kind of like each other would come down here and sit and talk, maybe hold hands, and possibly even smooch a little." She reached Nagler's side and stared into his eyes. "Well, it's a plan. Why are you so skeptical? The lunch part or the smooching part?" she teased him. She reached up and kissed him. "I see your face. If you cheer really loud when we do this, I'll put your name on a park bench," she said and laughed.

She was always doing that. Disarming him with a smile, pulling him out of the shell he retreated behind, anything to keep some distance between himself and the world.

That was the part of a plan she was developing just before she left Ironton, but her ideas ran headlong into the announcement by Mayor Gabriel Richman that he was going to build a shopping center on the Old Iron Bog.

It wasn't that she opposed the shopping center. It was just as the manager of a program designed to revitalize the downtown area, she had to tell the mayor that the state would rather see all that effort and money maybe spent filling in the twelve acres of empty parking lots in the center of Ironton and not the Old Iron Bog.

Nagler recalled everyone in town at the time thought the shopping center was just a campaign promise, something Richman could tout in his next election run when he would need some whiz-bang, shiny toy he could present to voters so he could say he was working for them.

Six months after Lauren Fox told the mayor what he did not want to hear, funding for her job was removed from the city budget and she was gone.

Gone without a trace. Gone without a good-bye.

Nagler shut his eyes against the pain. They had talked nearly every day for two years. What started as a strong attraction had shifted into companionship; at times growing, at others... unfulfilled. They met in the corridors of city hall, in her office, on street corners, at ballpark ribbon cuttings. God, she was kid. That's what had raised all those eyebrows, he knew. She was a kid, maybe twenty-four, and he had been forty-five. And then gone, all the questions hanging in the air like wishes.

No, he said silently.
I can't do this again.
She's gone.

No one they both knew had heard from her. Vanished. *Bury all the old memories. That's what I'd do. All the confusion. All the disappointments.*

He stopped in the street and shook his head at the chaos around him, at a city broken, pulled apart and stunned. *I wonder what the mayor will think about the headless horseman,* Nagler thought.

****

After he left the medical examiner's office, Nagler headed back to the Old Iron Bog to ponder the scene in full daylight.

Wasn't any better. Not even after three hours of sleep and maybe six cups of coffee.

The yellow tape was still there, shredded, clinging to bushes and twigs, ripped open like a débutante's white party dress in some bad Hollywood teen murder flick, shredded as she stumbled and fled the unseen attacker. The tire tracks were there, squashed into the soft mud, more indistinct now that several more hours of mist had fallen. The daylight had not lifted the gloom; it sat with its same gray emptiness just like another bad idea.

Mulligan, the medical examiner, said she was approximately five-eight, a hundred-twenty pounds. She didn't appear to be a junkie, but they had no toxicology test results. There was no sexual assault.

"She wasn't dumped before the rain came. Given the injuries, there wouldn't have been any blood and the body would have been more seriously degraded," Mulligan said. "So, like those kids said, sometime last night."

In his mind Nagler scanned the streets in the north part of Ironton near the Old Iron Bog. Lots of homes, but a number of older warehouses, machine shops and storage sites left over from the days when manufacturing took place, back alleys, narrow streets, lots of dark, out of the way places worth checking.

He walked along the narrow dirt road unfulfilled, side-stepping mud puddles, pondering the scene in the middle of the night, his head down, kicking clods of dirt. He examined the flattened grass and wide dig marks in the mud where the kid's truck supposedly drove out of the bog. The grass was bent in the right direction — toward the exit road and then Mount Pleasant, so that part seemed plausible. Then he turned and stared at the spot maybe fifty feet away where Chris Foley said the body had been found. "Can't be," he muttered to himself. "It's too far." At the time the kids had said they were here the storm was had still been raging with heavy rain and high winds. After a week of listening to that storm, he knew there was a sound to that rain, a pounding, a steady relentless beat – one-two-three-four, one-two-three-four, one-two-three-four – of water pounding wood, cement and brick, with crescendos of a splash against window glass, a clap as the wind jabbed through your heart like a fist. In the bog the song of the storm would have been accompanied by the harsh brushing of reeds as the wind raked through the tall, waving grass and cracked naked branches on the ground. No. The air would have been filled with sound; hell, the air was sound.

No. Those kids weren't fifty feet away. They were parked right there in that big clearing. At night in the rain, he had not noticed how large and solid the clearing actually was. There was enough brush to partially hide the truck if they backed it in, he imagined. Those kids didn't come upon the body. Whoever dumped the body had come upon them in their truck.

Let's see. The kids were here – Nagler moved to a stand of tall grass and brush at the deep edge of the clearing and noticed depressions at his feet that could have been tire tracks. The headlights of the approaching vehicle at first would have played off the tops of the marsh grass and the kids might not have seen it. The grass would have been moving violently in the wind and the light would have seemed almost otherworldly for a moment; when the light became more solid as the second vehicle got closer, Nagler guessed the kids would have rolled to the floor of the back seat of the truck and pulled a blanket over them, probably hoping whatever was driving down the road would pass by without noticing them. Then what? The second vehicle stopped and the headlights illuminated the front of the truck. Why didn't they look? They panicked, Nagler decided. Saw the other vehicle, couldn't believe that anyone else would be here in the middle of the night and in the middle of that storm, and hurriedly dumped the body and drove out. Nagler re-examined the bent grass at the edge of the cleaning. He lifted a few stalks with the toe of his shoe and noticed they seemed to be broken on both sides. Giving up, he knelt on one leg and groaned as the squish of the cold mud slid through his pants as he carefully shifted some of the grass. It didn't take long to see that the uniformity of the top layer was deceiving: The lower layers were smashed and tangled, bent in all directions. A vehicle had driven over the grass twice. Once inbound, and once outbound. Even though the road was a couple of feet away.

Nagler stood up and shook the mud off his pants leg but still felt the wet spot on his knee. It had been a panic move. They'd driven in, seen the truck, dumped the body, said whatever the kids said they heard, and in their hurry to escape, drove straight over this patch of grass, did a quick turnaround, and drove over it again. Somewhere there is a vehicle with grass in its grill.

The exact time of death was just a guess, Mulligan had said. But it was within the day before she was found. Had those kids lied, or were they just scared?

Nagler was examining the ground again when he heard a door slam.

At the head of the road, parked with its big fat cargo butt half in the travel lane was Gabriel Richman's gold Cadillac Escalade and stumbling down the muddy road was the mayor himself.

"Mr. Mayor."

They shook hands. "Frank. Nice pants."

Nagler smiled. "Yeah, just checking on something and needed to get a little closer to the ground than I had planned."

"What do you think?" Richman asked.

"I think some unfortunate kid got caught up with the wrong gang and they sacrificed her," Nagler said. "We'll find out soon enough. Something like this, something this messy... someone talks."

Gabe Richman was gazing off into the distance and an awkward silence settled. His eyes were dark, his face unshaven. He, like his city, had been without sleep for three or more days. He was not a tall man, or large in anyway, Nagler knew, but Gabriel Richman seemed shorter, smaller, pulled in at the shoulders as if his body was collapsing around itself to fill the hollowness within.

Nagler said, "Some storm, huh?"

Richman broke off his gaze.

"Yeah. Record-setter. We've got three hundred people still living at the high school and the rec center. Hundreds of homes and businesses are damaged and need to be inspected. Power is out everywhere, so no one can get back in. The city's sewer plant was knocked off line, but thank God, Smitty got a crew in there. There's a natural gas leak down on River that the company won't be able to get to till the water recedes. Either that or they shut off the whole city.   You can see the gas bubbling up through the water and the air down there smells like rotten eggs, so heavy it feels like it's going to explode."

Nagler had rarely heard such bitterness in the mayor's voice. Politicians never sounded angry. They sounded discouraged, the words spilling from downturned mouths to seem sympathetic; they sounded hard and resolute so to be seen as the leader. And here was Gabriel Richman with a voice full of anger and frustration, a helplessness, rising in his tone, speaking as if the storm and the damage it had caused happened only to him. Nagler wondered if Richman doubted his abilities to lead the city out of its current mess. He had certainly never faced anything like this before, but then few had. A career built on making promises is pretty light stuff, Nagler decided. A flood like they'd had could carry it pretty far off course. Still, Gabe Richman had been at all the flood scenes, huddled with the emergency management teams, the fire and police chiefs, and visited the hospitals and emergency shelters.

"You've been everywhere," Nagler said. "Get any sleep?"

Richman kicked at the dirt.

"Tried. A little here and there." Richman sighed. "We've got at least six houses so far along the river that will have to be condemned because they were shifted off their foundations – and God knows how many more – and the west side is an island because the river ripped up a couple hundred feet of that old downtown parking lot and left behind a pile of debris that is acting like a dam. It could take weeks to dig it out."

Richman ran his hand through his hair and yanked up a handful as if he meant to pull it out.

"The fire department was rescuing families on Richards Avenue with a rowboat. A rowboat, Frank. The river is blocks away, but there was so much water..." Richman closed his eyes and let out a long breath. "A god damn rowboat," he said softly.

Richman walked a small circle and then repeated it. It seemed to calm him.

He looked at Nagler and then across the bog, shook his head and smiled weakly.

"I hated this place as a kid, Frank." he said softly. He turned back to Nagler. "Hated this town." The words exploded from Richman, air finding a vent, emotion delayed, released.

Nagler winced.

"That something you want to tell me, Gabe?"
Richman smiled sourly.

"It's not a secret," he said and laughed, his mood suddenly lighter. "This swamp became a symbol for everything that was wrong in Ironton. I grew up watching this city die. Factories closed, stores moved out. People out of work. It wasn't the place I imagined it to be and I could feel myself being sucked into the hole that is at the center of the city, giving up like everyone else. They were all so angry when I spoke about the future; they said the city had none. Get out while you can." He scratched his bearded chin and frowned. "I was too young. I believed them. My own hometown was killing my dreams. This town was old George Richman's creation. You've seen the photos. The department store with the line of horse-drawn delivery wagons. The dress shops, the theaters. The old mills. People worked hard, raised their families, and made dreams come true. And I wanted that. But the dreams were gone, the mills shut down, the great passenger trains just photos on the station walls, and the big highways just too far away to be useful as an economic factor. The politicians at the time began to blame my grandfather. Lived for himself, paid off his friends, made them all rich while the town declined."

Richman waved his hand in the air, as if dismissing the bog, the weather, the girl's death, the world.

"I don't know. The truth was that this was not going to be an iron center for ever. The mines were played out. The mills were old and inefficient. The owners just took the profits and failed to invest in the mills. In the end the whole industry collapsed under its own weight. The world changed after the war and Old Ironton was not ready for it," he said, softly. "We waited too long."

The mayor rubbed his hands on his pants to loosen some sand.

"When I went to college I realized that lots of places were like Ironton. Places that found themselves running behind. That's why I wanted to build that commercial center here. To show people in this town that dreams can happen. If it had worked, Ironton would have been a place to remember again. I told myself that I could fix this. This town is in a lot of ways my family's legacy. I have to fix it. Besides, we would have gotten rid of this old place, a symbol of the city's failure."

Richman spat. "And now this." He laughed. "I know it seems like an odd time to raise the past, but we've meeting for months on an economic plan. I go into that office every day thinking that we will say the right thing to the right people and we make the deal that will get things moving again. I can't tell you how heavy all this feels: The dreams, the responsibility, the failure and now this damn storm. Do me a favor, Frank, wrap up this bog case as quickly as you can. Let's give that girl's family some peace and maybe make some good news for a change."

He rubbed his eyes with the palm of his hands like he was grinding the sleep out of them.

Then Richman laughed, but it did not disguise the weary bitterness in his voice.

"When are you supposed to do it? When are you supposed to remember to dream about the future?"

Richman grabbed Nagler's hand and shook it hard.

"I'll see you, Frank. Have a meeting with the business administrator, some feds and a couple of guys from the state. Hope I don't have to beg. I'm not in the mood."

Nagler said he's keep the mayor informed of any developments in the case.

"So that whole shopping center plan is dead, huh?" Nagler shouted after the mayor.

Richman turned back to the cop, his face wrinkled in a peculiar quizzical frown as if Nagler had just found the magic box.

Richman brushed his hair back and waved a hand in the air.

"Maybe for this place," he said and waved at the bog again. "But maybe not dead. The city could use it and someone will make a hell of a lot of money when it happens. Need to find the right place." Richman laughed. "Maybe it'll get me re-elected," he said bitterly. He turned and walked back his car.

Nagler glanced up at the Escalade as the passenger side window slipped down a bit.

Behind the dark glass, for just a second before the panel slid closed, Nagler thought he saw a blonde woman. In the next moment as the image sharpened, he was sure it was Debbie Glance, the planning board secretary.

Nagler looked his watch. It was nine-thirty in the morning.

Debbie Glance. The Cadillac drove away with a scratching of dirt under its tires.

CHAPTER 4

"Post that online yet, Dawson?"

Jed Upton, the day editor, tugged at the sleeves of his pinstriped shirt. He was more fashion plate than editor, a shill for what had become a three-wagon traveling show as the corporation drained away profits, cut staff, and swore that the Internet would be their salvation even as the electronic termites ate away the underpinnings of the enterprise.

That was all that mattered now. Getting the story online - posted on the paper's website – so the anonymous commentators could tear the poor girl apart before they turned on themselves.

Hits, clicks, unique visitors, an invisible and uncountable audience upon which the Jed Uptons of the world based the future of his newspaper and the fate of his company.

Dawson thought he would do better to try to count fairies.

He yelled back, "It's up. Let the feeding frenzy begin."

The newsroom had returned to normal. Reporters, photographers and editors who had been trapped in homes without power had returned. They had been reporting from their cars, using cell phones that were dying as fast as they could thumb type while their batteries would draw power.

Upton stopped by the reporter's desk. "What's next? How about something on the old bog?"

Dawson squinted up at the editor. "How about we follow the crime? The cops will have more this afternoon." Upton was not impressed. So Dawson asked, "Like what?"

Upton hated to be questioned about his story ideas, because back in the day, he was a hotshot big city reporter, don't you know.

"No one knows anything about it," Upton said. Dawson knew that meant that Upton did not know anything about it. "How long has it been there? Has it always been a swamp? Maybe there's a sunken village there and maybe there's some survivors?"

Dawson just shook his head.

"Sunken villages? The paper going to pay for an archaeological dig?"

Dawson tried not to laugh.

"Maybe we'll find Fred Flintsone and Barney Rubble. Let's see," he said in his best fake-newscaster voice, "Geologists said the Wisconsin Glacier began to retreat many thousands of years ago. The water rushing off the melting ice formed miles of mucky land, including the swamp upon which sits the City of Ironton. The scientists predict that the city will one day simply sink below the surface and never be seen again."

Upton waved his hand walked away with a scowl. Another close encounter with a reporter.

One of these days, he's going to fire my ass, Dawson thought.

He glanced around the huge, empty room. The paper would be moving to a new, smaller office in a month. The owners contracted to have the paper printed elsewhere and delivered by hired trucks. The move had cost a hundred jobs. Once the paper had been one of the largest employers in the region. Now it was one of the smallest with just eight reporters, a couple editors and a few advertising reps.

They gave up on the business, Dawson told Frank Nagler one day. It got hard, so they quit. The Internet gave them one more flashy toy but it drained the company of income so all they could do was cut costs, processes and people.

Dawson returned his attention to the body in the bog.

He had checked the website. That was the predictable headline they wrote: "The Body in the Bog. Cops probe tale of headless woman."

Maybe she was someone's girlfriend and the wife caught them in bed. Like some corporate executive, or a state senator. That'd be juicy.

But something like that would already be in the wind: He would have already received a dozen calls and emails. Maybe even heard about before someone died.

Probably just some runaway. She might not even be from the area, he thought. The Interstate was known for a couple famous unexplained deaths of young women who had been kidnapped elsewhere, killed and dumped along the highway that ran from New York to Pennsylvania and eventually to the West Coast.

After he had returned to the office Dawson had checked with Nagler, who said there were no local girls reported missing yet, and a check of a national database had so many women with similar descriptions to be essentially useless, since the locals had no head to match against a photo.

As he picked up his notebook and stood up, a flash box popped up on his screen as he was shutting down the computer. The state's U.S. Attorney was holding a televised press conference at two in Trenton.

He'd just held one, Dawson thought. Busted some small time mayor in South Jersey for taking a bribe.

Sold his soul for like two grand, Dawson remembered. Cheap soul.

****

Dawson headed out to Barry's, an old lunch place on Warren, for his usual, a Cuban sandwich, coffee and a load of crap from Barry.

The restaurant was a hole in the wall with one long counter with nine chairs and five tables crammed against the wall. It was half filled when Dawson arrived, as usual, but one end of the counter was piled with brown paper bags for take-out. With the power still out in most offices, Barry's was one of the only places to eat downtown.

The door opened to Barry's bellow: "Hey Jonny, get these outta here. What am I, paying you to look good?"

Jonny, a thin Colombian kid of nineteen with slicked-back black hair and a killer grin, grabbed the bags. "That's exactly why you paying me, old man."

Dawson and the kid nodded hellos in the doorway and then Dawson stepped into that simmering air of the diner, assaulted by a dozen aromas swirling together yet distinct, like a good gumbo or salsa.

"Hey, mister reporter man," Barry yelled. "So what you got? What'd your paper say, a body in the bog? What is she, some chicka, a little Latin hottie, huh?"

Dawson waved him away. "That's disgusting, you old fart. Have some respect, for Chrissakes. She's one of your ex-waitresses. Was gonna spill the beans on what a crummy boss you are."

"You're wrong. They all love me. Tony, give me a Cuban."

Barry placed a cup of coffee, silverware and a napkin in front of Dawson, and leaned in. "So what is this?" He tossed his head back slightly, raising his chin.

Dawson dumped milk and three sugars in the coffee and stirred it around.

"Don't really know. Just some unfortunate kid." He tipped his head, grimaced and swallowed some coffee. "Why'd they cut her head off? That seems pretty brutal for this county. She might be a dump from the city."

Dawson's Cuban arrived.

"Could be," Barry said. "These kids here, they hear stuff. But they ain't heard anything on this."

Dawson raised the sandwich.

"But you hear about the shit in the fourth ward?"

Dawson placed the sandwich back on the plate with a grimace. Now what? The fourth ward. Even though Ironton was mostly Democratic, there was always shit in the fourth ward, some stupid party infighting. A couple of elections ago the party chairman ran a slate of candidates against his own incumbents which gave the Republicans an opportunity. They ended up winning most of the council seats and drove Gabe Richman crazy, calling for studies of everything under the sun, blocking all his plans, even for street repairs.

"So, what's up?" Dawson asked.

"The Trenton Street Club wants to expand the parking lot out back. But there's a house on the lot they want. They want Richman to declare it blighted, knock it down," Barry said. "That way they can claim the lot through eminent domain."

Dawson rolled his eyes.

"I'm guessing the house is occupied," he said. "What, some Hispanic family with three kids?"

"And they're claiming it's a crack house with mattresses in the cellar and families living in the attic that's been all chopped up." Barry looked out the window and cursed. "Ain't no crack house. I know the lady that owns it. She's been there forty years. Nice old lady. Goes to St. Stephen's. But the old mayor, he got a bug for her house. Wants it to be like the old days, when he could get the city council to approve stuff like that."

The old mayor. Howard Newton. The Trenton Street Club was his power base, ran it like an old political boss. Everyone paid homage to Howard Newton.

"What's Richman think?" Dawson asked.

Barry shrugged.

"I think he's trying to avoid it. He doesn't need Howie Newton asking for stuff right now."

Dawson shrugged. Same old, same old. He stirred his coffee and picked up his sandwich as Barry began to turn away.

"Hey, one more thing," Barry said as he turned back.

Dawson put the sandwich back down.

"Now what? He pointed both hands at his sandwich and made an exaggerated mock-angry face. "Can I eat my lunch?"

"Who's stoppin' ya?"

"What?"

"Tony's got a brother-in-law. Bit of a screw up," Barry said as he leaned against the counter.

"I'm supposed to be impressed? We all got brothers-in-law."

"Well, I'm sorry for you."

"Feeling's mutual."

"So, anyway. Bank was going to take his house. You know, a foreclosure. So he gets a lawyer, works a deal with the bank, thinks it's okay, and goes to court at the county. When he gets there some other lawyer out-bids him. On his own house. So Dommie's lawyer asks the guy, what's up. He said his client's got him on a retainer to buy up foreclosed houses in Ironton. They fix 'em up and sell them quick. Make a hell of a lot of cash. Ever hear anything about that? Some corporation."

Interesting. Dawson raised an eyebrow. "Is it illegal?"

"Dommie's lawyer didn't think so. Just has a smell about it. You know what I think? We see in the news about all these big shots stealing millions? But the real crooks are the little guys sitting in some back office where no one notices them. They make the books say whatever they want and the go home and put the money under their mattress."

"That's quite a theory, there, Barry," Dawson said. "Why didn't we find the money floating through downtown when the river flooded?"

"Cause they left it at your house."

"News to me. Okay, I'll check around," Dawson said. "Where's the guy living, Tony's brother-in-law?"

"In Tony's guest room. Wife and kids staying with her family. It's driving Tony nuts."

"As if working for you is not bad enough."

Barry walked away waving a towel in the air. "Ah, eat your lunch, reporter man. Sounds like you got work to do."

****

Back in the newsroom, the three reporters and two editors on duty stood in front of one of the flat screen televisions the publisher installed to give the empty room the feel of a big city newsroom. Either that or an off-track betting parlor, Dawson mused. All they needed was a bucket half-filled with cigarette butts, a couple of winos and a green-and-gray checked linoleum floor.

The U.S Attorney had just announced the arrest of sixty municipal, school board and county officials from dozens of Jersey towns on charges of bribery, money laundering and conspiracy. What surprised Dawson was that none of them were from Ironton. *What? We're not good enough for your big-deal task force? Those Trenton guys, probably couldn't find Ironton with a map.*

"Holy shit," someone said. Dawson walked away shaking his head. *Man, it's everything at once.*

The attorney's office had turned into an informant some lawyer who got caught stealing his client's money. The guy met with the officials and offered them a bribe if they would rezone some land for his supposed development company.

It was so transparent it was comical, Dawson thought. But they fell for it.

CHAPTER 5

Frank Nagler looked at the charts one last time, and then looked over at Dan Yang, who was sorting papers into six piles.

Yang was a police forensic accounting officer Nagler recruited to examine the material delivered to him in a series of nine letters.

Nagler had created one giant chart out of more than a dozen sheets of typing paper taped together with lists of dates and department numbers and what appeared to be amounts, highlighting numbers that appeared more than once in a colored box, but there were so many of them the chart looked like Christmas wrapping paper. After he added one more sheet of blank paper, Nagler laughed. What a mess. That what's Lauren would have said, he realized, then looked down at the table and cursed.

That's what Yang had said, too, which was why he was sorting the papers into piles.

The first letter was simple enough. It said Nagler would get a second letter. It was written on a computer in a standard word processing format and printed on common white copy paper. All the letters were created in the same manner. After the fourth one, Nagler was hoping the author might have decided to use letters cut from magazines or newspapers just to liven them up. The postmark was no help: The mail was processed at a regional center where a generic postmark was imprinted on the envelopes.

What the letter didn't say was that most of the invoices that would come had been redacted. So while at times a few numerals of an account number were visible, most had been blacked out.

Nothing had an address, nothing had a bank name, an initial or any other mark except for wavering lines that appeared to be made by a medium black marker. The letters almost seemed like a joke, a tease. But every few pages, an account number was left uncovered, or a bank name was only partly obscured, just enough - Nagler cursed the invention of the black felt-tipped pen - to suggest that all this was really something.

"What's the point of sending all this stuff and then making most of it unreadable?" Nagler asked.

Yang guessed it was possible the visible information was the path the sender wanted them to follow. "You know, here's step one; step two will follow." Either way, Yang said he could detect a pattern.

"Look at numbers that end in 25." They appeared ten or twelve times up and down the charts: 125, 525, 825, 1225. "Dates?" Nagler asked. Yang shrugged; maybe. The number 9235 was listed twenty-five times. Could be a bank deposit or part of a bank or government account number. "Why the same number?" Nagler asked.

"Feels like money laundering," Yang said. Despite the random nature of the material there seemed to be a pattern. He had been able to circle the same dollar amounts listed under several different accounts, suggesting transfers. But the dates were missing. Still, a lot of money moving in and out of accounts. Yang said he had to plot the dates they could find before he could really determine a pattern or time-line, or find the starting point, the first transfer. Once that happens, the rest of it falls into place, Yang said. "Maybe," he shrugged.

"But where's the money coming from to start with?" Nagler asked. "Other departments? If that was so, I guess we'd find a budget line with little or no balance."

"Possibly," Yang said. "Could be from fees the city collects, tax payments that are shifted illegally, grants. We really don't have enough data here to draw any conclusion. Maybe that's the beauty of it. Random, decentralized disbursements. Hard to track. On the other hand, it could just be normal end-of-the-year budgeting."

"What do you mean?"

"Towns are allowed at the end of the budget year to shift funds from one account to another to cover shortfalls caused by the normal flow of government business," Yang said. "On paper, it would look just like this." He held up two stacks of the pages and shrugged. "We need more pages, numbers and dates."

"Oh, good." Nagler stared at the pile of papers.

"What if they did this deliberately?" he asked. "Blacked out enough of the numbers, leaving some for us to see, just as a tease. You know, a way to say, 'Hey, look… here's some hints, figure out the rest.'"

"That's possible," Yang said. "But why send all this without some key to connect the numbers we can see. Seems maybe they are making fun of us. You know? Hey, smart guys, here's some hints. Good luck."

Nagler scratched his neck. "It's like I thought - who'd I piss off?"

"Before the storm hit, the city had started replacing computers and adding new software to others to shift all the financial data to one system," Yang said. A lot of computers were damaged in the storm as well and because it involved the police department, he would be consulting on the project. "We're going through maybe three hundred computers one-by-one. We'll see what we find. I can get a complete list of the banks and accounts the city has used for, what, twenty years?"

"That's probably far enough back," Nagler said.

"And who are they?" Nagler asked. "A city employee or someone who stole some letterhead and has a computer? How can we be sure these forms are even real?"

"Another good question, Frank. Glad it's your mess."

Nagler smiled. "You're not getting away that easy. I could assign you permanently to this case."

"No thanks."

Yang said he'd talk to a professor he had in college. "Maybe there's some analytic software out there that could make sense of all this."

"Worth a shot," Nagler said. He looked the chart again. "So what are they doing with the money? Where are they stashing it?"

Yang looked up and shrugged. "That's the piece of it we don't have here. These accounts sort of circle around on themselves. But the money has to be going somewhere. It went out of City Hall to other accounts, maybe to cash. It has to be invested in a form that doesn't attract attention."

"Are they sending it off-shore?" Nagler asked.

"I don't know," Yang admitted. "You hide millions and billions off-shore. I don't think we have that much here, so far a few hundred thousand. Bonds, maybe, some stocks. Something common, every day. Maybe old coffee cans hidden in crawl space or buried in a back yard somewhere."

"What?

"A joke, Frank."

"What about real estate? Market's been really soft for a while. Maybe there's some good deals out there."

Yang nodded. "It's easy enough to set up a shell company or two and shift the properties around. When I was in college in Boston I had a landlord who did just that. He owned blocks and blocks of apartments and just before the city was going to come down on him for code violations or taxes, he sold the properties to himself operating under a different name. The city chased him around for years."

Nagler smiled. "Just like we're doing."

Yang laughed, "Yeah."

One set of numbers puzzled both men.

10.2167; 10.2171; 10.2245; 10.2246; 10.2301; 10.2319; and 10.2326.

The set of numbers were listed on a separate sheet of paper, typed in order on one line each. 10.2245 had a check mark next to it.

****

Two days after the woman's body had been found, the police lab had completed a preliminary analysis of the evidence gathered at the old bog, but had not added much detail to the general knowledge.

Anything left in the sand like boot prints or tire tracks was inconclusive because the sand was so moist any imprint was unclear. They had typed the blood droplets as A positive and were awaiting a DNA analysis, and the city, county and state police were checking the old warehouses and vacant lots in the area for anyplace that could be a crime scene.

And none of it meant anything because there was nothing to compare it with. No alerts for missing women or girls, or cold cases sitting in old files had given any clues. And that bugged Nagler to no end.

Everybody leaves a trail. So who erased this one?

The first night, after Chris Foley left, and while he spoke with other responders, Nagler eyed those walking about the scene, but could not recall anyone who seemed out of place. Everyone had seemed to doing their job as the scene called for it to be done. No one had been doing more watching than working and the only out-of-place comment he recalled was the one made by the rescue squad kid, but that was just adrenaline.

Alerts had been sent to high schools and to colleges to report any female student who failed to report for class at the start of school and a group of officers were going through old crime records, a lot of which were still in paper form, for any similarities.

To Nagler, the lack of a crying mother or worried husband or boyfriend appearing at the local police station might be a good indication that the woman was not local, even though he initially thought she was. The body itself was not enough to go on.

So we dig. Still, you might notice in two days that your daughter or wife had not come home. Unless you killed her.

Nagler pondered all this as he watched two officers maneuver the small boat through the thickets at the old bog. They would be out there for a few more days, poking the weeds, scooping up baskets of muck on the chance that as the water level in the swamp settled, evidence could be found.

It was just too clean. Okay, he could maybe understand not finding any clothes in the bog – They were probably in a black plastic bag somewhere, tossed into a restaurant trash can or placed alongside a curb somewhere on trash day, just one more bag of stuff. And the amount of trash that had been piling up on sidewalks as homes and businesses were being cleaned out seemed staggering. The city deployed squads of front-end loaders and construction dump trucks to scrape the streets clean.

But why no other evidence, Nagler wondered. Broken limbs on trees, a cigarette butt newly discarded, a snatch of fiber from a coat, a bag snagged on the swamps grass, or anything that might have fallen from the car. None of that had been found. So the search continued: Maybe it ended up in the brackish water, blown there by the fierce wind or washed off the road by the flood.

But it was the question why that bugged him the most. Why kill this girl? And why so violently? What secrets do you know that someone wanted hidden so much they took off your head and hands?

Nagler wanted the Old Iron Bog to give him that answer. What did you see the other night, you old swamp, that you're not telling me?

****

Nagler heard the voice before he heard the footsteps.

45

"Reliving past glories?"

It was Jimmy Dawson.

"Actually I'm just waiting for you," Nagler said. "Surprised you weren't here earlier, you know, before all the good seats were taken. What's up?"

"Poking around as usual," Dawson said. "Upton was yelling because we didn't get any video of the search the other morning. I told him that badly lighted footage of shadowy figures wandering around in the dark recorded from the road with a cell phone camera would not have made compelling viewing. And there was the obvious problem that none of the actual video cameras had been charged due to the power outage. He didn't seem to get that this wasn't reality TV and the cops and the camera crews were not going to do it over for a better take. But he didn't care. It's all about traffic on the website. I could see that a good piece of video might draw some attention, but it's not about quality anymore. Just get them to open that file and get a few more unique visitors."

Nagler looked at Dawson. He had never heard him sound so discouraged.

"What's up, Jimmy," he asked. "Doesn't sound like you."

Dawson scanned the old bog.

"Couple weeks ago, the new kid, Havens, comes into the office in a big fuss and runs over to Upton and they had a big old time viewing a video Havens made. He apparently went on a drug stakeout with Ortiz and Martin and ended up chasing some drug dealer through the back alleys of the old silk mill."

Dawson stared ahead. His voice was flat and expressionless. Didn't sound like Dawson at all.

"I watched the tape, Frank. The kid was running, so the camera is bouncing all over the place. Video is all jiggly and out of focus. Gave me a headache. You can't tell where he is or really what he is doing, and he is out of breath so you can't understand what he is saying, but they thought it was Academy Award winning stuff. I asked him what all the running was about, and Havens really didn't know. They never caught anyone and the rest of the video is Havens and two cops sitting in a police car talking about the Yankees."

Dawson look at the ground, kicked at some of the sand. "Don't know, Frank. The business may be passing me by. It used to be about talking to people, telling stories, providing facts and letting taxpayers know how their leaders were spending their money; about watching and anticipating where they would screw up. It used to be about life in the city, about the people who made the city what it was and those who were trying to tear it down. Now it's just a business for Tweets and twits."

Nagler looked at the ground. He was wearing boots this time. Sleep, he said to himself, is a wonderful thing. "I'm not sure about that, Jimmy." But then said nothing else. Nagler knew that he'd been there, too, had that same thought.

Dawson said, "You know, Frank, when I asked you about Lauren Fox the other day, it wasn't a joke. It was a real question. I know you two were close."

Nagler just sighed.

"She left town, Jimmy. In a big hurry. Foley wondered if she maybe had stolen something, but all her city accounts had checked out. Every dollar was accounted for. Because she left in a rush, the chief assigned a detective to trace her, but they followed her last paycheck to her parents' home, and after that there was no trail. As I recall, I thought the probe went on a little longer than was necessary for an employee who quit her job suddenly and who had not committed any crime."

"But what about you, Frank?"

Oh shit.

There was an edge in his voice when he answered. Jimmy ought to know better. "Did it hurt? Yeah, what the hell? We weren't getting married or anything, but it was fairly serious. It was just the uncertainty, I guess. The sudden disappearance. But I don't want to talk about it. She left town without saying a word. I haven't thought about her or her exit in months because it just pisses me off."

Dawson took a few steps away.

"Look, I just know that you seemed pretty shaken at the time. I was asking just in case, you know, you heard from her."

"It took you two years to bring it up?" Nagler was now laughing. "Thank you for your concern."

"Jesus, Frank." Dawson shook his head and frowned. The pair fell into an awkward silence; distant road noise like a chattering wind settled in.

"Why did you bring her up?" Nagler asked.

Dawson shrugged. "I saw her name in some old stories I was looking at for background on the storm follows. She had some good ideas, but they never went anywhere. Seemed like a bright kid. Wonder why Richman didn't like her."

All it took was a crack, Nagler thought. One small incision of unwanted knowledge slipped under the wall and everything crumbled. He had successfully blocked thoughts of her from his mind for most of the past year, not asking the questions of why and wherefore, sidestepping any reference to her, even avoiding the places they once visited together as part of her job, just to make sure that no trace of her would again rub off on him; no scent, no scene, no random word spoken by a stranger, no imaginary glimpse of her hair or a face that could be hers would crash the wall he had built.

After a minute, Nagler asked, "What do you know about Debbie Glance?"

"Debbie Glance?" Dawson shifted his weight. "She's been around city hall for maybe ten, twelve years. Started in the tax office, worked in the mayor's office for a few years and now is in the planning board office. Why?"

"She was riding around with Gabe Richman the morning the body was found, after the storm cleared. I came back up here and he was on the bog road and she was in the front passenger's seat. She cracked the window just enough so I could see her. I think she did it on purpose."

"Gabe Richman and Debbie Glance? Holy shit," Dawson said. He was paying attention now. "Gabe Richman and Debbie Glance. Wonder how long that's been going on?"

Nagler shrugged. "I'd say for a while. It was nine thirty in the morning. You don't just start screwing around that early unless you've built up to it."

Before Dawson could say anything, one of the cops in the boat yelled out. "Hey, detective. Nagler! We found something."

Nagler started running toward the boat, with Dawson trailing. "You have to stay there," Nagler said. "You'll get the damn story. See anyone else out here?"

When Nagler reached the boat, the officers were standing on the road, holding something in a plastic bag. It was a woman's hand.

Foley met Nagler at the medical examiner's office as Mulligan carefully examined the shriveled, white hand with long, slim fingers. Nagler decided the hand wasn't white at all; it was beyond white, drained of all color or shading or life.

The medical examiner quickly compared the cuts at the wrist to the right arm of the dead woman, but it was impossible to determine if it was a match or even from the same woman. The real problem, he said, was that the hand had been in the water for several days. "Tests," he said. "We need tests."

What attracted their attention was a gold ring on the hand's third finger. It was a lion's head gently hammered into a thin sheet of gold less than a quarter-inch round. Even after what might have been three days in the Old Iron Bog, the ring looked expensive.

Foley said, "You were there when they found it, Frank?" Foley was oddly withdrawn, Nagler thought. His voice was flat and hollow, when possibly it should have been upbeat, given what they had in front of them. This was potentially a big lead in the case and Foley was acting skittish and nervous when it seemed to Nagler that he should be gratified that something that could be viewed as progress in the case had emerged.

"Yeah. They said it was in the water about four feet off the side road that headed to that spot you showed me," Nagler said. "What are the odds that the rest of her might be in that swamp?"

Foley jumped in. "We need to be sure, so let's wait until any and all possible tests have been run. We don't want to give whoever did this a hint we may have made a break, and we don't want to give her family bad information." He glanced down at the hand, then at Nagler and Mulligan and then again at the hand. His lips were pursed and his eyes cold.

Mulligan cautioned, "Gentlemen, we don't know if this hand belongs to our Jane Doe. We ought not to jump to conclusions."

"But –" Foley began.

"Sorry, Doc," Nagler said. "I wasn't thinking about saying anything to the press, but what are the chances that there is another girl in pieces in the old bog? I searched several databases and there aren't a lot of young women missing right now."

****

Foley and Nagler left the medical examiner's office but stopped in the parking lot.

"That hand should help us," Nagler said.

Foley shrugged. "We'd better hope so. Or there are more bodies in the old bog than we know about. I know you don't want to think about it, but -"

Nagler interrupted Foley. "Yeah, I know. Charlie Adams. Not yet, Chris. Not yet. But think about this: Why did the killer leave the ring on the hand? Mulligan might be right, that we don't want to jump to conclusions about whose hand it is, but why don't we just for the heck of it assume that is belongs to our bog girl? It would be our first concrete lead."

Foley nodded. "Okay, right. With the storm and all the damage, and the slow recovery, it would be great if we could wrap this up. Records show there hasn't been a dismemberment of a young woman in the New York region in more than five years. There have been a few drug killings, but they've been shootings. I hope this is not the start of something. Let's get on that ring. It seems to be our best lead now. Even if Mulligan is right and the hand does not belong to our victim, it could lead us somewhere. Eliminate a few possibilities, if nothing else."

Nagler agreed. "Let's hope. I'll check old theft reports and show the photo around to jewelers and department stores. With luck there's some trademark on it. They probably made more than one."

Then he said, "Saw the mayor at the crime scene the other morning. He looked like hell."

"Richman?" Foley asked. "What the hell."

Nagler stared at Foley as the other cop scrolled through an email list on his phone. What the hell? That was a little odd. "Yeah," Nagler said. "He was clearly exhausted, but seemed genuinely concerned about the victim's family. Maybe he was just distracted."

Foley looked up from the phone. "Maybe that's it. He's been up for days with this storm." Then he looked at Nagler. "But he's right. Let's get this one done." He reached over and shook Nagler's hand. "Have to run, Frank. Another disaster clean-up meeting."

"Sure," Nagler said. "You okay, Chris? You seem a little, I don't know…"

"Just tired," Foley snapped. "Too many meetings, too much to do and too little to do it with."

Nagler nodded. "One thing. Anyone from your emergency department talking to homeowners on the east side? Some folks told me they were threatened with eviction by a city employee."

Foley smiled. "You talking to Sam Rothwell? I heard he said that."

How did he hear that? "Yeah, heard it from Sam, but heard it from others, too." He lied.

"Nothing to it. We've been following up reports of gypsy contractors and phony insurance agents offering deals to some residents. We're on top of it. Gotta go."

"Richman was up there with Debbie Glance. Any idea why?"

Foley stopped and turned. "She works in his office, helping him with the recovery effort," he said. "Why would that be strange?"

"Because it was the first thing in the morning," Nagler said. "Do they always meet on the way to City Hall, in his Escalade?"

Foley leaned into Nagler's chest. "What are you implying, Frank?" Foley said in a voice that came from the authoritarian side of his soul, carrying the suggestion that maybe the wrong rock had just been overturned.

Nagler's spine tingled. It was an odd response.

"Nothing. Just asking."

Foley stepped back and looked at the ground then glanced in both directions.

His voice was softer, less edgy. "Gabe has known Debbie since high school. We all have. Like everyone in this city. It's really a small town. The Richmans helped her out after high school when she got into a little trouble with drugs. She had a hard life then. When Gabe got into politics, and then when he got elected, she helped with his campaign finances. She's got quite a head for accounting. Then he gave her a job at city hall. Yes, I know. You're not supposed to hire your friends, but show me a politician who hasn't, and I'll put him up for sainthood."

Foley shook head. "There's nothing there, Frank."

Nagler smiled. "Didn't say there was, Chris. Just thought it was a little odd. Isn't that what we do as cops? Look at things that don't make perfect sense? I get that she works for him, but if they were going to be at the same city hall meeting, why was she riding around with him beforehand?"

Foley stared at Nagler with narrow eyes.

"I don't know, Frank. There's nothing there. Forget about it."

Then Foley walked away quickly, poking at his cell phone and placing a call.

Nagler smiled to himself. How interesting. It might not be related to anything else other than what it seemed – the mayor getting a little on the side – but it was still interesting.

****

The police released a photo of the ring to the papers in hopes that someone might recognize it. Nagler also showed the photo to some jewelry stores and several department store jewelers who said it was not theirs: Too expensive. Only Manny Calabrese at Ironton Jewelers offered any help.

Manny Calabrese's family arrived in Ironton in the late nineteenth century as part of the great European immigration. It seemed as if their whole Italian village moved and settled all at the same time on Richards Avenue, where they planted grapes for wine, tomatoes for eating, built St. Anthony's Church and opened businesses downtown. Manny looked like a merchant. Gray slicked back hair, a heavy gold pinkie ring on his right hand, wide blue suspenders held up pants that grew a waistline to match his own. A phone and a pencil in the same hand, in constant motion. And the killer ability to sniff out a deal. Nagler decided it was the eyes. Manny Calabrese could spot value or a fake from a hundred feet.

"It's handmade, easy, Frankie," Calabrese said. He always called Nagler "Frankie," but in Manny Calabrese's world everyone was Bobby, Joey, or Nicky. He even called the mayor "Gabey." Drove him crazy. At a business luncheon when the city was presenting Manny an award, one of those affairs where everyone one is "Mr. Mayor," "Madam Councilwoman," or "Chief," Manny Calabrese called Richman "Gabey" a dozen times, as in "Hey, Gabey, come over here. I want to thank you for this award."

Calabrese examined the photo through an eyepiece.

"Look at that lion's head. That work has not been machine pressed, but carefully crafted. I'm guessing twenty-four karat. If I could examine it, I'll bet there's a serial number and the artist's initials. That I could track. Keep this?" Calabrese waved the photo at Nagler, who nodded yes.

"This is a ring bought by a beautiful woman, Frankie."

Nagler laughed. "How do you know that, Manny?"

"Because it would make her more beautiful," Calabrese said, winking.

Nagler shook his head and said he'd check the ring to see if there were any identifying markings.

"You do that, Frankie. I'll show it around. You take care."

Later on, as Nagler sat before his computer with a blown up copy of that photo in front of him, he began to see what Calabrese meant. It didn't seem like the kind of a ring that a young girl would be wearing unless she had rich parents and they spoiled her. And it didn't seem to be an heirloom; too modern.

It also did not seem to be the kind of ring that a boyfriend or even a husband bought without a lot of help. It was a little too fine, and for a boyfriend, seemed to be a little too expensive.

It was the kind of ring, Nagler decided, that a woman would buy for herself. Someone who understood her own sense of fashion, and yet had a conservative sense. This was not a showy ring, but a simple, confident piece of jewelry, bought by someone who knew herself.

And was probably single. Otherwise the clueless husband would have bought it, but only after she dragged him to the jewelry store and pointed it out, Nagler mused. What did that make her, thirty or so? Someone with a little experience in the world, maybe?

"So how did you end up in my swamp?" Nagler said to no one in particular.

With not much else to do, he scrolled through a series of photographs in the local paper's computer archives, stopping to enlarge any hands of women visible in the photos. After scanning about a hundred, he decided that too many women wore rings.

The next image on his screen was of a ceremony at town hall from about three years ago, a classic ribbon cutting, with a line of eight participants on either side of banner declaring, "Congratulations!"

53

At the end of line to the right of the photo was Lauren Fox.

He drew a box around her face and watched as it emerged larger and slightly fuzzy on the screen. Even in that poor display, Nagler again understood her beauty. Her delicate face was finely drawn, a narrow nose and deep, dark eyes; he recalled that she always seemed to be smiling.

No one in Ironton had quite seen anyone like her in some time, Nagler recalled. She kicked into gear programs and ideas that had been discussed at city hall for decades but no one had taken time to shake off the dust. He remembered thinking she showed how hide-bound and favor-driven the city had become. That had to induce fear among the flock.

With himself as her guide, she walked down the back alleys of sections of the city that even police officers would only enter if they had a partner. Nagler would caution her about the characters she was going to meet, but, she would say, that was her job.

He glanced again at the ceremonial photo. Lauren stood at the end of the line, grinning so proudly he could nearly feel her pleasure. She leaned slightly to her left to get in the frame of the photo and her hands hung at her waist, her left hand clutching hard the fingers of her right hand. He enlarged her hands, but the result was too pixilated to determine if she was wearing a ring.

He leaned back in the chair and, whether he wanted to or not, recalled the first night he took her out in an unmarked patrol car so she could better understand the city. It felt like a stake-out with a rookie cop, Nagler remembered.

They drove slowly through the lower east side until they parked in an alley between two empty stores. The street seemed quiet. A few cars passed by, but with all the stores closed except for one bar, few people walked around.

Lauren sat at attention, Nagler recalled. Every movement seemed important, and she cast her wide eyes up and down the street.

"You do this a lot?" she asked softly.

Nagler laughed. "You don't need to whisper, Lauren. No one can hear you."

He imagined she blushed.

"How do you do it, Frank? What are you looking for when you

watch the street?"

It was a good question, and he said so.

"We know there is a certain amount of drug activity going on, and we know most of the players, so we look for new ones. We take the reports we get from the state and federal drug agencies for new drugs, new packaging, new dealers on the regional level. Anything that might show up here. And we look for strays, you know, people paying a little too much attention to vehicles, businesses or homes - ."

"Who's that guy?" Lauren interrupted.

"By the bar on the corner? That's a drug dealer."

"Wow. Are you going to arrest him?"

Nagler chuckled softly. "No. See the other guy? Just coming out of the bar? That's an undercover cop. He's sort of taking names and numbers. We're going to do a sweep in this neighborhood in about a month."

Lauren stared intently through the dark street toward the bar as if trying to memorize every detail. "Wow," she said softly.

At the desk, Nagler smiled. Most of their tours were not that dramatic. He just tried to show her areas that needed the most attention and introduce her to the local block leaders, especially in the ethnic neighborhoods. She learned, and learned quickly. She came back with questions and data, and data and questions, and little by little turned all the new information into grant applications. Streets began to get cleaned up, porch railings nailed back into place and painted. New windows appeared on old homes. A street festival or two began to fill what had been up till then just another hard, sunbaked Saturday; streets filled with color, laughs and music, and the air filled with the aromas of barbecue, spicy chicken and smoked sausage.

When did the appreciation become friendship and the friendship become attraction? When did the smile of encouragement become the smile of affection, the chatter slip into an awkward first silence, then soft, silent stares? When did her face begin to fill his dreams?

He closed out the photos on the screen.

I don't want to remember. But he did. He had held those hands, pressed them softly to his lips and felt their gentle caress on his cheek. I don't want to know, he said in answer to the question that had not been asked. I don't want to know where she is. Nagler turned off the desk lamp and shut off the computer screen as if that would drive away the image in his mind. The unasked question hung in the air like mist, and he pondered it in silence.

CHAPTER 6

The U.S. Attorney was talking about corruption in the State of New Jersey everywhere there was a camera, a microphone, a reporter, or a voter.

It was never "New Jersey," Dawson thought. It was always "The State of New Jersey," just as in Washington, D.C., it was "The American People" who have spoken or not spoken, approved or disapproved, according to the politicians, when most of "The American People," Dawson knew, were at home watching football.

The Attorney needed to rent a bus and hang a big banner on it declaring the "End Corruption in NJ" tour.

Still, nailing sixty officials was pretty impressive, though it was like throwing chum on the water. Like sharks drawn to blood, politicians are drawn to money. Did they have to make it that easy?

"We will end this corruption," the Attorney declared. "The people of the State of New Jersey deserve no less. I am disgusted that sixty elected representatives of the people decided they had a greater right to sell their office to the highest bidder than they did to fix the streets, help the senior citizens, and take steps to lower taxes or simply act in an honest manner. They sold their office for a couple thousand bucks. Who are these fools? My office will make sure they never serve the people of the great State of New Jersey again."

The people of the State of New Jersey.

Dawson looked away from the television as Howard Newton laughed at the scene being broadcast.

"The poor people of the State of New Jersey," Newton coughed out. "They elected these assholes, again and again. What do they think is going to happen? The people of the State of New Jersey. My God. Biggest bunch of sheep there ever was."

"Said the man who had been elected to office five times by those same sheep."

Newton waved a hand at Dawson. "Bah. What do you know?"

They were on the shaded patio of the Trenton Street Club. Dawson had come to ask Newton about the house that Barry told him about, but the television was on and the cable news reporters were following the U.S. Attorney everywhere.

It as odd he was there, Dawson chuckled softly. Newton, the old pol with the shady reputation, and him, the supposed muck-raking reporter. *How many times had we squared off? But we needed each other, didn't we?*

Newton was probably eighty-five, Dawson figured. He never told his age to anyone. His face had settled into a mass of splotches and moles that might have been cancerous. That probably accounted for the oversized Panama he always wore, that and the shades. Always shades, even indoors. The scars on his nose traced back to his boxing days when Newton was a small middleweight with an up-yours chip on his shoulder that got him into more trouble inside the ring than he ever faced outside it.

He fought on guts, not skill, and after a round of being pounded by a whirlwind of punches, his opponents inevitably sized the kid up and leveled him with a combination or two.

He had shrunken inside his clothes like a punching bag that leaked stuffing, and when sitting in a chair silently as he was now, he was scarily corpse like.

Dawson always noticed Newton's hands. The leathery brown skin was wrinkled and bulged with veins. The knuckles were broken and bent, but his nails were perfectly manicured. The index finger of his right hand curled around a fat Cuban cigar like it was a wad of hundreds.

Beyond the line of evergreens at the end of the yard, Dawson could see the peaked roof of the house Barry had told him about. The club's yard with a perfect green lawn was lined by trees and shrubs centered in garden patches of flower beds that were rotated seasonally. The landscaping bill for the place was probably more than he made in a month, Dawson thought. But knowing Howie Newton, he paid nothing. Got it in trade. An exchange of services.

Because that was what Howard Newton could deliver: services. Help with a permit, a building inspection, working papers for some underage kid, a job in the road department that suddenly was opening on Thursday; a little environmental clean-up problem at your auto repair place.

It was the whole subterranean wink-and-nod culture that laughed in the face of the U.S. Attorney and his gang of sixty saps who managed to get caught. They all knew how the game was played but just got so full of themselves they thought no one would ever notice.

Howie Newton had been doing it all his public life. A little at a time. Just enough not to get noticed too much.

Dawson had written countless stories about Howard Newton. He had been investigated or sued dozens of times. The state had been in to look at the city's books two or three times when he was mayor. Somehow the books were always square.

Dawson gazed jealously at the green lawn and peaceful yard. All that greenery took a lot of fertilizer.

Dawson laughed to himself, amused that it was so easy to jerk the system around to one's own advantage. During the Depression when Ironton was really in the dumps, a city mayor, who also served on the county commission, had all the city's main streets renumbered as county roads so the county government had to plow and repair them. It wasn't illegal, and in a way it made sense. But it twisted the rules and gave to a few that which was denied to the many.

When everyone did it, the system crashed.

"So, Howard, I hear you're interested in that house out back for a parking lot," Dawson said.

"Parking lot?" Newton asked. "Where'd you hear that? Not a parking lot. Just the other side over there is that empty Italian joint, Dominic's? There's a fast food company wants to buy it, but they need a bigger lot to get it past the planning board."

Dawson interrupted.

"So you'll get the property and become good friends with the fast food guy's real estate attorney ..."

"What the hell - yeah." Newton shrugged, then waved the cigar in the air.

Had to love Howard Newton. Right out there.

"What about the homeowner. What's she think? Maybe she wants some of that fast food money?"

"Old Maria? She's got cancer and wants to sell out so she can go back to the old country and die in peace. Asked me to buy the place last year."

Newton leaned forward in the chair and placed his hands on his knees.

"What? I'll give her a fair price, more than it's worth," he said.

"Did you even mention that fast food company?"

"Crap, Jimmy, she'll be dead before they make her an offer, and they'll low ball her anyway. She'll do better with me."

The pair sat in silence for a moment. The television channel had returned to its regular programming.

"You're surprised, Jimmy," Howard Newton said. "You always seem surprised; as long as I've known you. Need to stop being surprised; it'll clear up your vision. Look at things from a different direction sometimes."

Dawson wondered, am I?

Newton gazed over the lawn.

"I know you think I'm a crook," he said. "Go back and look what I've done. I helped people. Their sons needed jobs, the daughters needed to get into the county college but their grades weren't so hot. So I helped."

"Oh, hell," Dawson said. "That's so much bullshit. You were mayor for twenty years, made what? Three grand a year? As far as I could find, you never had a regular job in your life. But you always had a new Caddy, your house was half again as large as your neighbors', and your son has a job for life in the sewer department. Come on, Howie. That's Mob stuff. You must have something on nearly everyone in town."

Dawson stopped. Why am I railing at this old man? Known him my whole life and he's never been any different. He'd steal your lunch while you were in English class and sell it back to you an hour later.

The old man was silent for several minutes; his fingers rolled slowly over the smooth edges of the chair's arm.

"It's what we learned, Jimmy." The voice came from a smoky distance. "What our grandfathers learned to survive. They were all working for the big boss who owned that mansion on Blackwell with the five turrets, the wide porch and thirty fancy windows. They worked fifteen hours a day in dirty overheated buildings handling hot metal with no protection. They got burned, lost hands, arms, got crushed by a load of iron, branded by the dripping slag, and if they faltered, the shift bosses ground them into the dirt. If they were lucky, they lived to be fifty.

"They'd walk past that house behind the iron gates – made with iron they had forged – and knew that it was their labor in that hot, stinking iron mill that had made the man rich. And he was going to keep it all."

He slowly lifted the cigar. The tip glowed red as he drew air though the tobacco. The air filled with the dense aroma as a slim stream of smoke leaked from the side Newton's mouth.

"So they set up an alternative way of doing business, because, hell, they had no money, but mostly they knew they could not trust the mill owners or the bosses or the bankers, the landlords or anyone who had control over their lives. So we all did favors, and some of the favors got big. It was how we fought back against a system that was killing us, one in which if we played by the rules, we had no chance to succeed."

The old man placed the cigar on an ashtray, stood up and put his hands in his pants pockets.

"Did that make us corrupt? Don't think so. Made us traders. Trade something, get a little extra for it when you trade it again. It was all so small time. But you know what? People didn't lose their homes to the banks. If they got behind somehow it was made right. And when they got hurt on the job and the factory boss threw them out, their kids got fed, and the house got fixed. Then they did a little work for you. Look at that flood last week. Those people will be paying off those repairs for years because the insurance companies who sold them home insurance didn't tell them that it didn't cover water damage. What the fuck did they think a flood was anyway?"

Dawson stood and walked to the edge of the patio. "The crooks are wearing the suits, Jimmy, sitting on city councils," Newton said. "Seems so innocuous. They write an ordinance to tear down a building so only their friend's company could qualify, look the other way when their brother's kid wants to be a cop or stack the land-use board with their golf partners. They twist the law into knots to justify anything they want. That's who the Attorney General caught. For them it's like breathing. They don't think anyone notices. Then there's the guys with three cell phones and nine hundred dollar suits. Listen to them. They sell so much bullshit, they forget who they sold it to."

"But when that something you traded wasn't really yours, isn't that corrupt?" Dawson asked.
The old man turned, his mouth working.

61

"You tell me, Jimmy. You tell me." The raspy voice had an edge, the lips drawn tight. "What's it mean when a lobbyist for the oil business sits in a committee room and helps a Congressman write a bill about oil regulations? Or when the bankers cook the books in a way that even other bankers can't figure it out? The U.S. Supreme Court gave human rights to corporations and said that money is free speech; said big companies can cheat women out of equal pay. The big stores pay so little or schedule employees so they work a little less than full time so they have to get health insurance from the government."

Newton pointed a finger at Dawson.

"That's corruption, Jimmy. Big time, in your face, stop us if you can corruption and they have the money, the lawyers and the rules to make it stand up."

Clouds overhead shifted and Newton was suddenly standing in full sunlight; like a bat he shuffled back into the shade of the patio.

"They make rule after rule to shut that door of opportunity for the little guy. Get their hands around the throats of the middle class and squeeze. They make deals that only benefit themselves and their money men. The cut taxes for the rich and screw the poor. Remember that congressman who wanted to get rid of Medicare and let the insurance companies run it? That would put old folks out of their homes, take food from their mouths. These assholes act like the Great Depression happened to somebody else.

"They won't be happy till they grind everyone else under their wheels, the grinning bastards. Eisenhower said fear the military-industrial complex. These guys make the military-industrial complex look like a carnival, such is their immeasurable greed."

Newton returned to his chair and shut off the television.

"And you're worried about me buying an old lady's home so she can get out from under a monthly mortgage payment that's more than what her immigrant parents earned in a year? Bah."

"There's a lot of people exercising their free speech these days, I'd say. And that holier-than-thou U.S. Attorney has a list of friends as long as your arm and they're all going to come calling one day."

Newton adjusted his shades and Panama hat.

"We all know evil when it shouts at us, Jimmy," Newton said. "We all know corruption when the dollar amounts are huge and the villains smile pretty for the cameras. But it's the small men in the background who are the most dangerous; it's when they are the most bland that corruption does the most damage," he said, his voice soft like a hiss.

When Dawson left, Howard Newton had settled back into that corpse-like state, sitting stiffly in his chair. The only sign of life was the occasional rise and fall of the Cuban cigar in the corner of his mouth. The sound of Newton's voice stuck to Dawson like oily sweat.

****

Back in the newspaper office Dawson sat before his blinking computer screen alone in the vast room. He hadn't turned on the lights so the room was lighted by the dim safety lights. There was an unholy silence.

He had just finished his Sunday political column. Jed Upton was not going to like it.

Tough shit.

He wrote:

"It's as easy as breathing, to ignore the truth and color the lies in pretty shades so that no one questions what they hear; as easy as breathing to spin the grand tales that enthrall, that remove all doubt because they are so large. As easy as breathing to walk away when all the dreams go pop and the sky is empty, filled with darkness.

This is a time of small men.

Small thinkers, small doers, men of small ideas, constricted intellects paying tribute to ideas that were small when they originally surfaced and were rejected.

Small men who think that nothing would ever change, small men who have beaten back the margins so that there are only two answers: Yes and No.

Small verbalists who construct sentences that begin and end with the same thought, strings of words so tightly wound that a cry for help couldn't escape.

Small men who shrink as the problems grow larger. Small men who are never right because they are also never wrong.

They descended on Ironton a week ago to see what was left behind when the flood passed through. Yes, it's bad they said. Yes, indeed, people are still out of their homes, still living in schools, what a terrible

63

thing.

All we need is some money to get started again, the residents said. All we can offer is vague promises, the small men said.

The problem, they said, is that you rely too much on the government to do everything for you. You need to be more self-reliant. Do more for yourself. It'll make you feel better.

You should be like me: I don't need anything, the small men said. I have my truck and big screen TV, my three-bedroom house in the suburbs and a lawn tractor the size of a Volkswagen to cut my lawn.

And if someone tries to take it away I have my licensed handgun and will use it to defend my castle.

Where did these small men come from?

We created them, fed them, and encouraged them with our undirected anger. Erected monuments to them because we needed an idol, something flashy to distract us while we sank into a collective stupor.

We became blinded by our own self-satisfaction, and as soon as we did, they had us.

Otherwise every middle class homeowner and job holder would be in the streets when teachers, librarians, clerks, street cleaners, public engineers, accountants, crossing guards and the occupiers of all those little jobs that hold our society together are attacked as greedy, tax-sucking bums.

But they are not attacking me because they're union, and I'm not.

I'm an insurance adjuster, a car salesperson; I sell pizzas, run a local hardware store, a bodega. I'm a carpenter, a plumber. I'm an independent business owner. You aren't talking about me. You're talking about them.

And everything they do makes my life harder. Or at least I think it does.

And while the little guys fight among themselves for scraps, the small minds who make the rules tilt them in their own favor again and again.

The millionaires being ripped off by the billionaires. And everyone lost their homes. Guns don't kill people; people kill people. Cigarettes don't cause cancer. I've smoked my whole life and I didn't develop cancer. Here, have one; take my pack. If a nuclear bomb is dropped, hide under your desk. Build a fort; build a shelter. Stock up on food and water. Buy an arsenal. Teach your kids to shoot. Build a fence. No one gets in. They'll never get me.

Hate sustains evil. But I'm not evil; I'm a magician, and you'll believe anything I say or do.

And so it was.

The magician's trick in the end is to get the audience to look where he wants us to look while he switches coins. And we're all suckers for a good magic trick."

***

Three days later, Gabriel Richman launched his re-election campaign.

He used the building that his grandfather erected as a department store as a backdrop where a few hundred supporters waved placards that said simply, "Gabe for Mayor."

The downtown streets had been cleared of storm debris, the power lines had been replaced and the only reminder of the flood was the thirty-foot high pile of dirt, rocks and concrete created when, to ease the flooding in the west side of town, an earth mover brought in by federal agencies dug a channel through the debris that had been deposited in the river.

The receding flood left a torn and wounded landscape, like a photograph of a familiar place with sections raggedly cut out. It was all tilted, leaning; wrong and smeared with a black stain that seemed permanent.

Dawson recognized many in the crowd. A few department heads, the public works crew, city hall secretaries and half the city council. The rest of the crowd seemed to have come from the junior high school meeting of the Young Democrats or the nursing home around the corner. They waved the signs on cue, cheered a little – a couple of times in the wrong place in Richman's speech – but generally acted like they wanted to be elsewhere. The high school band played cheerful marches and Richman's theme song that he had stolen from the Clintons, Fleetwood Mac's "Don't Stop." The crowd, except for the senior citizens, sang the chorus, and Richman's microphone picked up the off-key voice of an enthusiastic supporter.

One person who acted like she wanted to be there was Debbie Glance, Dawson noted. She grabbed Richman's arm several times, took his hand in hers and raised it above his head to the cheers of the audience. She cheered loudly, clapped with enthusiasm, and smiled broadly while the mayor's wife, Marlene Richman, stood nearby and did her best to support her husband. Dawson thought he could read something into the postures of the two women, but in fact, Marlene Richman never appeared with her husband at any public events other than at the start of a campaign. It was like Gabriel Richman wanted to remind the voters that he was still married. It was important, Dawson knew. Marlene Richman's family started the city's first bank. But today, more than most, Marlene Richman wanted to be somewhere else.

In truth, no one wanted to be there. Richman, always a snappy dresser for public events, played the part. The conservative blue pinstriped suit was appropriately serious, and along with the muted red-and-white tie, gave the impression of a serious man taking a serious step in life. Dawson had covered each of his previous campaign kick-offs and the charge in the air was sparkling, alive, the cheers thunderous and continuous. At those events, Richman, a man of average height and build, seemed larger than life, heroic, even, no doubt a leader, an unquestioned visionary. His voice boomed across the crowded streets, rose and fell in song, ripe with passion and soft with caring; the words of the speech rang like great thought and filled his voice with a richness it never had any other place or time. Listen to me, it said. I am. Follow me.

And they did, through four terms. Dawson realized that Richman never accomplished anything lasting in his previous terms, but had not done much damage, either. Dawson guessed he continued to win because he seemed to be a decent man, an earnest public servant, a trusted soul whose family had a long-time stake in the city. Maybe he was what the city needed all those years after the Howard Newtons of the world played three-card Monte with the city budget.

But now his face was tired, his voiced ragged. All the trappings of a big-time political event were present; all that was missing was something to cheer about.

"These have not been easy times," Richman shouted to the

crowd. "Our city had already been hit by an economic storm as the nation and world slid into a recession. Many of your friends and family lost jobs they had held for years. Many of your neighbors who worked for the city also lost their jobs."

A slight hiss slithered through the audience at the mention of the job cuts.

"I am not standing here today to say I am proud that we had to lay off workers," Richman said. "Many key services you expect your city to provide have suffered. Projects have been delayed. I am sad to say that your lives are not better. And then the skies opened up and washed away the hopes and dreams of many families. We mourn for those who died in that storm. Our hearts fill with compassion for those who were injured, whose homes were lost and whose businesses were damaged. But you are not alone. I have been in meetings with state and federal officials to remind them that this city – that you, it's citizens – need help, and they have promised to send help. They will send the funds and the workers and the ideas that Ironton needs to rise again."

The line drew a short but spirited cheer, mostly, it seemed, from the city staff.

"We will rise again. Just as we have done before." A slightly larger cheer.

"You all recognize the building behind us as the old Richman's Department Store. My grandfather built it, and for years it was the center of commerce and pride that this city felt. It is a symbol of what this city has been and is a reminder of what it can become again."

"But what many of you might not know is that this building was the spot where a great fire was stopped before it consumed the entire city. All the wooden buildings were burned to the ground. But what stood was this solid brick structure. They fought the blaze from the top of this building and beat back the flames. The city was saved right here. Right here, the city rose from flames and looked again into the future. Just as we will today. We will stare back at those flood waters and say, No, you will not take our spirit. You might wash away our homes, you might damage our businesses, but you will not take away our dreams."

The crowd began to murmur as Richman's voice rose. The fatigue was gone from his face; it seemed lighted from within.

"I know you all will remember this. Three years ago I said the city would build a new shopping center on the Old Iron Bog," Richman said, smiling. "Well, you all know how that turned out."

A chattering, tittering laugh rose from the audience. Yes, they knew.

"Got my head handed to me on that one," Richman said lightly, shaking his head. "But I learned from that experience. I asked questions of experts, and learned how to better prepare for such an undertaking. For one thing, I learned we need to put our plans on more solid ground."

The line drew sharp laughter, a smattering of applause, and even a groan or two from the city workers in the audience, who might have been the only ones who got the oblique reference to the Old Iron Bog.

"What I also learned is that we can never give up," Richman's voice began to rise and fill the open street. "We must always move forward. So I'm going to tell you today of our new plans. And, yes, my opponent will say it's just an empty promise, and some of you will say that you've heard it all before, but if we do not dream, how do we accomplish anything?"

A cheer rose quickly and fell as a few campaign signs waved above the crowd.

"In the next few months the city will begin legal action to take over the old stove-works complex. It was the place where all your fathers and grandfathers worked, once a proud symbol of the greatness of The City of Ironton," Richman shouted. "The company that owns it has abandoned it, and sadly it is now a symbol of the failure, yes, you heard me, the failure of this administration and others, to take on that challenge of wrestling so valuable a property from those who have no stake in the future of this city, no interest in your future. Well, no more.

"While our city has been torn, seemingly tossed into a big bowl, spun around and dumped out, while our streets have been ripped up, our parks ground into dirt, our schools and homes slammed by trees, and wind and rain, we will not stand by and despair."

Richman was screaming, his voice filled with fervor, his eyes wide and blazing as he pointed into the crowd. "Today is the day we begin to recover. Today is the day we gather our wills and step back into the light! Today we rise. Today we stand. Today we live again!"

Richman waved his fisted hand above his head and shook it at the cheering audience. They began to chant his name. "Rich-man! Richman! Rich-man!"

And Gabriel Richman smiled back and waved and bowed and pointed at individuals in the crowd and applauded them; he laughed and smiled and waved and acted as politically important at he could.

Richman turned to find his wife, but first turned left, when she was actually standing to his right. It was just a slight step forward, Dawson noticed, but Debbie Glance caught herself at the right moment and instead raised both hands over her head and cheered. Richman stood waving at the crowd with his arm stiffly around his smiling wife's waist.

As the Richmans left the podium, Dawson wondered where the mayor and Debbie Glance got together to screw. And how he could catch them.

****

Dawson was not the only person watching Richman and Debbie Glance. From the back of the crowd, Nagler leaned on a lamp post, drinking coffee and watching the pas de deux that pair performed. They turned at the right moment, stepped away in unison, smiled together and, it seemed, almost bowed together. He had run into her at city hall a few days after the woman had been found in the bog and he stopped her in the hallway at town hall to ask her how Gabe Richman was.

She stammered an answer. "He's fine, um, haven't seen him today. He's touring the damaged sections of the city with federal inspectors."

Because he had not paid her any attention, Nagler never noticed how thin Debbie Glance was. She was not a large woman by any means, but she seemed unnecessarily thin, sickly thin. Her eyes jittered around the room as they talked. She wore a white cotton sweater, which only struck Nagler as odd since the past few days had seen the return of hot, humid weather more typical of July than late summer.

"How'd those meetings with the feds go the other day?" Nagler asked.

Debbie Glance blushed. "What meetings?"

"The other day, when you were driving around with the mayor near the crime scene in the bog. Wasn't that you?"

"Oh, that day," She smiled and looked away. "Gabe was giving me a ride to work, and went by the bog, you know, just to see. My - my car broke down."

"Sure," Nagler said. "Nice of him."

"He's a nice man," she said as she walked away.

"Know what, got a question, maybe you know." Nagler said. "All the police records that were in the basement storage that got moved when the storm hit, where'd they go?"

"Newark. Temporary storage. Why?"

"Something for an old case. It'll keep. Thanks."

That last question just jumped into his head. Something was going on between those two, he thought. What might not be as important was why.

Before him, the election crowd had thinned out and he turned to leave.

"You know it's a joke, don't you, Frank?"

Nagler turned to see the bloated, red face and to smell the whiskied breath of Bartholomew Harrington, Ironton's favorite pro-bono attorney. He had been someone, as they say, back in the day. Fresh out of law school, Harrington challenged the state's housing and development rules, taking a couple of cases to the state's Supreme Court. He took on cases for homeless families, shop keepers being pressured by national chains to sell out cheap, challenged developers trying to flatten blocks of homes for condos and won a reputation for leveling the playing field for the dispossessed.

It didn't hurt that he was tall, handsome and had an actor's speaking voice and timing. Nagler had seen him in Ironton's city court turning the simplest eviction case into high drama, swooping around the courtroom, displaying evidence with a flourish, but with enough restraint that no judge ever stopped him, and no prosecutor accused him of grandstanding, even though he was.

Simply, he cared. More than once he had called Nagler or Dawson seeking a favor for a client who had come to him with a problem that was not fit for court, and more than once Nagler had made a few calls.

Then it all changed for Harrington. Nagler had lost track of him, thinking that maybe he had just moved on, left Ironton for a bigger stage. But now he was back. He was heavier, drunker, less a showman than a shadow.

Mostly now, Harrington filed endless requests for public documents and gave rambling speeches at city council meetings that left those in attendance looking away or shaking their heads in embarrassment. A few times, Nagler asked around to see if anyone knew what had happened to Harrington, but no one was willing to venture an opinion, maybe out of kindness, such was Harrington's general appearance. Maybe the lights just went out and Bart Harrington was now playing the role of Ironton's crazy uncle, but as Nagler turned to stare into the man's face, the eyes he saw were not those of a crazy man, but were filled with anger and passion.

"Hi, Bart," Nagler said.

The man was wearing the same herringbone tweed jacket with the brown elbow patches Nagler last saw him in. His wild gray hair poked out of the side of his Yankees cap like weeds. Under his arm was a brown folder held together by a thick rubber band.

"This whole thing is a joke," Harrington repeated. "Gabe Richman hasn't had an original idea since he married into money, and I'm not even sure that was his idea."

Nagler shrugged. "It's an election year. They say a lot of things."

"Not Richman," Harrington said, the words biting the air. "I've looked at the paper trail for the stove-works. It's been sold and resold, packaged and repackaged thirty-five times in fifty years. The owner is a ghost company and the documents of sale are a series of dead-ends, switchbacks and circles because no one wants anyone to know anything about the site. It's not a surprise that the city hasn't collected taxes on the buildings in decades or that no one has tried to sort it all out. Richman will never do it. Someone is telling him what to say." Harrington looked over his shoulder, like a spy. "Someone is pulling his strings, Frank, and when they stop, something is going to change. Something disastrous will happen. I can feel it."

"Come on, Bart." Nagler felt suddenly weary. There was enough to worry about without some new Bart Harrington conspiracy to consider.

"Look around, Frank. The city's a mess. Look at the faces of the people. They're tired. They're angry. Why hasn't something changed in such a long time? Because the powerful don't want it to change. Some-

71

thing changes and they start to lose control. Something changes and they lose their payday. But something is going to happen and all that festering rage will pop like a boil. Soon. It'll happen soon. Someone will make it happen, you'll see." Harrington's face was clenched, his eyes narrow and darting about. He looked like he was out of his fucking mind. Harrington turned away, and then turned back. "I have some information for you, some files I've found. I'll get them to you."

"What...?" *Everyone has files for me. Jesus. What am I, a library?*

Harrington reached over with both hands and grasped Nagler's right hand and shook it.

"Be well, my friend," Harrington said. "Don't get caught on the wrong side of the mess." Then he left, stepped around the corner heading to the train station. Nagler took a couple of steps toward the corner but Harrington had vanished, slipped into the street like wraith. Nagler glanced in a couple of directions to see if he could discern Harrington's gray hair streaming from under the blue cap that would be bouncing above the heads of any others along that sidewalk, but saw nothing.

What the hell was that, Nagler wondered.

CHAPTER 7

Nagler thought Ironton finally exhaled.

The sun was shining, the emergency shelters finally closed and the power had been restored. Some of the federal relief money had arrived and homes were being repaired, a few more businesses opened and the city patched streets, hauled debris to the old landfill where it was being prepared for disposal. Nagler stopped to watch the high school football team practice. The cheers and the smashing grunts echoed around the field, as the coaches' piercing whistles stopped the action. The team's first home game was in a few days. It was the kind of thing, he knew, that would offer cheer and community and spirit and take everyone's mind off the recent disasters. The game had been delayed because the field had been flooded, but the local branch of a national hardware chain donated the materials and the labor and the field was repaired.

Still, he thought, it was too quiet. Life on mute: No one was yelling at kids on bikes racing between walkers to get off the sidewalk, arguing over the Giants or Jets at Barry's, telling the cops on the beat about the dumbass out-of-state driver who made that U-turn on Blackwell; complaining about the trash men leaving their cans in the middle of the street; no one slapping down the newspaper, saying, "Why don't they just take all my money?" No one laughing. No one crying. It felt like those dark days after the winter solstice; the days are getting longer, the sunlight lingering extra minutes each day, but no one noticed until that day in late January when the sun seemed to be hanging in the sky later than normal and they looked at their watches and smiled. That was the day Ironton was awaiting, Nagler thought, that day of redemption.

But mostly Nagler was at the Old Iron Bog, walking the narrow sandy paths looking for something that made sense. The boat searches had been reduced to one a week, working a grid in one last effort, even though they had produced no real evidence.

How could this be staged so well?

He stood again in the open clearing where the body had been found, looked at the remembered angles of the vehicles, the flattened grass, now growing tall. *Why here?*

Whoever had dumped the body knew the city's attention was diverted by the storm, but it was just their bad luck – and our good luck - that those kids had been out there screwing. Most puzzling was the lack of any new report of a missing woman. Did that make her a prostitute or someone who entered the country illegally? He contacted the groups that track missing and exploited children, but the medical examiner had said quite clearly she was not a child, but was mostly likely in her early twenties, although she could have been missing for years. Even the hand that had been recovered proved less than illuminating. Mulligan had said he could not be certain it was the same woman. First, the bone cuts did not match as well as he'd hoped or needed for a positive identification, and because the hand had been submerged in water for whatever time it was, other tests had proven inconclusive.

Mulligan explained the cuts that removed the hands of the woman in the bog were smooth and most likely done with a sharp instrument like a saw or large cutting instrument, while the cuts on the other hand were cruder, leaving a more ragged cut that also showed bone chips, suggesting a smaller, knife-like instrument that required several attempts to remove the hand. Further, he said, the flesh on the single hand indicted a recent removal, otherwise it would have only been bone, the flesh degrading as it sat in the water. But removal of a person's hand was not by itself a fatal wound, Mulligan said.

What are you hiding, you old, cold swamp, Nagler asked himself.

Finally the thought that had been rattling in the back of his mind for days, the one that had popped up the very first day as he maneuvered his car through the rain-filled streets, forced its way to the top of the list: We've been here before, seen these patterns and deaths.

Twenty years ago, in the first big case Nagler ever investigated, they found Charlie Adams, a sixteen-year-old, had raped and murdered nine women, disposing of their bodies in old buildings, the railroad depot downtown, in the river and the Old Iron Bog. His victims ranged from two women in their seventies and eighties, to four in their thirties and three in their late teens or early twenties. He removed the eyes from the older women, disemboweled the younger ones and removed hands from the others.

And he didn't care, Nagler knew. At his hearing when he admitted all the crimes, Charlie Adams's voice was ice, worse than one of those computer-generated sounds that greeted him at the city parking garage, his vacant stare, a taunting, chilling mask devoid of humanity in a way that said, I win. The assurance with which he described the acts elicited gasps and tears from the victims' families.

But Charlie Adams hadn't killed this woman - he couldn't have. He was still in state prison and would be for at least another decade. He had been sentenced to life in prison, but the law at the time called for the possibility of parole after thirty years. Nagler had testified at a few motion hearings regarding Adams's case, as his lawyers found creative ways to get it back before a judge, a way maybe to get him out of jail on some technicality.

Just to be sure, Nagler had called the prison to see if Adams was still there, and he was.

Once jailed, Adams had never spoken about his crimes, nor granted any interviews to journalists, so the History Channel never produced a show on him.

That was the other thing that Nagler didn't want to think about: That somehow there was a Charlie Adams copycat, and they had just discovered the first victim. Nagler thought that was far fetched. Even the local press stopped following the case after Adams went to prison. A couple of stories appeared, but no one ten years later wrote a "Where is he now?" feature and no one did a jail house interview.

Guess they didn't want to stir the monster in his cave.

A chill spidered up his back. He hadn't thought about Charlie Adams in years, and now that he had, all the gut churning returned. All those nights. All those nights, the stakeouts, the hours standing on bridges, shining flash lights into dark buildings, the dead uncertainty as if the fear and suspicion of the city had cast itself into a shadow in the dark, a branch shifting at the edge of a light on a dark alley; a crack, a step, grinding sand.

The other detective assigned to the Adams case was Chris Foley. Nagler recalled that was one case where Foley's one-two-three method of investigation paid off. At a time before computers, Foley maintained immaculate records of the movements of the victims in relation to Adams' whereabouts and even produced a map that was used in the trial to show how Adams stalked his victims and ambushed them. His exhaustive inventory of the various scenes and apartments provided key evidence used to convict the young killer.

But it didn't have anything to do with Adam's capture. Nagler caught Adams disposing of some of the clothing belonging to his last victim. It was at the far end of the rail yard, where the river flows through a steep-sided gully, deepens, and then takes a sharp turn as the water slams into a wall of solid rock. The action sets up a swirling eddy that slows the river's flow before it again drops down a rock cliff. In the autumn, when the river was at its lowest level, the smell of the rotting vegetation earned the stretch of the river the name Smelly Flats. The only access to the spot was along an old canal trail used mostly by junkies, lovers and the homeless.

Even then Nagler knew it was as much luck as skill that caught Adams. He and Foley had guessed that even though the six victims had been found in different locations, the last three had been dumped in more easily accessible, although not obvious, locations. The first three had been left in abandoned buildings and when found, their bodies had decayed considerably. The next one was found along the rail road tracks and was discovered quickly, perhaps too quickly, because the fourth woman was dumped deep inside the old bog and was only discovered by a junk dealer illegally dumping auto parts.

Nagler guessed the killer was not getting enough publicity from the discovery of the bodies, so changed locations to get more front page news.

The next couple of bodies were found floating in the river, one near city hall, and the outcry was loud and harsh. The police chief yelled at Nagler and Foley for an hour about how they had better catch the killer soon, and even the mayor at the time, old Howie Newton, held a press conference declaring it was unacceptable that so brazen a killer would sully the reputation of the great City of Ironton by leaving a dead body near city hall. Nagler recalled that Jimmy Dawson cracked that he didn't understand Newton's complaint: The mayor had made it a habit to bury as many people at city hall as possible.

It seemed that the publicity splash of that killing forced Adams to retreat. His next victim was again dumped in the old bog alongside an entry road much like the recent victim. Nagler remembered thinking at the time that the killer was trying to find a middle ground to his locations and it must have occurred to him that anything that looked like a pattern would eventually lead to his capture. So the next body was found near the stove-works in the west side of Ironton.

Foley argued that the next body would be found in an old building because the waterways had become too visible and with the increased police patrols, it was going to be more difficult to move around without capture. Nagler, instead, argued that the killer was playing a game and each time he placed a body in an obvious spot, it fed his ego and fueled the notion that he was beating the cops at their own game.

Two days later, Nagler was proven right: A new body, this time, and for the first time, a naked body, was found near city hall, and that night, with his ears still ringing from another of the chief's tongue lashings, Nagler was standing on the bridge over the rail yard when he saw a boy carrying a bag walking along the old canal path. When Nagler caught up to Charlie Adams, he was burying a bag of clothes in the Smelly Flats.

Nagler was hailed as a cop hero and was forced to spend as much time trying to escape that moniker as he did trying to work the next case. He made a point to bring up Chris Foley's part in the police work, but even Foley acknowledged that no one cared about his role. "It was your hunch, Frank. That's what caught him. I was glad to help," Foley told him.

While the press stopped following the story, Ironton's citizens, relieved of the nightly terror that the vicious killer was still on the loose, hailed Nagler. They asked him to speak at their churches and schools, to accept awards of heroism and bought him cups of coffee at Barry's. They hailed him on the street as they drove by: "Hey, Frank. Great job!"

He would wave back, or shake hands if he was stopped on a sidewalk or in a store.

None of the well-wishers noticed his sadness, or his dull, worried eyes. They never saw them, so filled with their own joy and relief; had they asked, Nagler would have said it was nothing, fatigue.

There had been no crimes like it in Ironton's history. As part of the investigation Nagler read pages of old newspaper stories and talked to some retired police officers who still lived in town, and none had seen anything like Charlie Adams' killing spree. There had been murders. Drug deals or robberies gone bad, domestic fights that became armed attacks, gang initiations.

But he found nothing that had the ability to grab the city by its throat and cut off its collective breath.

Ironton, like most of the canal and iron towns of the county at one time, was a boiling cauldron of ethnic pride, drunken rage and lawlessness. Neighborhoods, more like encampments of Cornish, Irish, Swedes, Germans, Italians, Slavs and others, made up the towns. After days of hard work in the iron mines or at the forges and foundries, they met at the bars, and drunk and filled with homeland pride and a poor workingman's rage, it was never surprising that often the next day a body was floating in the canal. Nagler's grandfather told him the stories, he recalled. The work underground in damp, sweating mines. The rhythm of iron pounding on iron as they carved out holes in the sweating walls for blasting caps and dynamite; nervous fingers. Then the coolness of fresh air as they again broke the surface, once more alive. "We grabbed civilization out of those rocks with our fists," his grandfather said.

And so they had. Nagler thought. Old Hurd's forge, and soon Oram's and a dozen mines. Canal boats tied for the night at the basin, warehouses of goods flowing east to west, mules in rope pens, braying; campfires, and roasting meat; soft songs floating on the smoky air; then soon the towns grew along the river, brick streets and iron rails as trolleys rolled through to Lake Hopatcong where the swells built their summer homes. And shops and ice cream parlors and vaudeville at the Baker Theater, the iron money rolling in, transforming the village, while the rich men built their mansions and the poor men huddled in cold water flats. Then George Richman built his fabulous department store and sold the beautiful women fashions from Paris, and handmade silk suits for their men and marveled their children with mechanical toys and sparkly things that had just arrived by rail from New York City; the department store that filled the streets with a squadron of white horse-drawn delivery vans and draped starry red-white-and-blue banners from its three floors of windows, the place for that first suit for the young man, Maria's white confirmation dress, a pair of hard-soled shoes and the wedding gown with the long train for the family's first daughter.

Nagler, like anyone who grew up in Ironton, knew about George Richman. He was credited with transforming Ironton from a grimy, one mill town to one of the largest manufacturing centers in North Jersey. He owned iron mines and iron mills and the railroads that connected the two. But more, he attracted companies that could turn his iron into other products and soon the city was home to a dozen mills making kitchen pots and farm implements, stoves, then shoes and coats and ladies' stockings; everything the growing world could want.

George Richman was also the politician to marshal Ironton's city charter through the Legislature, creating the modern city from a section of a neighboring township.

There was nothing that George Richman couldn't do, it seemed. *Except predict the future.*

The mines played out and steel replaced iron as the building material of choice, and soon superhighways, shopping malls and subdivisions buried the old mines; weeds grew up through the rusted rails, the canal was filled in and paved over, its existence noted by a brass plaque screwed to the back side of an old warehouse. The fall, oh great Troy, is deep and far.

Nagler never knew how sorry he was supposed to feel for Gabriel Richman. His grandfather had left a legacy that would never be repeated; never again in New Jersey would there be so much virgin territory to claim, so much to invent, create, or destroy and exploit. Once there was a place that paced the world, a place center to the commerce and culture, a place that thrived and grew and redoubled again and again, a place so special strangers smiled when they heard its name, businessmen spoke in awe of its industrial might, asked how could it be done, and wondered how they might get their share; a place of laughter and dreams.

That was not the place where Gabriel Richman dwelled. He was stuck alongside the road with the wooden wagon with the broken wheel, trapped in the place of hollow eyes. He didn't have the smoky, noisy mill upon which to build his city's dream, he only had its memory; he didn't have the great shopping center with its transportation hub to boast about, he only had the faded billboard. He didn't have a grand department store with horse-drawn delivery vans and starry banners, he only had the Old Iron Bog and it sucked below its dark surface all his dreams and visions, only to leave him standing on its muddy, overgrown road haggard and lost, staring into its dark waters asking why.

Nagler laughed. And here I am, asking the same swamp the same question.

Where have you buried your dead?

CHAPTER 8

"Did they really think they'd get away with it?" Dawson asked.

He and Nagler were crammed into the last table in the far back corner of Barry's, their usual window seat taken over by an elderly woman and her eight shopping bags. The entire front of the diner had, in fact, been taken over by her shopping bags as she pulled out items from one bag, folded them carefully on the table and placed them in another bag. Everyone in the place was watching her, even the kitchen help. Out came a white dress for a young girl, then matching shoes, as the woman smoothed the fabric, or rubbed out some imaginary spot, then a pair of blue pants for a boy, which she held aloft with one hand as she ruffled through two other bags for a shirt. Then she shuffled clothes from one bag to another, pausing long enough to write a few words on the side of the bag, in between sips of tea. She finally stood to leave, wrapping the handles of four bags in one hand, then putting them down, shuffling in one apparently lighter bag, then with her free hand, grasping one by one the handles of the other bags and with her long-handled purse draped over one shoulder stepped sideways out of the restaurant smiling; in the street she paused and the diners watched her head bob up and down a few times as she apparently adjusted her unruly burden before she walked away.

Nagler put down his coffee cup. "Get away with what?"

"You know, the Attorney General Sixty, the elected officials they caught in that bribery sting." Dawson held up the page of the paper with a list of those officials who had accepted a sentence, about half of the sixty. Some got thirty days in jail, some half-a-year. All were fined and made to agree they would never seek public office again. Some of them were just working guys and probably lost their jobs, Dawson guessed, but a lot of them were lawyers and accountants, which meant, conviction or not, they'd never be out of work.

"Think about it. You're sitting at your mayor desk one day, all important and such, trying to figure out how to get your brother a job at the road department, and in walks this stranger who offers you ten grand to throw a planning board vote his way. And you say yes! You don't even question who the guy is because he's got a reference from one of the councilmen, who also took the cash, and he got a reference from some local banker. Don't you ever wonder about that?"

Nagler smiled briefly. "It was good police work. The bribes were the right size – not too small to be an insult, but not so large that it couldn't be hidden successfully – marked bills, recordings of all the sessions. Just a good job."

"What would you do if you had a case like that?"

"Follow procedure," Nagler said.

Dawson paused a moment. "Yeah, you would." He glanced over at the empty window seat, now vacated by the shopper and her eight shopping bags. "Why does this type of thing seem to happen in Jersey more than any other place? Every election, every public contract, seems to have a money trail attached to it. You hear about Marbury, that town in South Jersey? The officials had a scam that went back a quarter century. Every mayor, council member, school board member and administrator bought into it as they extracted bribes and paybacks from contractors. Seems it was a rite of passage: You only got to run for office if you agreed to continue the game. And they stand there and smile at you so sweetly. But there's nothing behind their eyes, just the blandness of evil."

"How'd they get caught?"

"Someone talked. Maybe they didn't like their cut."

"Why is that so different from politics as usual? These guys get elected passing cash from one campaign account to the other. Vote for my bill and I'll make a contribution. Don't vote for my bill and you'll never get a dime and I'll run someone against you in the primary."

Dawson laughed. "You sound almost as cynical as I am. But what do you expect from a state whose best known public figure is a fictional mobster and the state motto is 'Fugetaboutit!' Where you can be elected mayor, county director and a Legislator and keep your day job at the local school, a place you can get elected in some of these small towns by just getting your entire neighborhood to vote for you. A state where every wide spot in the road and railroad warehouse became a town where the local government has so many departments it takes four votes by different committees to plant a tree. A state that has more school districts than towns and more ways for the politicians to steal your pocket watch than anyone else can imagine."

"But what's it say when we idolize a guy like Tony Soprano who thrives on murder, extortion and drug dealing?" Nagler asked.

"Maybe we like his initiative and go-get-'em attitude." Dawson tried to lighten the mood.

"Yeah, crap," Nagler said. "Then why did we stand and watch the banks plunder neighborhoods with crappy loans, or invest in poverty and death when they red-lined black areas of cities, or applaud so loudly as smart action the federal budget cuts to food and housing programs even while the politicians who cast those votes made sure the money for their family farm was approved. We have institutionalized greed and self-interest. Problem for me, Jimmy? I have to work for whichever of these people get elected. You don't. It's gotta stop somewhere."

Wow, Dawson thought. "What's up, Frank? You're, I don't know, a little moody?"

Nagler picked up his coffee cup, swirled the last of the cold liquid around in the bottom and placed the cup on the table again.

Nagler smiled. "Yeah. Too much unsettled stuff. Can't figure out why we have so little on that dead girl in the bog. We've chased national leads, statewide information, everything local. I guess I don't want to be that old New York detective who is still trying to solve the Lion Lady crime. Remember that one? They found the body of a young woman out west off the Interstate. The guy took the files when he retired and spent a decade walking the scene, tracking down witnesses and revisiting every detail of her death to no avail. As much as I admire his dedication, I don't want to be him. I mean, no one has their head cut off for no reason. Either she knew something or someone, or we're tracking a butcher, but if that's the case, why has there been only one death?"

"You sure there's only one?"

"We thought of that. Nothing matches locally. Illinois and Florida are investigating a couple of mutilation deaths, but they aren't connected, and the detectives in each state I spoke with are pretty certain they were close to an arrest."

Nagler paused and glanced out the window into the glare of sunlight reflecting off the bank window across the street; the window shimmered like fire.

"I was thinking the other day that it feels like someone is deliberately blocking access to the information we need. But that gets tricky because if it is true and it is internal and you mention that suspicion to the wrong person, word gets back and more information disappears."

"Isn't that how the power structure protects itself?" Dawson asked.

"Yeah. It's a question of who has the most to lose," Nagler said.

Dawson stood up to leave. "Just want you to know, Frank, that I didn't do it."

Nagler laughed. "You sure? Anyone vouch for your where-abouts? I bet if I asked your editor, he'd sell you out in a minute."

"Yeah? Well don't ask. I'll see you."

When Nagler returned, the lobby at city hall was lined with tired home and business owners waiting to see the federal officials and the tax assessor. An agreement had been reached to offer buyouts to the owners of the two-hundred homes deemed uninhabitable. Some were just gone, others lost porches to water, roofs to trees or were twisted off the foundations. Others were just in the way, built years ago in the river's flood plain and rebuilt and repaired numerous times.

"Hey, Frank. Frank Nagler."

Nagler turned to the voice and saw Mattie Washington in line holding a red folder overstuffed with papers.

"Hello, Mattie," he said and she kissed his cheek. Mattie was a retired police dispatcher. For years her voice had flowed out of the radio in Nagler's car, sending him out, using a self-designed code, to check on that "Little hoochie-coo down on Broad Street," a local hooker, or the "baby hoodies" on Main, a teen-ager gang, or the "sew-ers" behind the old mill, the junkies cooking up their works so they could inject the drugs with rusted needles.

"Gonna take a buyout, Frank," Mattie Washington said.

"Hard choice, huh, Mattie?"

"Not as hard as I thought," she said. "It's just a house, an address on a street. I lived in a dozen places before we settled there. I don't need to be memorializing my first apartment, know what I mean? I got my family and my friends, that's what matters. Besides, we got pulled out by the fire department and spent a week at the high school. Ain't much left of it. The house was half in the neighbor's yard. Always wanted to retire to Florida, Frank. Have a house on the beach and have the grand-babies visit during school break. Just a little place with a patio and some shade and a view of the great wide ocean where I could just sit and ponder life and drink iced tea and not have to listen to my doctor complain about my weight." Mattie Washington laughed. "That woulda been something. But now I'm staying here. The settlement ain't bad. But you can be sure I'm gettin' a place on high ground."

Nagler shared her smile. "You can't leave here, Mattie. Where I am going to get all those hot tips?"

She shook her head. "You see my boys out there, you tell them if they get in trouble they can just go turn themselves in. I don't want no part of that mess."

"I'll do that Mattie."

He reached over and embraced her. "You're a good woman, Mattie. If you need anything, call me."

"Since you mentioned it. There has been a lot of traffic on that old canal trail leading out of the railroad yard."

"Down in the Flats?"

"Yeah. We think it might be gangs that have been raiding the busted up houses. Copper's worth a lot these days. Maybe they're stashing it down there."

"I'll check, Mattie. You take care."

****

When Nagler got to Dan Yang's office the wall was filled with charts.

"You're killing me, Dan," he said. "More charts?"

"Sorry, Frank. We started clearing some of the newer computers and found some of the best information yet." Yang said. "We were able to identify some departments and their actual account numbers, and even better, some funds that were attached to spending bills passed by the city council. We've got a clear path for about twenty questionable transactions."

Yang said he would be able to find the originating entries, but they were having some problems recreating files because some of the software on some of the older computers had been corrupted and no one had yet found the time to drive to Newark and paw through box after box of paper files.

Still, Nagler was impressed. "That's great, Dan. You're sure?"

Yang explained the information on several lists. There were or-dinance numbers that approved spending, account numbers where funds were deposited and others that showed where similar amounts were moved from account to account.

"You know how I said that this could be normal accounting at the end of the year?" Yang asked.

Nagler nodded. "I remember something like that."

"Well forget it. The timing's all wrong. I checked when these ordinances were approved and the votes were taken in March, June, August, not after November when the budget-balancing would occur."

"So this shows that city funds approved for one thing were pos-sibly being used for something else?" Nagler asked. "Is that the big crime? Doesn't seem like it."

"I think it's the tip of the iceberg, Frank. This is fairly sophis-ticated. None of this information was stored on one single computer. There were connected files that showed one path for these funds that might have been the path the city council intended, and another set of ghost, look-a-like files and dummy references, essentially a second set of books that showed how the funds were hidden. What we need it to find is an end-use, a public works project like a road repair that was funded but not completed, or some equipment that was supposed to be purchased that never was bought, something like that. That would pro-vide the proof of fraud."

"Show me how it worked and then give me your best list and I'll start checking them out," Nagler said.

"Here's one. The city council approved about three grand for a recreation project. Instead of being allocated directly to the rec depart-ment, the funds are in a planning board account. Then, here, they were moved to public works, and then to community development. A lot of money was shifted through the community development account, which was odd, because the state was supposed to approve all the spending from that department. Remember that number on those letters and in-voices that appeared so many times? 9235? It's the account number for the community development office."

Yang, searching the charts for more information, didn't notice that Nagler's face was flushed and that the detective had placed one hand on a desk for support.

"Wait a minute," Yang said. "Wasn't that the office run by that woman who left suddenly, Laura, Lorraine…?"

"Lauren Fox," Nagler said.

"Weren't you and she…?"

"Yeah."

After Yang left, Nagler started at the piles of paper and the charts and wondered. "What did you have to lose, kid?"

CHAPTER 9

Ironton was a city of alleys.

The big highways passed to the north and south of the city and the main local streets followed the river and the hilly terrain.

What connected all of them were the alleys, warrens of dead ends, a network of narrow potholed passageways that carried the gossip of the neighborhoods from house to house, block to block, until it passed from the Italians to the Irish, through the Germans and back, so changed, so lost in translation it had become new again.

The alleys were where the household commerce took place. While the front porches stood guard over the main street, doors locked, shades drawn like deserted rooms in some dead train station, the back doors squeaked and slammed a hundred times a day as the family's kids ran off to school, off to baseball practice, or off to Cheryl Johnson's house, where she promised Bobby DeLuca she'd give him a blow-job.

The alleys were where the garbage trucks waddled down the street, barely clearing the fender of George Stein's new F-150, and where the snow plows, not so careful, nudged a few garbage cans into the light poles as they dug out a path.

Where the homeowner marked off their proud territory with fences. Some were slatted, a few were tall barricades, with a double-latched gate; a few others were new, white picket fences, the signs of progress and change.

But mostly the fences were rusted or green plastic-covered chain link. They drooped in the middle section where the boys had used the fence as a brace as they took the shortcut, or leaned at the corner post near the driveway where Nancy Jackson backed her father's Impala into one or two while leaving for school.

It was one in the morning. Nagler was walking the alleys where he grew up, a section of Ironton wedged between the stove-works complex, where all their fathers worked, and the section of the city where old Bowlby, a former mayor, began to think like a governor of a Southern state and declared he was seceding from Ironton.

He didn't, of course. While his neighbors were unhappy the new waterline skirted their five square blocks of rebel territory, they knew they would never get city water if they weren't part of the city. Still, that minor dust-up a hundred years ago had marked the neighborhood as rebel territory, some untamed section of streets, inhabited by those willing to stand up to authority, even if it wasn't exactly the way it happened. But all good rebellions were just a notion. And the notion stuck. When asked where he grew up, Nagler would say with pride, "Bowlbyville," not Ironton.

Nagler had been out on the streets a lot lately, wandering darkened alleys of childhood memory, past the still darkened, flood-damaged homes, leaning in the half-light against the granite face of the train station before dawn, waving off the commuter train that slowed as it rolled east, standing on the Sussex Street bridge just watching the river flow, as if the rails, the streets and the water held clues that could calm the cauldron of thoughts, questions and feeling that boiled in his head.

He had done the same thing as a rookie detective. The quiet streets allowed the dull stares of suspects, the wailing of wives, the curses of husbands, fathers and cops to settle out until he was able to clearly see the details, the reasons and the crimes.

9235.

The number was burned into Nagler's memory. Lauren Fox's account. What were you doing, kid? He asked Yang to dig out as much detail on that account as he could find on those computers. The mandate for that department was quite broad, Nagler recalled, and could have included recreation equipment, roads, furniture and building supplies. She seemed to be handling eight projects at once.

He stopped and looked into the dark street ahead. Isn't that just wishful thinking? Just because she was beautiful and you were falling in love with her doesn't mean she wasn't capable of stealing, he chided himself. Leaving the way she did was bad enough. How many hidden reasons were there, he asked himself.

And Dawson wonders why I'm moody?

That wasn't what had Nagler walking all night – that was just a case, a complicated one to be sure, now even more complicated, but just a case. At some point he would have to tell the chief he had a conflict of interest, Nagler knew. But not yet.

He had the sense that he was pushing back against an invisible tide, standing alone while some unseen darkness crept just out of sight, around a corner, down an alley. It wasn't just the storm or the dead girl in the bog, or the lying politicians and shifty businessmen – They existed in some form or other all the time. It was like we stepped off a ledge, he said to himself. All the things that bound us together have been torn apart. Instead of smiling at our neighbor, we scowl; instead of helping, we complain, we blame, we hate. Then we close a door, step again into the darkness, letting the silence fester.

Then there was Bart Harrington, wandering the street like Jeremiah, pointing to the sky with a crooked finger, warning of damnation.

Nagler wondered what it was about the storm that brought Ironton's old characters out to the streets again. First there was Harrington, who no one had seen for six or seven months. The storm rearranges the city and there he is.

And then there was Howard Newton, the old mayor. He rarely left the Trenton Street Club anymore. Some of it had to be age. Newton was never seen without a cane, dark shades and that white Panama. He walked slowly, pausing between steps at times like he needed to catch his breath. Nagler had read all Dawson's stories about Newton: The slick politician just skating by, one step ahead of the investigators, apparently cheating, but not cheating enough to get caught. Nagler guessed that if Howie Newton was out and about, something was up. And then, there he was, standing in front of a battered downtown store surrounded by a collection of eight hundred dollar suits, all waving documents, the white Panama bobbing up and down as he spoke and pointed with his cane.

Newton had some sort of a property investment company. Someone was going to buy a lot of damaged property for bargain prices, and maybe Newton was that person. Let it go, Nagler walked on in the other direction. Then again, Howie Newton never really changed. Maybe the city never changed.

And worming his way through all the mess was Charlie Adams, the city's evil spawn. Nagler woke the other night in a cold sweat as the image of Charlie Adams' round, hairless face emerged in a dream: so satisfied with himself, eyes half-closed, challenging. Come inside if you dare.

But Nagler had dared. He had ventured inside that tangled mind to find cause and motive and means, to sort through the complications, to get one step ahead so that when Adams emerged one last time, Nagler

90

was there. But Nagler didn't want to go back there. It all got too close to tearing up the rights and wrongs, ripping up the rationales that held us all together. Maybe, that was why the current city atmosphere is unnerving and yet feels so familiar. When it was easier to express rage and hate than it is to accept reason, when it was easier to divide than gather, easier to kill than it was to be safe, then the ground has begun to tremble. When Charlie Adams walked Ironton's streets the city huddled behind locked doors clutching guns. We are there again, Nagler thought.

****

His old house was on Lincoln. It was a nasty, hilly, narrow alley that more often than not was blocked by the wreck of a stolen car left there by the Hansen twins, the neighborhood's thugs. That was their signature: Any car they stole was driven through the railroad yard downtown and then through as many crappy back alleys as possible to reduce the vehicle to scrap. When it stopped running, they left it.

No one said they were the brightest crooks. Nagler smiled. He was the cop who caught them on their last spree when the old Jeep they tried to bury in the Old Iron Bog got wedged above its axles in mud. Just because it has four-wheel-drive, he remembered thinking at the time, it's still not a tank.

Lincoln ran down to Mullen, then over to White, then to the highway. It was always dark, even in the daytime as tall maples overarched the homes, blocking out the sun. At night two streetlights a block apart cast more suspicion than light.

There were no sidewalks when he lived there, just two narrow, worn-down pathways on either side of the street that carried the men of the neighborhood to the mill, clean from an overnight bath, blue denim shirt, hair slicked back under a wool cap; and then back home at night smelling of ash and coal, hair dusted with white powder, faces black with oily grime, the blister on the left heel a little more raw where the cardboard inserted to stiffen the sole had rubbed through the sock.

Each trip to and from the stove-works made the men five dollars richer. Five dollars closer to death.

Each day they molded doors, stove tops, stacks and panels for the Perfect Cooking Stove, a cast iron kitchen stove that was the star of many kitchens. During the wars they made small heaters designed to give foot soldiers some carry-along warmth.

This was Ironton at its peak. A dozen iron mills, foundries, cutting and stamping mills operated along the river and rail lines; in the hills to the north and west mines has been dug into the rich deposits of iron ore that had supplied George Washington with cannon balls, and then with better technology, had been tapped to unimaginable depths so that the hills contained a lattice work of mine shafts and tunnels that generated the wealth that propelled the county into the twentieth century.

That only mattered to young Frank Nagler when he watched his father leave for the mill each morning and return each night. As he got older, Nagler measured the state of his world against the condition of his father's nightly return from work as it transformed from the homecoming of the young, fit worker who carried his young son on his shoulders the last block to home while the boy breathed in the dust, ash and sweat of his father's labors, to the middle aged man who limped on a bad ankle as his son took up his lunch pail and sometimes had his father lean on him to make the walk easier.

Nagler, like his friends, watched the stove-works grind the life out of his father so that when it shut for good, the boys were relieved their fates had been changed.

Nagler stopped by the stove-works that night. It had been a mile long complex of thick walled brick buildings that lit up the night with forge fires and ever burning lights and drove away the silence with metallic screeches of metal wheels turning and grinding and the heavy slammings of boxcars, ore cars, cranes and iron parts.

Now it was a wreck of empty shells, the peaked roofs rotted to dust, the windows shattered by rocks and pistol shots, the bay doors of loading docks rippled with waterlogged paneling.

Feral cats kept the rat population down.

Lauren Fox wondered why Gabe Richman had not proposed to build his shopping center here. She said it was a project the state would have funded.

A neon street light a block away flickered to life, brightened and flashed, then darkened. The cycle was repeated about every minute. It made the alleys between the forty-foot walls even more sinister; wind crept through broken windows, water dripped.

It was late September so the homeless crew that lived under the railroad bridge in the summer would be settling into the main building where a long section of the roof was intact. They were mostly old vets, a handful of guys who fell hard for whiskey and drugs, people who lost their jobs and then their homes, or mental patients let loose when the state decided it no longer wanted to warehouse sick people.

There were always a few families. Dirty faced kids playing in the dust of the old mill as their mother sorted the black trash bag of clothes she picked up from the Salvation Army. Nagler called the county when a family arrived; they could not survive the winter outside. Why do we allow this, he asked himself more than once. Why is this accepted? Even at the end when Ironton's mills closed one by one, families weren't living under the bridge or inside the shell of an old factory. Someone offered help.

I guess we just don't care. The politicians don't care, the schools are under attack and the feds just arrested scores of public officials for stealing. The words were bitter in his mouth even before he said them.

"Welcome to America in the Twenty-First Century."

A camp fire cast grotesque shadows on the far corner wall as a dozen or so figures moved through the dark, a laugh breaking out of the low murmur like glass shattering in an echo chamber.

When his eyes adjusted to the darkness, Nagler saw several tents made from plastic tarps, a clothesline draped with pants and towels, ice chests and coolers, a make-shift fireplace made of old stones and strips of metal with a battered cylinder of aluminum as a chimney, and an assortment of lawn chairs, each occupied by a body marked by a moving red flare that brightened and faded as they took a drag.

When he got closer, and some of the homeless men perceived he was a cop, they froze.

"Hey," Nagler said. "It's me, Frank."

"Brother Nagler."

The voice emerged from the deepest corner of the site. It was Delvin Williams. "Del," Nagler acknowledged his old friend, who was walking stiffly out of the darkness. The men shook hands and exchanged a brief embrace.

"Been a while, Frank."

"Yeah. Too long, Del,"

They went to high school together. Del's family lived a couple blocks away and as boys Del and Frank were inseparable. When Del's father died in a mining accident, he dropped out of school to work and eventually became a porter on the Phoebe Snow, a luxury train that ran between New York and Chicago that always made a stop in Ironton.

Nagler would see him at the downtown station, sparkling in that white uniform with pants creases so sharp you could cut paper. Del was so proud of his job, and was so good at it that when the Phoebe Snow was taken out of service, the Lackawanna Railroad presented him with a silver medal.

But Del liked to drink and liked the needle and eventually all the bright lights faded into a blur. He'd been on the streets for maybe fifteen years, probably more, Nagler guessed. He avoided the social workers and cops, choosing to camp out under the bridge, and in winter finding a place in one of Ironton's empty buildings.

"So what brings you to our camp tonight, Frank?" Del asked.

"Just walking, Del." His voice was small in the cavernous shell of a building. "Was close enough so I thought I'd come by see how you're doing," Nagler said.

"Well, Frank, I'll tell you I'm the fucking King of England," Del Williams said with a smile. "Couldn't be finer." Then he laughed until he coughed, and then coughed until he nearly choked.

"You're not well, Del, are you?" Nagler asked.

"Doctor in that hospital van said it's probably lung cancer," Del Williams said, and waved his hand at the darkness. "Can't fix it, probably have six months. He told me he'd get me into the hospital, but I said no. I'd have to give up my luxury suite." Del laughed, but looked into the darkness of the building with hollow eyes. "Next time you come on by, Frank, you'd better poke me because as Mercutio said, I might be a grave man."

Nagler felt helpless. He knew there was no way to talk Del into a hospital stay.

"Can you handle the pain, Del?" he asked.

"Man was born into pain, my friend. This ain't nothin'."

Lung cancer. Add the malady to the weight Del Williams carried, maybe three hundred and fifty pounds. A memory of Del as a high school basketball player flickered across Nagler's mind. Thin as a rail. It was said he could slip sideways through a press and double-team like a shadow, a knowing grin on his face.

Now he was sitting wrapped in three sweaters reclining on a torn plastic lawn chair in a hobo's camp with a couple dozen other men and women either too oblivious of the outside or too afraid to go back, a glaze over his eyes, a body torn and huge, poisoned by choices he had made, forced down a chute that got more and more narrow until he convinced himself like the others had, that this was the way to live and they proudly, defiantly, dared the outsiders to lure them back. The chute became too small, the choices too narrow and the nod too good. It's easy to feel forgotten when you wander off alone.

The corner of the mill was silent; no one even shuffled. Outside, an early commuter train rattled by, long empty cars with lights that flashed through the open wall, wheels clattering on the rails, clack, clack, clack, till it swung that last turn into downtown, wheels squealing on the curved rail.

"Someone find my friend a chair," Del Williams said, and when it appeared Nagler sat next to his friend and caught up.

"So how's that fine lady of yours, Frank? How's Martha these days?" Del Williams asked. "Last time I saw her was maybe on one of those return trips from Chicago on the Phoebe Snow. I think I met you and Martha at the steakhouse and the three of us had a grand old time telling stories about the neighborhood. Remember that?"

Nagler forced a smile in the dark. There never was a meeting downtown, or drinks at the steakhouse. It was just Del and his memories jumbled up, flaring, fading, every place he had ever been, everything he had ever seen at the edge of his damaged mind like sunlight slipping away.

"You came to our wedding," Nagler said instead.

Del Williams laughed again. "I surely remember that, I surely do. That girl could daaaance. She was a marvelous girl, Frank. You tell her ol' Del was askin' for her."

"I certainly will, Del. Thanks for asking."

Nagler's looked quickly at the filthy ground, so Del would not see the pain that suddenly filled his eyes; he shifted in the chair so that the slumping of his shoulders was not obvious, so the echo of sorrow in his heart remained hidden.

He doesn't know she died. Nagler glanced at his friend leaning back in the chair, eyes closed in whatever state of grace he had found. *He doesn't need to know.*

An hour later, as Nagler stood to leave, Del Williams grabbed his arm.

"Saw your friend Mister Chris Foley out here the other day," he said. "He was walking around the place with some woman I think works at city hall. She was taking a lot of notes and they was pointing at the tracks, the bus garage and this old place and taking more notes."

"He say anything to you?" Nagler asked. *Foley?*

"Naw. I asked him what's up, because, man, this is our home, and he just said the owner filed another tax appeal and the city was going to fight it, somethin' like that. He gave me twenty bucks, though."

As he crossed Main back into the neighborhood, Nagler heard Jimmy Dawson's voice. He was telling a story about Howard Newton and some deal he had pulled off on the east side.

"The only thing that has lasting value," Dawson said, "is land. They aren't making any more of it."

****

The streets settled into a pre-dawn, holy quiet. A stillness so deep the sound of a car spinning its wheels in gravel three blocks away filtered through the dark streets; a quiet so dense the tapping of Nagler's shoes on the cement sidewalk sounded like a crack of steel against steel.

The house was a few blocks up and over. He knew the route so well he could walk it blindfolded: Out the back door on Lincoln, through the Harrigans' yard, down the narrow walkway that led to the stairs the city put in so people could get down the hill to stores on Washington. Then a jog up to Elm, through the grouchy lady's yard, which got easier after her stupid pit bull died, and there it was.

Martha Shannon's house. 14 Elm Street. White with blue trim, one center gable and a slick tin roof so steep it would kill you just to try to climb it. Her room was on the second floor on the right, with two windows, one front, one side, and pink curtains.

Frank Nagler sat behind her in second grade. She had the neatest handwriting, and long straight red hair that she held together with a silver barrette. When they walked home from school she filled the air with vivid stories of her day. They stopped and spoke with every-one on the streets: Old Mrs. Drake, whose husband died in the war and whose children never called; Mr. Adams, who was always washing his car; Bobbi Jackson, who had two kids by the time she was twenty and worked nights cleaning offices, but waited at the corner of Main Street for the little one to get off the school bus and run into her arms, jacket flapping, papers slipping from his tiny hand so he had to stop and pick them up and dropped his lunch box, and just before he was going to cry she scooped him into her arms and they laughed all the way home.

The first time Nagler held Martha Shannon's hand was in the third grade. It was the softest thing he had ever touched and he knew he would hold it forever.

The early sun glinted off the topmost window of the old Shan-non home. It had been vacant for years when the last owner lost it to the bank. The fence leaned to the street, a porch railing rested on the stairs and the glass in a couple windows in the upper floor surrounded the perfectly round entry hole of a small rock.

Her parents moved away years ago. They were probably dead now.

More than once on one of these night prowls he took the three concrete steps, walked around the pile of leaves and branches, opened the unlocked front door and stood in the dark hallway where he had waited for Martha Shannon to go the Baker Theater for the double bill, or waited for Martha Shannon to change sweaters one more time be-cause, Frank, the green one just really didn't go with my skirt, silly. Sometimes her mother would walk in from the kitchen, still wearing a white apron, wiping a pot and sweetly chide her precious daughter, "Hurry, dear. Frank's still waiting, Martha." Or her father would walk through the hallway to share the conspiracy, just to say, "Her mother made me wait, too. Can't hurry them, no matter what." Frank would just say yes, sir and smile and when they left the house, he'd roll his eyes at Martha as they walked down the street.

He stood in the hallway where he had waited, hopeful and thrilled to even have the chance to wait for her so many times before, so many, many times for dates, school, football games, walks, or trips to the Old Iron Bog. He laughed to himself when Foley talked about the kids in the car who called the police about the woman's body. Thirty years ago those kids were Frank Nagler and Martha Shannon, huddling naked under an old quilt, the scent of her lavender perfume mixing with the musty quilt smell, the taste of her mouth and the softness of her neck and belly still fresh in his memory.

The hallway held all those ghosts, the trapped sounds of their young love woven into the dusty spider webs that clung to the corners of the ceiling, silent witnesses to all the times they kissed and then jumped apart when the floor above them creaked or a light carved a slice into the darkness. Or stood facing opposite walls when they argued over something they never remembered. But then they made up when he would ask, "Are you okay?" and she'd say yes, and she'd ask "Are you?" And Frank Nagler would gaze deeply into her green eyes, hesitant to answer because they had been at this point before and sometimes he said he was okay when he was still sore, but he would gaze into her green eyes and the little hurt would be drawn out and he'd slowly nod his head and say, "Yeah."

The hallway where he stood nervous and stunned on senior prom night as 17-year-old Martha Shannon slowly and elegantly descended the stairs in a red satin gown with thin straps on her pale shoulders wearing a smile as wide as tomorrow, trying to be as cool and adult as possible when she really just wanted to shout, half crying, "Look at this dress, Frank. Isn't it beautiful? I want you to like it so much. I got it just for you." A gown that hugged her body and billowed around her legs as it ran to the floor, a gown like Hollywood actresses wear to the Academy Awards. A gown that had been her big secret for weeks, and had been so secret that she yelled at him for even asking about it; a gown that comically knocked Frank Nagler back against the front door, his knees so weak he grabbed for the door handle.

A gown so red and so perfect on the girl he had loved since the third grade, he cried.

It was the hallway where Frank Nagler reached out to steady the ambulance gurney that carried Martha Shannon Nagler down from the second floor bedroom around the tight platform turn to the first floor, where the medics put it down and with a jerk popped out the wheels; where they slowly passed through the front door, toward the ambulance with the pulsing red and blue lights that shined off the darkness, pausing to lift it above the concrete steps while he stood transfixed by fear and pain and dread until one of the men said softly, "You need to come, Frank," and he walked out of the Shannon house for the last time and into the back of the ambulance.

He kneeled beside the gurney and held her hands as carefully as he could. The leukemia that had been diagnosed at nineteen had come back, eating her away for the past four years, until all she could do was rest in bed. Nagler the young cop was at her side every night as she told him about all her visitors in as bright a voice as she could muster, that in the last few days had become a whisper.

The ambulance bounced through Ironton's streets and Frank Nagler held onto his wife's gurney and tried to gently brush from her forehead her red hair, now thin and sparse and streaked with gray, all the while whispering, "it's okay; it's okay."

She gazed up from the pillow, eyes soft with love for her husband, then dark as pain flowed, then unfocused as the last moments they had entered and passed, her eyes worried not for herself, but for her husband, helpless in his grief, searching her eyes for solace that she could not offer, and trying to pass to her what strength he could find, what words he knew, what prayers, what hope, what love; something that would last.

It's okay.

It's okay.

****

The grave stone was red granite, as close as he could come to the color of her hair.

She'd died in October and the cemetery was carpeted in fallen leaves of red, orange and yellow as a chilling early morning wind blew in from the iron hills.

He stood at her grave long after all others left. They had tried, honestly tried, especially the priest, to transform the death of his young wife into some metaphor for the grace of God, who would comfort and keep her for however long - and Frank Nagler just didn't give a damn.

As the cold sun crept past the hills, Frank Nagler stared at the grave and waited for his heart to break, but sorrow did not emerge, instead, for just one thin moment, there was joy.

"We were a celebration, weren't we, kid? A star blazing across the night sky, leading all the way as they all followed. You and that great mane of red hair, so red the sun would blush, a laugh so pure it was like singing. Oh, how they loved you. Loved to be near you. And I was so thrilled by you and so humbled you would be with me. But we cut a path, took no prisoners. They would just see us and smile. What could they do? Man, I loved you so and it filled me with a passion for life that I can't explain. Everything was alive; everything was new, and would be new as long as you were here with me. I will always love you, Martha Shannon Nagler."

Then just like that, his heart closed. He felt the change as his body stiffened and his mind stopped spinning. He absorbed the cold, welcomed it, made himself in its image.

The tears of the early day were gone.

He knelt beside the grave and ran his hands over the soft soil.

"Good bye, my sweet love, my sweet Martha."

It's okay.

It's okay.

It's okay.

She died when he was twenty-four. Standing over her grave, he felt his youth slip away. He welcomed the hardness that circled his heart.

****

He stood above her grave watching the golden-red sunlight creep through the cracks in the gravestones and trees, casting elongated shadows that melted into the grass as the sun rose.

Martha's grave was the last stop on all of his nightly rambles. He didn't know why. He just wanted to be as close to her as he could, to have her as close to him as he could get her. For years, even after she died, there was no one else Nagler felt close to.

On this night Frank Nagler just told his wife, "There's a lot of trouble brewing, kid. Someone is stealing money from the city. And there's other stuff. I was doing okay, you know, then Dawson, you know sometimes he just says the wrong thing; so Dawson mentioned a name and I've been in a funk ever since. You know, Lauren Fox. I told you about her. We fell hard for each other, you know, but it sort of never took. But she opened me up again, Martha. I was grateful for that. You don't know what I was like after you died. I didn't know who to be mad at, so I was mad at everyone, and then no one. Just mad."

He stopped talking to himself and shut down his mind.

"I love you, Martha Shannon Nagler," he whispered. "It's important that you always know that."

A delivery truck grinding up Locust stalled and then started up again with a cough and bang. The driver ground the gears and the truck lurched up the hill.

The sounds shook Nagler out of his reverie. He paused over the grave for one last moment, then turned and slowly walked away. He pulled the collar of his jacket tighter, sealing himself off again from the rest of the world.

Outside the cemetery, back on the sidewalk he asked himself, why would the owner of the stove-works file another tax appeal? And why would Chris Foley, a cop, be out looking at the property?

They went bankrupt years ago and it seemed to him the city decided a couple years ago it couldn't locate the owners. They were in Minnesota or Wyoming or someplace else. Manitoba. Seemed to cause Gabe Richman a lot of grief.

Who'd know that stuff? Nagler asked himself. And he didn't like the answer.

Debbie Glance. She was the planning board secretary.

As he left the cemetery, Nagler considered what he knew about the woman. *She's been seen in the company of the mayor early in the morning, and I'll bet anything that the city hall woman Chris Foley was walking around with, the one that Del Williams saw, was Debbie Glance.*

Debbie Glance and Chris Foley. Debbie Glance and Gabriel Richman. What's all that mean?

Nagler found himself again leaning on the stone rail of the Sussex Street Bridge. A bright purple band of sunlight split the leaden eastern sky; the city peeled back the night and stepped into early morning.

In the daylight it seemed easy to forget and move on. The downtown streets were filled with commuters and shoppers again. It hadn't rained in a week. But the suspicion came back at night. The black river flowing under the Sussex Street Bridge chattered on the loose rocks and a tree limb trapped in a pile of storm debris flapped back and forth in the current, flashing through a dim spotlight, then vanishing into the darkness again; flashing, then vanishing; flashing, then vanishing.

Nagler watched the swaying limb, caught in the hypnotic motion, the sound of the night fading. The river flowed on and his mind drifted.

He shook his head and startled, looked up and down the street as if there had been a shout, a cry, a scream, when there had been none. He closed his eyes and let out a long breath.

In that instant, he knew that Bart Harrington was right. Something was about to blow.

He saw that he was standing near the riverbank where Lauren Fox had described the park she wanted to build. *The best days are the ones when I don't think of you.*

CHAPTER 10

Nagler knew he had reached Yogi Berra's fork in the road and was going to have to take it. Why hadn't he taken it before?

Because he didn't want to, because he didn't need to. Because he convinced himself that Lauren Fox's departure was only about him and their dalliance with affection, about the look in her eyes from across the room, the sly smile then the distance that grew. Because we see what we want to see.

But now he had no choice. Dan Yang's research overturned what he thought he knew about Lauren, her office, and what he thought about all those invoices.

The fork had become two piles of paper on his desk: One was copies of the invoices and data the Dan Yang had provided, and the other was printouts of newspaper stories about actions taken by the community development office. Something had to match, or fail to match.

Homes had been painted, porches and roofs repaired. Counselors were hired to speak about nutrition and home finance, teen pregnancy, drugs; soccer and football coaches motivated kids. Volunteers cleaned vacant lots, park benches were repaired and painted. All this activity, Nagler thought, some of which he didn't even remember.

A thousand dollars here, five hundred there. New fences, new porches, seven hundred to a new business, five grand to a homeowner on a ten-year, zero-interest note.

There were dozens of stories, small items, photographs of events and Lauren was in all of them. Little by little the events came back to Nagler. At first he was present because he had been assigned to show her the areas of need, and later because he wanted to see how she was doing, and later still because the progress of one project at a time had produced so much of the kind of street-by-street improvements the city needed to begin to raise the blinds, open the windows and step back into the street without fear.

Nagler pushed the papers away on the desk, stood up and walked around the room with two fists full of hair as if trying to yank it all out.

It didn't make any sense. There was too much activity. Lauren Fox would have to work all day and all night to arrange the projects and then fix the books so all the transactions and invoices matched so the cover-up would not be detected.

He stopped pacing and stared at the piles of paper.

Maybe this was the true fork in the road: There were too many departments involved, too much money in small amounts passing through too many accounts that required too much access to too many separate parts of city government for this to done by one person. With the crack in his heart widening, Nagler had to admit that if Lauren Fox was involved with this mess, she was part of a conspiracy, a thought that offered no consolation or satisfaction whatsoever. There was more than one of "them." Wonderful. If Lauren was involved in this, did she come with the idea in her head, ready for implementation when she got settled in? Was she that persuasive that she was able to round up co-conspirators in an instant? Or was it the other way around: They approached her with the scheme already in operation and convinced her to join?

Maybe that is why most of the dates of the transactions and invoices are blacked out. We can sequence the money flow but not reconstruct the entire time period.

He leaned on the back of his chair **and dropped** his head. The first time they kissed was at the high school. Lauren had waited behind as the crowd left the room. As they walked into the hallway, he took her hand and their fingers locked; she looked straight ahead and smiled. As they passed a door that led to an unlighted courtyard, she turned to him and smiled and then pushed open the door. There, in the dark, his arms holding her slim body as she wrapped her arms around his neck, they leaned against the cool brick wall and made out like teen-agers.

What did he want to believe? What did he have a duty to doubt?

He shook his head and the warm image of Lauren Fox dissolved. Something wasn't right, something just didn't feel right. No one could be that sincere and that phony at the same time, he thought, yet, he had to hold those two thoughts in his mind at the same time.

Then there was the nature of her departure: Sudden and without explanation. Not even Gabe Richman had much to say about it, even though his displeasure with her program was well known within city hall. Did Richman find out that the money was being misappropriated and told her to leave in a deal that made sure no one knew about the transactions?

And if she was stealing the money, where did it go? She drove an old Volkswagen Beetle and was always complaining about how she hated it, yet never got rid of it. She wasn't a flashy dresser and brought her lunch to work most days.

But even Dan Yang said that was the one part of the money trail they had yet to find. Maybe it would be in some of the other computer files they had yet to read.

Nagler left the office, bought a coffee at Barry's and walked over to the park near city hall. The picnic table he chose for a seat had been purchased through a grant that Lauren Fox arranged and had been installed by volunteers. Children ran and played on the lawn as traffic stalled and moved at the traffic signals, the air filled with grunts and roars and laughter; the life of a city.

If you took the money, I hope it went to something like this after the city froze your accounts, or to paint a home, buy uniforms for the Little League, that you spread it around in a thousand places in the city that made someone smile or made one little thing better.

He finished the coffee and stood near the trash can watching the kids play before discarding the empty cup. That stuff is real, he thought, that park, the table, new paint on the gazebo, the laughter of children, traffic on the street, even the nose-wrinkling fumes from the badly-tuned diesel truck. Lauren Fox had a part of bringing it here, but until he could answer a question not yet formed would he be able to say it was all good.

It's that easy, is it? That easy to decide based on some incomplete reports that the woman you were falling in love with was a crook? Are you that angry?

Was it easier to believe that than to imagine that this all was a setup, a diversion, a ruse? That someone had used Lauren's accounts as part of a crime?

"I don't know," Nagler said. "For the time being I have to believe both."

He sat again, placed his elbows on the table and ran his fingers through his hair. *Man.*

At that moment he truly understood the fork in the road: For him to prove Lauren Fox was innocent, he was going to have to presume she was guilty.

****

The lobby at City Hall was a madhouse when Nagler returned from the park. Two circling groups of shouting men and women ringed the room and two patrolmen pushed back against the surge of bodies, creating space. Voices echoed off the hard ceiling, distorting the words, but not the sounds. "Stand back!" A patrolman shouted at three men trying to rush past him. A hand shot out of the crowd and knocked off the patrolman's hat as he called into his radio for back-up. Nagler pushed his way into the crowd and was pushed back. "I'm a cop, goddamn it. Let me through." Nagler shoved bodies out of the way, waving his badge in the angry faces, and caught an elbow in the ribs. Nagler spun around and found himself face-to-face with Jimmy Dawson.

"What the hell is this, Jimmy?" Nagler yelled.

"Gabe Richman was here talking to those in line for the home buyouts and his opponent Bob Yearning showed up with this." Dawson held up a flyer with a couple grainy photographs of Richman and Debbie Glance sitting in Richman's Escalade and the banner, "What the mayor does with his free time."

Nagler scanned the flyer, noting only the word, "Lovebirds."

He looked over the top of the crowd and saw Richman and Yearning leaning on the wall at opposite sides of the room. They were each surrounded by several men and women, possibly election staffers, Nagler guessed. The election had been in the background for weeks as Ironton and its residents tried to recover from the storm damage. There had been two rather polite debates during which the strongest charge Yearning made was that the city was not recovering fast enough because of a lack of staff in key city departments, to which Richman replied that those departments would be fully staffed if Yearning, as part of a brief Republican administration, had not cut the city budget by 15 percent and fired all the workers.

The brief skirmish appeared to be over. While Richman and Yearning glared at one another from the opposite sides of the room, the two patrolmen managed to get some of the crowd to move along.

Sorry I missed it.

The roar had diminished to a murmur of discontent, then to the shuffle of feet, soft shoes on wooden tiles.

He pushed his way through the exiting crowd and stood in a small clearing in the lobby, eyes ablaze, grinning wildly.

"Oh, what a thing is this? What a scene of madness!"

The voice startled the crowd to silence and stillness as everyone in the entire hall stopped moving. Even the clerks behind the thick glass barrier of the tax department stopped shuffling papers.

Nagler looked toward the main entrance to see Bartholomew Harrington, still wearing his herringbone jacket and Yankees cap, leaning on the door frame holding up a handful of paper. Nagler caught the eye of one of the patrolmen and shook his head, saying leave him alone. Bart was never dangerous, just theatrical, and Nagler didn't want the scene to become anything more than it might on its own. Jimmy Dawson moved to the edge of the crowd, grinning.

"Here we have the two," Harrington said as he moved to the center of the hallway. "The Richman and the Yearning, staring each other down. Over what? A woman in a car? Surely you do better than that, Bobby. Maybe you'd like to discuss the piles of tires and pools of dark oil in the woods behind your repair shop." The crowd murmured.

Harrington pulled out a sheet of paper and tossed it into the center of the room, where it fluttered to the floor. Dawson jumped out to grab it.

Harrington spun in a slow circle, stopping now and again to hand out one of the papers in his hands.

"We have a city in flames and a populous seeking leadership and hope and the best you can do is squabble over a woman in a car? Oh, Yearning. What are you yearning for?" Harrington pulled out another sheet and held it theatrically before his face. "Smaller government! What a unique plan. But that is big government? Was not World War II big government? The interstate highway system? The cure for polio or the Internet? No, for you big government is a program that helps poor people heat their homes or use food stamps to feed their starving children. You say you will defund those wasteful programs, dear me. Is not big government also the program that provided you a zero-interest loan to expand your repair shop? And which you have not repaid? I have that flyer here somewhere? Ah, yes. 'From the campaign of Gabriel Richman'," Harrington read. 'What happened to the $50,000 loan

107

Bob Yearning received? He failed to pay it back. Three years overdue. Deadbeat Yearning. He yearns to be mayor. He can't even pay his bills. Don't let him near the city budget.' Paid for by the committee to re-elect Gabriel Richman."

Harrington tossed that flyer to the floor. "Ha! Oh such matters!"

"That's a lie!" Bob Yearning yelled. "Officers, why don't you stop him?"

Harrington turned silently to face the two patrolmen; he winked at Nagler standing at their shoulder. "Yes, officers, why don't you stop me? Is it because I'm freely exercising my right to free speech in the very place our government convenes?" The police remained in place. "I shall continue." Harrington pulled out another sheet of paper, studied it and tossed it away. "That is of no interest. Yearning, really? As mayor you will oppose dredging of the Mississippi River in Louisiana? How quaint. What's the Mississippi River ever done to you? Ah, here's the one. 'As a mayor I will trim the fat from the city budget'." Harrington waved the paper in front of the crowd. "Ah, yes. Overspending, the political opponent's perpetual complaint. My opponent is such a big spender. He plows the streets and collects the trash and makes the buses run on time. They said that of Mussolini, too. And we all know how that ended. Do you want to know how Bobby Yearning will accomplish that feat?" The crowd responded with a muffled, "Yes, tell us." "Let's see. Um, he'll cut fifty thousand from the welfare account, and seventy-five thousand from the school budget. Oh, he wants to close three parks and trim a million from the community development office…" Harrington looked up at the crowd. "Just what a city that was underwater for a week needs, one less way to recover. I'm mean, really. And I see here he wants to trim a half-million from the police department and fire ten of-ficers. The drug gangs operating on the east side of town will thank you for that. And of course, that will make it so much easier for the police to determine the killer of that young woman found in the Old Iron Bog."

Harrington stared at Gabriel Richman. "So, Gabriel, my friend, when will the police apprehend the killer?" Richman glared silently at Harrington and one of his staff grabbed his arm, holding him back and whispered something to him, after which Richman relaxed. Nagler watched the silent exchange. *Don't do me any favors, Bart. Jesus Christ.*

"And we will not forget you, Gabriel." A cheer arose from the crowd, at first a gentle ripple, then a few laughs, and then cries, "Yeah, Richman. What'd he do for us?"

Nagler wondered why the crowd had been so silent to that point. Maybe they were stunned that someone could pull off the act with such daring, or thought maybe it was just an act, and Harrington, a traveling player, the advance clown sent in to warm up the house. So they waited for the punch line or the straight man. Or the men in the white coats. But then, Nagler had seen this before: Harrington mesmerizing a courtroom audience and jury, the prosecuting attorney, head down, watching his case dissolve, running his fingers through his hair as Harrington spun tales, whispered conspiratorial details, roared the facts of the case as if it was the climax of a great drama, the end of the cycle.

And maybe, that's what it was. The end. Of what he wasn't sure, but it felt like the end. The end of it all, a message delivered by a man in a clownish suit as we stood in awe, awaiting our fate.

"So then, Richman," Harrington began again. "The man of promise, or correctly, promises. You promised to clean the streets and repair the parks. To build a shopping center on the Old Iron Bog, where if you recall my previous reference, there is a dead body. That might slow things down. And you promised to repair the sewer plant and install new water lines and build new homes and attract new businesses and settle the accounts with the owners of the stove-works, our neglected monument to waste and decay. Oh, Gabriel, the promises you made. You promised to lead us, to remember us, to heal us, to bring life back to the tired, dark streets, to bring joy back to the eyes of children and happiness to the voices of mothers, to remove from the city's eyes the shame of our downfall; to cast up the hopes and dreams of the vacant-eyed, to bring people and sheckles to our downtown, to bring back to life that full-throated roar that once filled the air of this city, that roar that said, we are here, yes we are. Oh where, Gabriel, did that roar go? Was it lost in your deal-making, abandoned in the eyes of your sweet lover, or forgotten in the haze of ambition? But it is lost, dear Gabriel, gone in a mist. The streets remain silent, the brick hulks of commerce still vacant. And what will you do? The sky has opened and delivered a torrent, and the earth has cracked. Your people cry out, lead us, Great Gabriel, lead us, but there you stand wrapped in anger, a puddle of confusion, wishing you could wrap your hands about my throat and shake the life out of me.

But you won't. You'll just stand and watch. Just as you have watched the city decay, watched your people despair."

Harrington held the remaining papers in his hand as he turned in a circle in the center of the lobby. "Here," he said. "Here are the lives of these two men who seek to lead you. Read and decide."

Then he tossed the papers in the air and as the crowd surged to grab the falling pages, Harrington slipped out the door like a magician.

CHAPTER 11

Nagler pulled his car to the side of the road and watched the sunlight shine dully off the gray-green water of the Old Iron Bog. The surface seemed as dense and solid as a conspiracy; the swamp played its part and gave up its secrets reluctantly. Bart Harrington's performance had set the blogosphere on fire with theories and complaints and insults after Dawson filed a story; and, oddly, police dispatchers received hundreds of new tips. The most obvious impact of Harrington's soliloquy was the insertion of the Old Iron Bog case into the mayor's race, which gave both political camps the opportunity to attack and defend the police. Richman's team had easily discounted the photo of him and Debbie Glance in the Escalade by displaying the original photo that was taken at a hospital fund raiser and showed both Richman, Glance, the council president and the hospital chief executive arriving at the site of a proposed new addition. Yearning's team had clumsily altered the photo to remove the others in the vehicle. That act allowed Richman to dismiss all questions about his relationship with Debbie Glance as just another campaign stunt.

Still, Nagler thought, *here we are.* The weeks of work on the case of the headless woman had produced nothing. The national announcement of her death had generated a few calls about missing daughters, but none of those cases matched the girl they had found. Nagler was just confounded. Couldn't be that hard. Just couldn't. And yet, he thought, staring at the damn swamp for the four-thousandth time, it just was. The discovery of the hand with the ring had not generated any clues, and his requests for files on any thefts or robberies that involved stolen jewelry had been slowed by the relocation of the files to Newark, just like Debbie Glance said. Foley stopped sending along the requests and at one point Nagler stopped by his office to ask why.

"Frank you've sent fifty requests," Foley said then. "We can't process them that fast."

"Let me go down there myself," Nagler said, impressed Foley had an exact count. "I'll go on a day off. Anything to see if we can close this case. What's the problem? I thought you and the mayor wanted this case closed."

"We do," Foley said. "Look, this not a reflection on you. I know you've been pushing hard on the case, but this turned out to be a tough one. You've pulled cases out of thin air. Maybe this is one of them."

Blow me off, Chris? "Was thinking the other day about Charlie Adams. Used the bog and the stove-works and other places as dumping grounds. I wonder…"

Foley cut him off.

"Of course I remember Charlie Adams," Foley said brightly; too brightly, Nagler thought. "He made you famous."

"Shit, Chris, that's not fair, and you know it," Nagler said. "If it made me famous, how come you got the promotions?" Nagler was surprised by the edge in his voice. He had never felt that way. So why now? The room was suddenly, deeply silent. Nagler waved his hand. "That was a long time ago," Nagler said softly. "Look, you did great work on that case, and you know it. We both did. That's why he's in jail."

Foley had his face buried in the papers on his desk, barely paying attention.

"Sorry to bother you, Chris," Nagler said, seeking a simple way out.

Foley carefully placed his pencil on the desk and slowly wiped his brow. He raised a hand and waved it forward and back slowly and closed his eyes. "Sorry. Frank… I'm just overwhelmed with all this. Could use three people, but we can't afford them. What were you saying about Charlie Adams?"

"I was thinking that since we found little useful evidence at the bog, we start looking in some of the other bodies of water in the city. Adams kept us running for weeks, remember? If someone was a copycat, I'm thinking why not? Maybe we send a search team down to Smelly Flats for a look. What could it hurt?"

Foley dropped the pencil on his desk and closed the fist on his right hand. "Why there?"

"Adams dumped bodies there. Besides we haven't looked there. Just a hunch. Not much else has worked."

"Yeah, maybe," Foley said softly, pulling away behind the paperwork on his desk. Then he looked up. "You heard about Bob Yearning's campaign flier alleging to show the mayor and Debbie Glance in the car together?"

"I was there. Didn't Gabe refute that?"

"Any ideas how Yearning knew enough to make a flier out of it?"

"What are you saying, Chris? Sure, I asked you about it, but so what? You suggesting I told Yearning that the mayor and Debbie might be catting around? Fuck you."

"Oh, no, Frank. Just wondering." Foley's voice was cold, icy; a threat.

Nagler remembered watching Foley at his desk reach over and open a file sitting there, and then look at Nagler almost surprised he was still standing there. "Anything else, detective?"

"No," Nagler replied and then left the room.

Richman and Glance, Christ, Nagler thought. But what stayed in his head for days was the word: Detective. Foley hadn't called him "detective" in years, if he ever had. Then Nagler recalled that Foley used the title when they were at the Iron Bog on the first night of the murder investigation, when he complained about clothes Nagler was wearing. Cops in the same department didn't refer to each other by rank, especially officers who had known each other for a couple of decades. Rank was used in public events, when speaking with officers from other departments or agencies, or if addressing a superior officer.

But Foley?

After the first night, a search of the entire swamp had been ordered and cops had been out in boats, or walking through the shallows with poles and cameras since that discovery, but nothing that appeared related to the headless girl was found.

They found a lot of footwear, a lot of beer cans and women's underwear, a countless number of condoms, some kitchen pots, about a dozen microwaves, car fenders and doors, broken mirrors, furniture, mattresses, and the strangest thing, an empty coffin. Dawson suggested they should be looking for Dracula. "If I wanted to find a pasty white guy, I'd arrest you," Nagler told him.

But no scraps of clothes or hair, no pieces of life they could attach to one dead young woman. That was what bothered him the most. Nagler could accept that she might have been killed elsewhere, even

113

miles away, and then brought to the bog for disposal. The big storm provided a great opportunity because everyone in town was huddling inside somewhere and the authorities were occupied trying to manage what was becoming a disaster. But it was also the perfect cover for a local killer. Darkness, heavy rain. No one was paying any attention.

We all were focused on the storm. It filled the Ironton's streets and homes, uprooted lives and held citizens in its terrifying grip. No one would have noticed a car, a car driving slowly, a person getting out, maybe, a body, then a sound, then more rain.

But why one hand? And one hand with a ring?

The medical examiner had been working with other agencies to find identification, and even to see if it matched the rest of the body that had been found, but had drawn no final conclusion. Tests and fingerprints had not given clues, and studies of past murders and missing person's cases had all been dead ends.

But there you were, Nagler thought as he got out of his car and surveyed the Old Iron Bog. Dumped in a vile and murky place like so much junk, and now unclaimed. Did no one love you? Did no one wonder why you have not called, emailed, or returned? Were you that alone in the world?

The sky grew dark as one last patch of light was swallowed by a rolling wave of black clouds. Nagler's mood darkened as the world at that moment changed from light to dark. The bog, the city, the gnawing sense that things he once took for granted were shaded and false, that people he knew were shells, frames that hid from sight who they truly were. For the first time in his memory, Nagler felt that he needed to be peering around corners as he walked down the street, needed to glance back every now and then to see who might be behind him. It was not fear - he'd been a cop too long to be fearful; cautious, yes, suspicious, always, apprehensive - but not fearful. Fear was standing above the grave of his young wife and sensing the world flowing away, leaving him standing alone; fear was stepping inside, and viewing the world from behind the gauze of loneliness that filled his heart and soul.

At the end of the bog's access road, three Ironton cops were securing to a trailer the small boat they had been using for week to search the bog. The search had officially come to an end.

Nagler shook hands with the group's leader, Sergeant Ramon

"Ray" Martinez, the city's official search squad leader. He had participated in search-and-rescue efforts all over the world, and was among the first to volunteers to work the World Trade Center site.

"Hey, Ray," Nagler said. "Nothing again, huh?"

"Yeah, Frank. I thought for sure we'd find something. Clothes, shoes, not necessarily her head or other hand, but some evidence." Her paused and looked over the bog. "It's too clean, man. Either that or this old place is better at hiding her secrets than we thought."

"You were here the first night when we found her," Nagler said. "What'd you think?"

"Thought it was staged," Martinez said. "Even in the rain and muck we would have found more evidence of the entry, disturbances on the bog shore, broken reeds, branches, something that indicated there was traffic in the crime scene. Once we got off the main road, it was hard enough for us to get around without slipping and grabbing at something, so I'd guess that if you were carrying a body, you might have slipped more than once. But we didn't see that, and I don't really know why."

"Good point, Ray. When I was walking around the scene with Chris Foley, we were both slipping and sliding a lot and at one point he snagged his jacket on a bush and complained that he had just got it back from the cleaners."

Martinez laughed softly. "Foley. I saw the two of you talking. I was about a hundred feet away, so I couldn't hear you, but I imagine he was telling you what he had been telling us for more than an hour."

Nagler scowled. "More than an hour? It seemed to me Foley hadn't been there that long. He had talked to the kids, he said, but..."

"He didn't talk to the kids," Martinez said. "One of my guys did. They were trying to get their car the hell out of there and we stopped them. We were gonna hold them until you got here, but they kind of blurted out their version of what they saw and heard and the girl said her mom was going to really mad that she was being interviewed by the police at three in the morning because she was supposed to be at her girlfriend's house. We did a quick interview, got their names and addresses, but Frank, it was pretty clear they hadn't seen anything, although they said they did hear a car and some voices. Their car was fifty feet away parked behind some thick brush. They were smart enough to park on a pile of concrete and asphalt, but the kid did say he'd been here a lot. They would not have been able to see who dumped the girl, nor would they have been seen."

"Foley said they heard voices and movements."

"Don't doubt they heard something, but I doubt they understood what they heard. It's normally pretty quiet here in the middle of the night, Frank. But it was pouring, and you know that rain, how heavy it was. Still the kids said they had one rear window partly opened so the car windows would not steam up on the inside."

Martinez and Nagler grinned.

"You ever come here as a kid, Ray?" Nagler asked.

"Never had a car." Martinez looked away, then laughed. "There was an old barn on Butler, up on the mountain. You?"

Nagler just shrugged and lifted one eyebrow.

Martinez said, "So Foley must have talked to my guy."

"Run it down for me, Ray."

"What's up?" Martinez asked.

"I had wondered why Foley was here at all, not to mention before I got here," Nagler said. "I got here in maybe thirty minutes from downtown because of all the detours."

Martinez laughed. "That's slow for you, my friend."

"Had trouble swimming upstream."

"Ain't that the truth," Martinez said. "Anyway, as I recall, patrol got here first after the kids called, maybe half past one. They verified that a body was there and called it in and secured the scene. Then little by little everyone else arrived. Me and one of my guys, fire department, the EMTs, the medical examiner's crew then you. Now I think of it, Foley was just here. I didn't see him arrive, but then there he was on the bog road. We hadn't even gotten our gear on at that point. " Martinez looked at the bog and shook his head. "I hope she doesn't win this round, Frank."

"When you talked to the kids, where was their car?" Nagler asked.

"On Mount Pleasant, just at the head of the swamp road. They pulled out after they saw the body. Why?"

"Just wondering. I was out there later in the morning looking at some damaged grass just off the swamp road. Makes sense the kids

116

might have driven over it." He reached over and shook hands with Martinez. "Thanks, Ray."

Martinez started to walk away. "Hey. Ray," Nagler called out. "Do me a favor. Check out Smelly Flats. I heard from some residents that there's been a lot of traffic on that old canal path, possibly stashing items stolen from some of the damaged homes. Maybe there's something there."

Martinez, puzzled, shrugged. "Sure, Frank. Let you know."

As he watched Martinez and his crew drive off, Nagler tried to recall his encounter with Foley that night. He thought of their conversation, examining the road and the spot where the body was found; recalled the point where Foley caught his jacket on the bush....

He was too clean, like he had changed clothes, Nagler suddenly thought. I was soaked. Everyone one else was wearing heavy rain gear and boots and gloves and Foley was in a jacket, a heavy one, but a jacket just the same. Nagler recalled the scene: The darkness and the rain, the bright lights filtered through a fog, the mud, and slipping - And Foley's shoes. Too clean and dry. They hadn't been able to walk across the road without getting their shoes covered with mud, and his had seemed like he had just put them on. But Foley said his city car was parked down Mount Pleasant. That would keep him dry.

Nagler scratched his head and stared out over the bog again. First Foley was wandering around the stove-works for some reason and now maybe made up a story about being at the bog crime scene. What the hell? Nagler stopped in the street and smacked his forehead. Staged. That's what Foley was saying the first night. That he was bothered the killers didn't toss the body into the swamp. Said it was odd the body was left out in the open.

How did he know that?

Foley's secretary told Nagler he was out with the mayor inspecting damaged homes, so Nagler drove to the east side of town. There was so much damage, he said to himself. In some blocks half the homes had blue tarps covering holes in their roofs, storefronts still had plywood for windows and handmade signs declaring "We are open" nailed to the doors. Crews with front-end loaders and dump trucks had growled through piles of sodden debris as if removing one more shovelful of junk would make it all better. Why is this taking so long, Nagler wondered. Weren't the feds here a month ago, with their hand-held computers, engineers and promises?

Along the river, which had risen up like a force and grabbed buildings and ground them to splinters, five or six cellar holes stared blindly into the sky, the homes above them tossed aside like toys. That was what's wrong, Nagler decided. Everyone is gone.

Nagler spotted Gabe Richman's gold Escalade parked outside an old warehouse a block off Trenton Street, Howie Newton's fiefdom. Nagler drove past the warehouse one time when he saw there was no one outside, then turned around and slipped his car into a space behind a box truck on the other side of the street. This didn't feel right: There were no damaged homes to be seen in either direction, just a few blocks of abandoned warehouses and machine shops left behind when Ironton's last wave of industrialization faded. Richman was the mayor, for crying out loud. He met people in his office. If it was a campaign thing, he'd meet at the Democrats' office. And if it was about showing some company bigwig a building open for investment, he'd do it with the press in tow, especially during an election campaign. No better publicity. He didn't need to sneak around, not here. It was a grimy, dark section of the city. There wasn't an officer on the force who didn't know these streets by heart, who couldn't point out a spot or buildings they had not been sent to after some tip or panicked emergency call. And yet, there was the mayor. Was this where Richman and Debbie Glance got it on, he wondered? *I hope not,* Nagler thought. *That would make it creepier than it already is. What are you doing, Mr. Mayor? What are you doing?*

Nagler knew he needed to get closer, but there was no way to approach the building without being seen if someone glanced out of a window.

So he waited. He pulled his collar tighter as the chill settled off the river like poison.

He wished he smoked. He never had, not even as a kid, just for the excitement of the forbidden experiment. Nagler just had this sudden image: A cop hanging around at night in the shadows of a dingy part of town, waiting for something bad to happen, or better, waiting for something unexpected to happen, something that would satisfy the unsettled feeling in his gut. A scene out of an old-style potboiler cop mystery or an old black-and-white movie. Cops in shadows, dirty politicians, a handful of henchmen, and somewhere an innocent victim, a stooge being set up to take the fall. And a cigarette, dangling magically from the corner of his mouth, just a small red dot in the darkness, surrounded by the haze of smoke that rose like the stink that floated up from the city and all the dirty deals and all the dirty men in their great, dark coats, with their hands in the pockets of honest citizens, taking every last dime... *And maybe a blonde,* he thought, letting the image spin away. A tall blonde, with a pouty mouth and a short, tight green dress, sitting in the front seat of his black Italian roadster; he looked over at her, her face half hidden in shadows, but he could feel the heat of her gaze -

Nagler just laughed. *I need to get out more.*

The door at the old warehouse opened and into the street stepped Richman and Foley.

Okay, that's wasn't a surprise.

That would have been Debbie Glance and Howie Newton. The four spoke briefly, the words lost in the distance. Newton waved his cigar in Foley's face, then turned away. The four then climbed in the Escalade and drove off.

That fucking gold car.

The next morning Nagler visited the warehouse again. The windows were covered with years of dust and dirt except where some hands had smudged the dirt when they opened the door, so he could not see much inside the building, except a few old machines and in one room a desk and filing cabinet with two of the drawers missing.

The loading docks had not been disturbed for a long time, that was clear, Nagler could see. All the doors had been sealed shut by paint and age.

The only thing that was out of place was a new deadbolt lock on the front door where the quartet exited the building. Who needs a new lock on an empty building?

****

When does the spinning begin, the slow turning that affects balance, that rapidly increases, changes sight, blurs the view. When does it go out of control? Is it gradual, or all at once?

Nagler felt he was in that gyre and that it was happening both

119

ways at the same time.

The following day he had planned to confront Foley about his actions on the night the woman's body was found, but the sight of Foley, Debbie Glance, Richman and Howie Newton together changed his mind. Instead, he began to follow the mayor on the several trips he took each week to the damaged parts of town. He was never alone – either Chris Foley or Debbie Glance was with him – and he always seemed to be speaking to a homeowner or shopkeeper about the condition of their property. When a homeowner came out to the street, Nagler watched Richman the politician surface: The mayor shook the person's hand and placed a consoling hand on a shoulder as they examined the dwelling. There was a lot of head nodding, a degree of pointing, of measuring marks up the sides of buildings, and at the end, shrugs. The scene was repeated time after time, with the same results. It didn't seem to be campaigning — there wasn't enough flair, and no press. What a great campaign opportunity. Mayor Richman consoles homeowners whose home remains damaged after the historic floods! Mayor Richman examines damaged (pick one) porches, windows, storefronts, vehicles. The sympathetic mayor shows he cares about the citizens of his hometown. What a guy!

And then the mayor departed and Foley alone walked the streets, knocked on doors and spoke with homeowners. Sometimes he asked them to sign a form and sometimes the look on their faces was hollow. The homeowner looked at the form, dropped the clipboard to his side and turned to his home and pointed. Foley would step beside them and nod his head. Sometimes he shrugged. Then he would reach for the clipboard and hold it out to the homeowner again and press the pen into his hand. Nagler read his lips: "It's okay. Sign here."

Nagler wanted to be closer, so he pulled his car out and circled the block where Foley was stopping at each house. The next intersection was shaded by tall brush, and he slipped his car in behind a panel truck parked illegally in the yard of the abandoned home on the corner. There was something familiar about the place, and as he walked through the junk-filled yard it came to him. It was a drug house that they raided more than a year ago. The home was just torn up, room after room of busted-out walls, filthy mattresses, broken glass and rotted food. He recalled the city filed a lien against the owner, but could not recall the outcome. Some of the windows had been boarded up.

As he stopped beside a shed he could hear bits of the conversation that was taking place between Foley and the homeowner of the large Victorian two houses up. The building seemed intact and well maintained, from what Nagler could see.

He heard Foley say, "We're just warning homeowners this could happen."

The homeowner, a young Hispanic wearing a suit jacket and dress pants, said something like, "According to whom?"

Foley said, "The city … from the emergency management department … Have to buy out some homes…"

He heard the home-owner's reply clearly. "We had no damage, Mr. Foley, just a little water in the cellar from a loose window. We're not in the flood plain - You may just have to sue us, I guess." Then he got in his car and drove away, leaving Foley alone on the sidewalk. Foley watched the car drive off and reached for his phone. Nagler could not hear his words, but it didn't take a genius to read his lips: "No sale." Nagler felt the world shift, the hole at the bottom of the swamp open. It didn't take a genius to recognize that what he just saw was a shakedown. A little official pressure, a friendly reminder to say, we get what we want.

After Foley left, Nagler walked the block and jotted down the addresses of the building where Foley had stopped. The ones on the lower end of the street were indeed damaged: Cellar windows missing, porches leaning where a post had collapsed, siding sheared off, doors and windows boarded up. Those were the ones where the city had pasted an inspection notice. But others showed no damage at all. Were they just in the wrong place? What about this block made them all so important?

Back in his car Nagler guessed there had to be some record, some paper trail somewhere. Foley had some authority as the emergency management coordinator. But Nagler doubted that those powers included telling homeowners they had to sell. He looked around. Why here? There were no main streets, just a tangle of narrow, short streets that connected with one another making a crosshatch of lots, all the same size, lined up one after another, classic housing in a factory town. The state road that followed the old canal route was eight or nine blocks away, but there was nothing here that would bring down all that traffic. The neighborhood was not near the river, not along a rail line, had no block-long factories left vacant and rotting. It was just a quiet section of a city, tucked away. Minding its own business. He drove around for a while, stopping at a dozen stop signs that slowed all traffic to a crawl, drove around cars parked on both sides of narrow streets when one side was supposed to be a non-parking zone, but who really cared; drove past neat homes with bikes on the porches; waived at kids who ran to the curb from the street where they had been tossing a football; absorbed the quiet of life, the pace of normal.

CHAPTER 12

It was raining again.

Man, we're cursed, Jimmy Dawson thought as he walked toward City Hall, head down through the cold, persistent rain.

A weak storm got itself trapped in the hills and valleys northwest of Ironton and squeezed three days of drenching, cold rain out of the sky. The state closed a main highway running to the northwest suburbs when a quarter-mile of rocky hillside let loose and blocked the road with boulders and dirt that buried a couple of cars and pushed a tractor trailer over a cliff. To the far north a series of old, man-made earthen dams gave way and the water followed the brooks and streams down the mountainsides to the east side of Ironton where riverfront homeowners had surrounded their homes with piles of sandbags squeezed in next to the big green trash containers that held the washers, freezers, floor tiles, wall paneling and sopping couches left by the last flood.

The streets were oddly vacant, this storm having finally driven everyone inside. In the last big storm, before the floods took the streets, residents and visitors tried bravely to carry on their business, until their umbrellas turned inside-out one time too many and that one last truck hit the water running curbside and sprayed the sidewalk where they were waiting for the light to change.

Or maybe it was a sense of doom. That was a newsman's thought.

He saw the headline: "State declares Ironton doomed." Forty days of rain fill basin. Citizens buy tickets for boat passage. Or maybe it was just October. Not cold enough to snow, but just cold enough to bring that nagging, damp feeling in your shoes, the coat that doesn't quite dry, the irritating throat scratchiness. A damp darkness that hints of depression.

There was a trembling underground. He could hear it in people's voices as he asked questions about any number of recent events, see it in their eyes.

The election, four weeks away, had added a level of panic to this undercurrent after Harrington's show at city hall. The more the politicians became active, the more things seemed to be wrong with the city. Corruption, I say, is afoot. And thievery. Dawson knew he was watching a campaign of innuendo, half-truths and accusations and precious little about how either man would work to put the city back on its feet.

Richman's opponent, Bob Yearning, doubled down on his messages, declaring he was as a tax cutter and corruption fighter. His campaign talked endlessly about how the Richman administration had allegedly hidden away thousands of dollars in state and federal aid that was targeted for the rebuilding effort. Yearning hinted that the money had been paid to Richman's supporters and stuffed into his own pocket. When asked for proof, he stuttered and tap danced and changed the subject. To Dawson, the attack sounded like something Yearning had read about on the Internet, not something he believed or could prove.

Richman fought back, even having a member of the governor's staff appear before the city council to explain that in fact, little money had been released because Congress was playing its annual game of brinksmanship and had not approved all the emergency federal spending.

But Yearning hammered away. He appeared weekly at some site where debris was piled and asked one simple question: "Why is this still here?"

Then he'd say, "It's here because Mayor Richman doesn't care about the lives of the citizens of Ironton. Mayor Richman is taking care of his friends. "

Dawson thought the approach as a campaign platform, even poorly crafted, was somewhat effective given that the city was on edge, since the storm and the discovery of the beheaded body in the bog. On the other hand attacking an incumbent's honesty was a political tactic as old as the hills, and unless Yearning came up with something else, he would in time simply sound like a shrill harpy. Yearning needed to provide solutions that Richman had not already floated, and his experience as the owner of a small auto parts store was a little shallow. Especially after inspectors did find piles of tires and a pool of oil in the woods behind his shop, just as Harrington said. But know what, he thought? Voters don't pay attention to those details. They want the flashy headlines on fliers: Cheater. Big spender. Crook. Cut taxes. Save the middle class. Support the troops. Save our jobs. Save the whales. And, of course, none of it ever came true, because even when you lost your job, it wasn't the politician's fault for promising to save it, it was your fault for having the wrong skill set for today's job market. It was, Dawson knew, just crap.

The one thing Yearning did that was effective was that he invariably pronounced Richman's name with two distinct syllables, pausing in between: Gabriel Rich Man. Mayor Rich Man.

Repeated a dozen times in a speech, the audience walked away hearing nothing else. Mayor Rich Man. Gabriel Rich Man. The mayor is a Rich Man. He is a Rich Man. You are not a Rich Man.

As he got to the porch at town hall, Dawson asked himself, what's that old blessing, if the creeks don't rise? He looked at the water flowing through the streets, watched the shimmering veils of water cascade off rooftops; felt the dampness intrude. Well, they're rising.

Dawson entered the small council room that acted as the municipal court and, like that day, a media room. The officials had not yet arrived so the only person in the room was a kid from Yourtown. com, a new Internet based news service that had invaded the area. It was a slight news outlet, a cross between an old-style weekly and a high school newspaper. It was mostly lists and calendar items and badly written opinion pieces contributed by readers. But that was the idea: To give citizens a feeling they controlled the news. The quality of the pages was in the layout and the design, not in the writing or reporting. Dawson had heard Upton complain about Yourtown.com a lot; they seemed to be winning the war.

Dawson nodded a greeting to the kid, whose name he recalled, Wilson Smith.

"What do you think this is about," Wilson Smith asked. He was setting up a video camera so the event could be broadcast live on his website, which meant, they would have this story first. He used to worry about that, but then he watched a few of the videos and realized the quality and sound were terrible and the "news" was just the talking heads repeating what they had just said without being questioned on the content.

Dawson said, "Might be something on the storm damage."

A door opened and Gabe Richman and Chris Foley entered the room. An odd pair, Dawson thought.

Dawson chuckled at the formality of these press conferences, as if Richman was going to announce he was running for President.

But it's only Wilson Smith and me.

Richman and Foley stood awkwardly in front of the dais, each clutching a few papers.

"Thanks for coming. I know we've not been holding these press conferences as often as you would like, and like I had promised in my last campaign that I would, but the lower floors of city hall were flooded and that's where the computer servers were kept and we had other damage. So I apologize. We have a lot of ground to cover today," Richman said. He seemed extremely nervous, Dawson thought as he glanced over his shoulder at the empty room. *Who exactly are you speaking to, Gabe.*

"Relax, Gabe," Dawson said as he settled into a seat in the front row of the pew-like benches with their hard straight backs and cushion less wooden seats. "There are only about five people watching that video."

Wilson Smith objected. "Our audience is bigger than that."

"Not by much," Dawson said.

"Excuse me, gentlemen," Richman said sharply. "I'll start now."

He looked the papers in his hand. Dawson chuckled and let out a loud breath.

"You will get a copy of these remarks after the conference," Richman said. Reading, he said, "The governor has announced that Ironton, like all towns in New Jersey, can expect a sizable reduction in state aid next year, possibly as much as four million dollars. We can't use any of the storm relief money for the operating budget. We have asked the governor to reconsider, given the damage that is still evident in town. But he said the state has been hard hit with the bad economy and he has to trim state spending. So, to offset that loss, and to build in some room in what already is a tight budget, I am announcing some staff reductions..."

"Layoffs?" Dawson asked. "What?" *Campaign gimmick.*

"I'll get to that," Richman said. "Most of these changes involve part-time municipal workers, but it will mean that two openings in the road department, a secretary position in the tax office, and the open water department director's position will not be filled at this time. More significantly, we will not be hiring the three conditional police officers we had previously announced. Two desk sergeants will be reassigned to patrol duty and one detective will be assigned to a supervisory desk post to cover the time made vacant by the other moves. We estimate this will save the city one-and-a- half-million in salaries and benefits. In addition, all employee bargaining units will be asked to accept no salary increase next year, saving an additional estimated one million."

"Who's the detective?" Dawson asked, although he believed he already knew the answer.

Chris Foley stepped forward.

"It's Frank Nagler," he said. "It is thought that with his years of experience -"

"What about his investigations," Dawson interrupted. "Who -?" "We've had some questions about that investigation, about the pace and the lack of progress," Foley said. "I'll be taking over the investigation of the Iron Bog death," Foley said. "I have some new information on that -"

"So, Nagler is being demoted."

Foley hesitated. "Not necessarily. It's an organizational move."

Dawson scowled. He absolutely hated that official voice, that neutral we-did-everything-by-the-book tone that officials adopted when they knew they were lying. *God, who did you piss off, Frank?* "What about that other case, the accounting thing?"

I'm not aware of that," Foley said.

"Didn't you have an accountant working with Nagler on some old town ledgers?" Dawson asked with sour impatience. *Come on, man, I know you're not telling me everything.*

Foley tisked and said, "We did have an accountant review the accounts of the old development director's office that was shut down a few years back."

"You mean Lauren Fox's operation?" Dawson asked. His skin was crawling; there was something so wrong here.

"I - yes," Foley said with rising irritation. "It wasn't an investigation, but a review of the books so we could file a close-out report with the state."

"Thought you already did that."

"It's not complete," Richman stepped in to say. His voice took on an edge, as if they had run out of answers on those sheets of paper they held and glanced at often. "Do you want to hear what we have on the bog death or not?" he asked.

"The report's not done? Been, what, two years? Why are you

running Nagler out of the department?" Dawson rose from his seat and walked toward the two men as he asked that question. He wanted to see them lie up close.

"That's not…" Foley started. He slammed the papers he was holding on the dais. "Look, Frank is an outstanding detective, you know that. But before he was a detective he was an outstanding rank officer with administrative skill. With the department cuts, we need him to provide that skill from now on."

Foley's face hardened into a mask, telling Dawson it was time to move on.

"So what about the bog death?" he asked.

Foley stared at Dawson for a long moment before he stepped back and began to speak.

"We have an ID," he said. "Her name is Carmela Rivera, 18, from the nation of Mexico. - "

"Aw come on, Foley," Dawson interrupted. "You said Nagler made no progress on the case and today, just after you announce you are taking over the investigation, you announce a major break. How, shall we say, fortuitous. Really, Chris? Just like that you solved it? I suppose next you'll tell us who is in Grant's Tomb."

Foley glared at Dawson, then looked away. He shuffled the papers in his hands, then looked up to speak.

"Yes, Jimmy, some of what I'm going to tell you resulted from Detective Nagler's work. But he is off the case. I'll continue now. Carmela Rivera was an undocumented immigrant who was coming here, we believe, to work. We identified her after a letter from her family was turned over to local police. Other evidence confirmed her identity. She had a brother in Boonton, who had moved here years ago, and she was supposed to live with him, but she never arrived at his house even though she left their home village three months ago. She got on a plane in Mexico City, but she never checked in with her family.

"With the help federal agents, New Jersey state police and immigration officials in Florida, it was determined that Miss Rivera may have been employed transporting drugs. They uncovered airline tickets from Mexico City to Miami and from Miami to Newark. We are investigating the possibility that a dispute with the drug smugglers resulted in her death. We feel that would account for the brutality of the crime.

Federal officials have identified a possible gang of drug smugglers with Mexican ties working out of Miami who bring drugs into New York regularly and who have been known to execute people in the manner we found Miss Rivera. And no, Jimmy, we cannot identify the drug gang."

"Where are the drugs?" Dawson asked. "Isn't it common for drug mules to swallow the drugs? The medical examiner said she had no drugs in her system."

Foley paused before speaking. "Can't say much about that. The federal drug agents are investigating that situation. But I'll say this. It is possible that the absence of drugs in her system might have been a factor in her death. OK?"

"How'd you ID her?" Dawson asked. "You had no head or hands."

Foley turned back. "The family said she had a small tattoo on her left wrist. We asked Dr. Mulligan to examine the body again and he found what at first he thought was a bruise, but enlarged, proved to be the corner of a dragon tattoo. We brought in an expert who reconstructed the mark and it matched."

Foley and Richman turned to leave.

"What about the ring?" Dawson asked.

"What?"

"The ring. About six weeks ago officers hauled out of the bog a hand with a lion's head ring on one finger," Dawson said. "You made a big deal of handing out a photo of it and we all ran it. Is it hers, Miss Rivera's?"

"Right," Foley said. "That's a, um, an ongoing investigation and I cannot comment on it." Foley and Richman moved toward the door to leave.

"So you've got another chopped up body in the bog?" Dawson shouted after them.

Foley stopped in the doorway. "Just can't comment, Jimmy. Thanks for coming."

Wilson Smith looked over at Jimmy Dawson, who was writing something in his notebook.

"Did you get all that? Can you explain what it means?" Wilson Smith asked.

Dawson just closed his eyes. At any other time in his career he would gladly helped out a kid reporter.

"No, kid, I can't. They're out in the hallway. Go ask 'em. I'm not going to cut my own throat."

Wilson Smith grabbed the camera and headed to the hallway.

As he walked out of the room, Dawson thought about the green, perfect lawn at Howard Newton's Trenton Street Club. How green it was, and how it got that way.

****

After Dawson filed a quick story for the web page on the mayor's announcements, he headed to the place where he'd find Frank Nagler. He was parked along Mount Pleasant, leaning against the car's passenger door, collar raised to the mist, gazing out over the Old Iron Bog.

They had been doing this stuff forever, running around Ironton at all hours of the day, standing in the snow and rain and brutal hot sun trading tips and information, telling stories or just complaining. Today, with mist and cold, he wished Nagler had picked Barry's.

Dawson knew he did most of the complaining, but that was the nature of his business. Listening to people lie to your face tended to sour your outlook on life. Frank Nagler had coolness about him, always did. When the police department was being slammed more than a decade ago over some phony charges about police brutality, it was Nagler who calmed everyone down. He carefully conducted hundreds of interviews, spoke with residents who had filed charges, with out-of-towners who came to city hall to protest the allegations, and worked all the details with the state police to end the case with a couple of letters of reprimand.

But there was also sadness about Nagler, and it was not just the death of his wife. Even before she died he seemed withdrawn. He was not a back-slapper, and in a department that called for camaraderie, no matter how forced, that was a mark against him. He went to work and did his job. Dawson could not remember a case that Nagler investigated that had been thrown out of court or challenged by department brass. His testimony in court was clear, detailed and well spoken. So it was not a surprise when he landed a big case like the body in the bog.

And it was an even bigger surprise when they took it away.

Nagler looked over as Dawson walked up to the car and smiled. "What do you want?"

"Ball scores," Dawson said. "Looks like the bottom of the ninth."

Nagler looked out over the bog. "You're too pessimistic, Jimmy. It's the seventh inning stretch."

"Foley kicked you to the curb, Frank," Dawson said. "Took your investigations, put you behind a desk. You're awfully calm for someone who basically got fired. Why aren't you ...?

"Yelling and screaming? On the over-night shift," Nagler said laughing.

"What? You're kidding."

"Lot of supervising needs to be done on the graveyard shift," Nagler said, laughing. "Did Foley tell you I found the brother in Boonton? The airline tickets? That I was talking to the feds?" Nagler laughed again. "I'm sure he didn't. It all came together in the last couple of days. How was he when he announced it? When I told him about it the other day he seemed surprised that I had tracked it all down.

Dawson started to ask a question, but Nagler cut him off.

"But, you know me, Jimmy. When have I ever been a screamer? You know. I don't scream. I get the job done. Besides, in this situation, embarrassing Foley could get me fired. Place is on edge. They'd need a scapegoat and it'd be easy to blame old Frank Nagler for rocking the boat. Besides after Bart Harrington made the case part of the mayor's race with his little act the other day, Richman needs to appear to be on top of things. What does a politician do when they have no real answers? Find someone to blame. Here I am."

Dawson started to reply, but Nagler cut him off.

"The worst part? I have to go back into uniform. I don't think I have one that fits," Nagler laughed.

Dawson tried again to ask a question.

Nagler nodded his head toward the old bog.

"Know how big this swamp is, Jimmy? A thousand acres. Left centuries and centuries ago. A thousand acres of black water, dead trees and unknowable debris, trash, and stuff, big enough to bury all the things we want to hide. And right over there," Nagler pointed in the general direction of a spot a couple hundred feet from where the pair sat, "in a space about five feet square, a mere fraction of the size of this place, two cops in a tiny boat conveniently found a severed hand with a gold ring on one finger. Isn't that odd? Did you know that the medical examiner cannot match that hand with the body that was also found here? They don't know who it belongs to and so they also don't know who the ring belongs to."

"What are you talking about? Foley said they matched it?" Dawson asked. "So, what, you think it was planted? Do you know whose ring it is? Did you tell Foley?"

Nagler just raised an eyebrow.

"So I was right," Dawson said.

"What?"

"At the press conference. I asked Foley about the ring and he started tap dancing about how that was still under investigation. So I asked him if that meant there was another body in the water, and he left the room. Man, something strange is going on."

Nagler stared out over the bog. The mist shrouded the western-most end in a blanket of gray; elsewhere stark broken trees, dead for years, poked branches through the murk. The center of the bog seemed darker, and wrapped in a brighter haze as if light was being funneled down some unseen channel underground.

"I was walking through the bog this morning," Nagler said. "There's probably four or five miles of roads and trails in there. Dead-ends that lead to sinkholes. A couple of them have grabbed the roots of a tree or two and are sucking them down to the underworld. A day like today you could wander on some of the roads and get lost easily, maybe lost for a good long time. The road sounds don't penetrate. You have no sense of direction. All there is is a swish of flowing water and the calls of crows warning each other about the danger of an intruder."

Dawson pulled his collar tighter and glanced at Nagler to see if his friend had been replaced by a French philosopher or something.

"Sure, Frank. What --"

"What's that got to do with anything?"

"Foley said he was bothered by the fact the girl's body was found out in the open like that, like it was meant to be discovered. Who would do that? Would gang-bangers operating out of Mexico, Miami and New York drive all the way out here to a swamp in Ironton, New Jersey to dump a body? You kill someone like that because you want to send a message. You don't drive forty-five miles in the middle of the night after a week of heavy rain just to find this place. Hell, in Mexico they hang them off bridges, litter the streets with bodies. So why didn't they drop it in the city near a flophouse where other drug mules might find it, or near some two-bit motel where illegals live? And why did Foley assume it was done on purpose? I was here the next day, in the morning. It seemed possible that the body was dumped in a hurry because the presence of the kids in their truck surprised them. Foley was so certain it was dumped there on purpose. One thing you learn is to never assume anything so you don't leave anything out. At the time I didn't think much about Foley's comment. Maybe I was just too tired."

"But you don't buy it."

"Was awfully convenient. Besides, he seem too certain," Nagler said. "When a suspect says something like that with that much conviction, you immediately think he's trying to send you a false scent."

Dawson sat stunned a moment. *Suspect? Interesting choice.* "Are you saying what I think you're saying, Frank?"

Nagler pulled his stare back from the bog and turned to Dawson. "I'm not saying anything, Jimmy."

Dawson tuned his face away because he was smiling. Then he turned back to face Nagler.

"You don't think that body is Carmela Rivera, do you?"

"It might be, but it doesn't make sense," Nagler said. "I know that girl is missing. They matched a blood type and a circumstance. The feds, the brother, all say so. She never made it to Newark, but she made it to Miami. Young girl, bright lights, big city. Who knows? It might be her, but the medical examiner can't say. So I can't say. What makes sense, given the apparent carelessness of the body disposal, is a crime of passion, or worse, just a senseless, brutal murder. Yet she had no other wounds, no defensive wounds, no stab wounds, gunshot wounds, no bruises. She wasn't raped, but might have been tortured. They cut off her head and her hands, which then fits the drug gang model. But it still sounds made up. Despite Foley's announcement, the feds told me that was just one theory they were looking at as they looked for Carmela Rivera, but they also said that this seemed to be more local than global. They hadn't actually traced her to New Jersey, although it seems like a logical destination. The brother seemed to be genuinely expecting his sister at his home. But what if she lied to him and her family? Then with the possibility that there might be another body in the bog, who knows. A serial killer? I looked back at the Charlie Adams murders to see what they might tell us, but this is not the same. This place does hide its secrets pretty well. Despite the authority that our friends the federal agencies can bring to a case, they told me they were as baffled as I was that there was so little information about this woman."

Dawson let the serial killer notion pass. He recalled Charlie Adams and covering the long investigation and trial. He was surprised Nagler bought it up. This was not the same, not at all.

"So you're saying Foley is lying?" Dawson looked at the ground and spit. What the hell is going on?

"Not lying. Protecting something," Nagler said. "Maybe it has some investigative purpose. Maybe he wants everyone to look away from what is really going on. Would make a nice newspaper story, though."

"Like what?"

For the first time in months, Dawson felt that old familiar rumble in his gut, the zing of nerve ending cranking to hyper drive as he tossed the details of a scene and story back and forth in his mind, following ideas down dark and hidden paths.

"I've got to get it from somebody besides you, Frank," Dawson said.

Nagler smiled. "I know a guy. I'll give you a number."

It began to rain harder, now a steady drizzle, but neither man made an effort to move off.

"This'll ruin your reputation," Dawson said as his face broke into a smile.

Nagler laughed. "What reputation is that, Jimmy?"

"The last honest cop."

Nagler shrugged and then squinted into the mist and stared out at the Old Iron Bog.

"That's not true. There's lot of others," Nagler said. "At this point, what do I have to lose?"

"Just saying," Dawson said as he began to move away. The mist and drizzle had become a steady rain. "But you know what they'll be saying before that?"

"No, what?"

"That we're not smart enough to get out of the rain."

They went to Nagler's car just as the rain intensified and pounded on the roof like ball bearings.

"So what do you think is going on?" Dawson asked. "Why do they need you out of the way?"

Nagler shook his head and cracked open his window a little. He wanted to tell Dawson about his theory that the body got dropped in a hurry because they might have seen the kid's truck; he wanted to say more about why he thought Foley was lying, but in truth he was not yet sure himself why Foley needed to lie. He wanted to tell the reporter about seeing Richman's gold Escalade parked outside that ramshackle factory building, and following Foley and wondering why it seemed he was shaking down homeowners. And wondering if all of this was like wandering through the dark warren of trails and paths through the Old Iron Bog that twisted and curled back, crossing one another or led to a dead end; and whether he had become so focused on the dark mess that the one piece of connective tissue was right in front of him and he couldn't see it. This was another fork in the road, but one he was not yet ready to take.

"Noise making," he said instead. "Foley wants to be chief, and McDonald is going to retire in a year, so if he takes credit for leading the investigation in to the bog death, he looks good. Gabe Richman is up for another term this year and even he knows the bloom is off the golden boy. He urged me the other day to solve this crime, so the family can get peace. Not much has gone right for him, and that overblown promise of building a shopping center on this place still hangs in the air. People still remember how damn cocky he was, how sure he could pull it off. Trying to be his grandfather, the biggest wheel in town. He'll never live that down, unless he comes up with another plan. City's dying, and Gabe Richman has no idea how to revive it. And now he's got the storm damage to deal with. They both need to be seen as taking charge, being the leader in a time of uncertainty."

"But it is still odd," Dawson said. "Has a funny smell."

"Don't disagree, but I guess that's why you became a reporter, huh?"

"Yeah, right. Upton will love this." Dawson said. "I was talking to Howie Newton the other day. Went to ask him what he knew about Richman and Lauren Fox."

"So how is old Howie?" Nagler started to say he saw Newton, the mayor, Foley and Debbie Glance together, but stopped.

"Still kicking, still dealing, still denying he's ever done anything wrong," Dawson said. "He's a million years old, and he knows more about the crap in this city than anyone. I'll be talking to him when he's in his grave, because even though he's dead, he'll still know. We'll find notes on his headstone."

Nagler laughed. That was about right. "So what's he say about Gabe and Lauren?"

Dawson leaned back against the car door. "He said she was asking about how the city's accounting system worked. She had grant applications that needed to show that the program would be connected to a city department, so she apparently needed some account numbers or the name of an employee in that department who might be in charge. Seems like pretty standard stuff. Howie said Richman went nuts for some reason, and assigned, you'll love this, Debbie Glance, to help Lauren out."

"Ha!" He slapped the dashboard. "That woman is everywhere and I have no idea why." *Debbie Glance.* Unbelievable. Then, Nagler thought, maybe not.

He paused a moment and considered. "Lauren had done a lot of work before I was asked to help her out. When I got there she was beyond the grant writing stage and working in the field. They felt she needed help getting into homes in the factory district. The slumlords didn't much like the city poking around." He looked out the window at the rain. "So what does Newton think got her fired?"

"This is the strange part," Dawson said. "He thinks she might have found something she wasn't supposed to find, but he wouldn't say what. He thinks she didn't get fired as much as maybe ran and hid."

Frank Nagler knew she had run away. He was supposed to escort her to an apartment building on the south side where housing inspectors found dozens of men sleeping on mattresses scattered on the floors of a three-story home. The men paid the homeowner ten dollars for an eight-hour shift on a mattress. Then someone else took their place. He remembered he got to her office but it was dark and locked and she did not answer her cell phone. Later that day he had gone back to her office and, shit, there was Debbie Glance tossing files into a cardboard box and a cop taking Lauren's computer.

He remembered Debbie Glance saying, "We've got a problem here, Frank."

Nagler rolled up the window and started the car. "Where you parked?" Dawson tipped his head to the right. "Hang on, I'll drive you over."

As Dawson started to get out of the car, Nagler said, "I think I've seen that ring before. I'll tell you when I'm sure."

Dawson put his hand on the door handle and looked back at Nagler, then opened the door and got out. He hesitated, then opened the door. "Something else on your mind, Frank?"

"No, just thinking about the night shift. All those drunks, junkies and whores. Watching the world pass by on that bank of monitors in the police station." He shook his head. "It'll be a gas."

****

Later that night a fire broke out in a section of the old stove-works. By morning twelve fire companies were working the fire that had spread to four buildings. By the afternoon of the next day, a half-dozen companies remained, pouring water on the piles of rubble to cool the hot spots as a damp, white, smoke-filled haze settled over the old factory. Three bodies were found.

The next morning after Nagler left the fire scene and drove through downtown toward his home to shower and change out of his wet, smoke-filled clothes, he saw Bartholomew Harrington on the corner of Main and Sussex standing under a large banner that read "End the fraud. Sign my petition."

"I really shouldn't stop," Nagler said to himself. "But with the city on edge again because of the fire…" And he pulled the car to the curb.

Harrington was busy arranging clip boards holding several sheets of lined paper and a collection of pens on a card table he had set up under the banner. As he approached, Nagler could hear Harrington was humming the climax of the "1812 Overture," the part with the militant strings and horns and the crashing percussion that sounded like cannon fire.

"What are you doing, Bart?"

"Oh, hi, Frank," Harrington said pleasantly. "I've filed a class-action suit against the city, the mayor, the governor and the state and federal governments. Over the lack of action on the flood repairs."

Harrington said it in such a disarming fashion, Nagler laughed. "Forget anyone?"

He shook his head firmly. "No, I don't believe I did, Frank." And then he went back to arranging the pens.

"What's that got to do with the banner?" Nagler asked.

"Not much," Harrington said. "The city has about five million in reserve funds. The petition is asking that they use that money to help homeowners and shopkeepers who lost everything in the flood. Use that money now and replace it when the federal funding shows up." He looked up again. "Someone has got to do this, Frank. Neither the mayor nor that idiot opponent of his, Yearning, will talk about this at their campaign rallies. I go to their candidate's events and ask the question, and they ignore me. Richman had me thrown out the other night."

"I'm worried about you, Bart," Nagler said. "Especially after the other day."

"Forget about it, Frank. That was nothing. Just spur of the moment," Harrington said, smiling and distracted. "You need to worry about yourself. I see they dumped you on the night shift." He just looked up at Nagler and raised his eyebrows, as if to say, "See."

"Yeah, well," Nagler said. "What's between you and Richman?"

"Not much. I just think he's a crook." Harrington shrugged.

"That's all? You stirred up a mess for me, you know," Nagler said. "And you've got Richman and Yearning running all over the place promising to cure cancer, end war, make us all rich and make our hair grow."

"Just like late-night TV salesmen," Harrington said, "and there ain't much difference. I can prove to you Richman is a crook, Frank. Just you wait."

Nagler felt the wet pants and shoes and smelled the musky smoke rise from his jacket. *Don't ask,* he told himself.

"Why?" Nagler heard himself ask.

Harrington smiled, and his eyes widened. "*Why* is not the question. *How* is the question. I'm in City Hall a lot and everyone ignores me. They talk and they don't think that I'm listening. I sit in the hallway on a bench with my head buried in a mess of papers and just listen. I think that if they knew I was paying attention they would stop talking. They remember who I was, how they were afraid of me."

"But they're not afraid of you anymore, Bart," Nagler said. "Not since you left, after...what did happen?"

Harrington stared at the ground, and then at Nagler.

"I just left, Frank." The distracted voice was gone. "I know everyone thinks I was drunk all the time, and you know, it helps me if they think that, but that wasn't it. I had gone to the state Supreme Court with cases, Frank. Argued before the state's top jurists. Then after that I found myself in traffic court trying to get some Hispanic teenager out of a drunk driving charge, and it hit me that I if got that kid off, or the next one, or helped some family beat their landlord over repairs, or even took on the state on some vital issue, it didn't matter. We – the kids, the poor, the workers, homeowners, cops, and the elderly - were just getting steamrolled by the authorities and the monied class. I had this vision of us all in a huddled mass while a tall, deep black cloud swarmed above us, and when it crashed down, we were all washed away, everything we owned or stood for, ruined. I had that dream again and again and the only way I could stop it was to get away. Saving the world became a full-time occupation and one day I realized I couldn't do it. So I left it for someone else to do."

"But you came back."

"Had to, Frank. I had so many phone calls asking for help. I realized there's no one else to take on this fight," Harrington said as he turned to speak with a woman who asked about the petition. Nagler just watched, torn between concern for Harrington's well-being, and worried that he (Nagler was sure) didn't have a permit for the sign, and police officers would come and forcibly remove him and the sign. Nagler laughed. That was exactly Harrington's point. Action brings repression.

"Go on, Frank. I'll be fine," Harrington said as he watched the woman sign the petition. "You smell like the inside of a charcoal filter, Frank. Go on. I'll be fine."

Nagler started to walk away, but then stopped. "You said you had something, some information for me. When will I get it?"

Harrington quickly looked in both directions.

"Not here, Frank. Can't tell you here. They're watching. But check your inter-office mail."

Nagler took a breath. I don't want to ask that question.

"Who is watching, Bart?" But he did anyway.

"Them." Harrington nodded toward two police officers across the street and half a block away.

This time Nagler didn't ask the question in his head. He didn't want to hear about listening devices, ear pieces, mind control or hidden cameras. *Yet after the stunt in City Hall, he might be right.*

He just walked away. "When you're ready, Bart."

CHAPTER 13

Nagler took a left from the main road, turning into the subdivision where Lauren Fox grew up. The houses were neat ranches, one- and two-story homes built in a neighborhood started after the war, set on large lawns, fully treed, yards with bikes, boats, a second car, a few camper-trailers, tree houses and a Winnebago or two. Some had rear additions or decks extending into the back yards. Barbecue units, canopies, satellite dishes tacked on the side of the house pointing to Jupiter. Lawn chairs, long green hoses, paved driveways. Life easy, calm and predicable.

Suburbia before the Wall Street and Internet money spoiled us all. Before we all became rotten kids.

Suburbia built by decent people who worked hard with modest aims and goals. Who wanted to be good at their jobs and friends to all those for whom they cared. Homes built by people who had known some sacrifice. The last of the war generation, the Eisenhower Americans whose dreams of glory died in Dallas, or were trampled underfoot when the Daley cops opened up the heads of the Hippies with billy clubs.

They sent their kids to school with the hope that what was kind and good in the world would stick and the hate and horribleness would fade. And that their children would make the difference.

Had they been deceived? As Nagler drove out of Ironton, the scenes from the stove-works fire flashed in his head. Not the bodies, not the rush and turmoil of firefighters, the EMTs holding clear plastic masks over the mouths of a half-dozen who got trapped when the side wall collapsed, not the sky turned red.

In that gray dawn, it was not the fire that gnawed at him and turned his stomach acid, nor the three deaths, for each of those was finite and done, but the piles of debris where that homeless crew lived. It was stacks of cardboard boxes and broken wooden pallets, now after the fire sopping wet and covered with more trash; a few shredded blue tarps were draped over clotheslines to make tents, plastic buckets positioned under holes in the roof to catch rain. Garbage lay scattered all over: Fast food bags, cardboard boxes for French fries, paper cups, foam shells that once held chicken or a steak, tatters of clothes, old socks and plastic bags.

He had only sensed the bad scene the other night when he stopped by, a dark, foreboding presence, and a shadow on the way to hell. It was so dense and confusing that it chased your mind away from what you knew was there.

In the full daylight, the mind had no place to go. The mad scene of debris and human wreckage was the bloody accident on the highway, the body smashed on the sidewalk after jumping off the skyscraper. We were horrified and fascinated at the same time. Move along, move along, the cops would say. But we had to look, had to look until we felt that sickness in the pit of our stomach. It was the only way we knew how to deal with it. But we didn't make it our own. We just watched, and wondered. Wondered how it could happen. Wondered how they could live like that.

But he chiefly recalled the eyes, dark holes burned into the faces smeared with charcoal from the fire, bodies wrapped in off-color sweats; the eyes stared nowhere; eyes that held no fear, hardened beyond pain.

Is that what the people who built these homes dreamed their country would become, he wondered. Did they even know such places existed? Not as long as their Golden retriever could chase squirrels in the back yard and their three-year-old could run through the sprinkler. Not as long as the smoke from Ironton's fire drifted in the other direction.

Frank Nagler did not like the coldness that was settling around his heart.

****

As he pulled into the driveway at 138 Maple, Nagler realized that Lauren had become the person her parents had hoped: Decent, forgiving, intelligent and kind. And she had made a difference.

She came to Ironton with no more than a half-million dollar state grant and a program that had no real structure except that which she would apply.

As liaison, Nagler helped guide her into some of the neighborhoods she needed to reach: The rougher ones, the ones with ten families in a home built for two, where sometimes the kids were passed around for entertainment, where the crack heads left their works in the hallways so they crunched under your shoes when you walked from floor to floor in the dark.

More than once he had seen her turn those soft brown eyes coal black and hard and back some reluctant landlord sputtering in Spanish about how he knew the mayor into his sloppy troubled house to point out exactly what damn violation she was talking about, what five families sleeping in the living room she wanted removed, taking that sweet suburban sensibility to a place no one in the town government that had hired her had thought possible.

Of course they really had not wanted her to succeed. They had been here before and bluffed their way past the state inspectors and latest do-gooders until they went away and filed a report that said, "Ironton never changes."

The local officials had seemingly become so used to their torn up streets and half-empty downtown, it had become a point of pride. So they celebrated the past, put up murals of miners and iron workers and held annual festivals that tossed about names no one knew except when they gave directions. For all of Howie Newton's bluster and myth-making about how he worked hard for the common man, Nagler recognized that during Newton's reign as mayor the only municipal project that was completed on time was the one that paved the streets in his own neighborhood.

Even Gabriel Richman was like that. His dreams were too big, giant structures with no foundation; a collection of words, ideas, concepts that had no shape, no center and no chance of succeeding. He, like the others before him, didn't want to do the legwork, did not want to lay that foundation. All that work took too long.

It was easier to make big speeches and find someone to blame when all the stick houses collapsed.

And into that mess walked Lauren. They tried to force her out more than once. They cut her program's shared funds until the state made them repay it. They lost her purchase orders. The inspectors failed to show up when she called. The paperwork always got lost. The families were back living in the attic a week later and the landlord who swore to the judge that he had seen the error of his ways was at the

Trenton Street Club's barbecue fund raiser by Saturday.

The Old Iron Bog was not the only thing in Ironton that stunk.

But Lauren persevered. He'd see her at the end of the day with that broad smile on her face as if she had just spent the day at the beach instead of in the mayor's office reminding him exactly what he signed up for when he agreed to have the state program in his town for five years.

What had she gotten into? What caused her to run? And who was she hiding from?

Nagler hoped a visit with her parents might help him figure that out. He wasn't supposed to be here, in fact he wasn't supposed to be doing anything but running the night shift, but it was not just Foley's disapproval that had stopped him. More than once he had started his car's engine, rolled out of the driveway and drove west from Ironton; more than once he had come to the split in the road where the left fork went to Lauren Fox's town, and the right fork turned to the Interstate and back to Ironton. More than once.

The two-story ranch was dark blue and had a large corner lot. A clothesline ran from the side of the porch to a maple tree in the back and a yellow blouse, a white towel and some men's shorts swayed in the breeze. Evergreen shrubs were clumped on either side of the two-car driveway and stone steps curled from there to the front door.

He cupped his hand to his eyes and peered into the garage where one car occupied the left hand stall.

What the hell?

It was Lauren's VW Beetle. Nagler recognized the duck sticker on the rear window, the symbol of some wildlife federation. That and the City of Ironton parking sticker.

A thin layer of dust coated the vehicle, and couple boxes had been placed on the floor between the car and the garage door. It had been there a while, Nagler understood. *Two years?*

It could not be that easy, he thought as he knocked on the wooden storm door.

Her mother answered, and in the dimness of the hallway that the sunlight had not filled, for a moment Nagler saw the familiar image of Lauren: The dark hair pulled back over her forehead with a barrette, the thin nose and lips and an endless pool of brown eyes that had drawn him into their depth more than once, brown pathways to a soul whose beauty and pain he had only begun to understand when she left.

But in the full light of the day Adrienne Fox proved only to be the rough sketch of the stunning woman her daughter would become. Maybe age and the recent events involving Lauren had taken away the underpinning of that face, but as he studied it he knew that her mother's face had always been rounder, softer, and the eyes, though the same brown, less well defined, as if the light that filled them from within was always less focused, less bright. Her mother was smaller, slighter and now, clearly, more frail.

"Is it alright that we talk in the backyard," Adrienne Fox asked. "Lauren was always there, reading." Her voice had a hollowness that was left after the substance of the world had been yanked from people's lives, after they had been told their loved one had disappeared. The mouths of the survivors moved, the words floated out and drifted away in the breeze, broken bones of thought caught in a throat and coughed up.

Nagler wanted to start with the car, but backed off. Her voice, so weak. *How to discuss her daughter without making it sound like I'm assuming she was dead?*

"I know you have questions for me about Lauren's exit from Ironton, but first do a mother a favor: Tell me about my daughter, Mr. Nagler," Adrienne Fox said. "Tell me why she was so wrapped up in you and you in her and yet the two of you parted under such strange circumstances."

That was not where he wanted to start the conversation; it was the question Nagler had been avoiding for too long.

"What do you mean strange circumstances?" he asked.

"She left Ironton without saying good-bye to you, isn't that right?" she said. "It seems to me that Lauren leaving the city at all could have been considered strange, correct? She only hinted at events and circumstances, so I don't know details. But she asked us for help, something that she had never done."

I'm nervous, Nagler thought, amazed. *Christ.* He felt his stomach flutter. *I've interviewed killers, for crying out loud and this scares me to death. Maybe I could pull the cop thing. Just the facts, ma'am. Nice dodge.* He closed his eyes and let out a short, sharp breath.

Foley would be pretty upset to find out he was here, but Nagler didn't care. He found himself reevaluating his positions on Foley, and not because Foley had busted him to the desk on the overnight shift. It was a lot of things: The odd behavior at the bog crime scene, the tour of the stove-works, the trips with the mayor and apparent shake-down of that homeowner, the general coldness that had settled in between them. Nagler wanted to report that incident, but in the current atmosphere he had to keep it to himself. *But if you are about to bust someone in rank, you might stop being so friendly.* There were a lot of things that just didn't add up. And now Lauren Fox's mother wanted a report card. *Man. How'd I get myself here?* But maybe it is time for this, too.

He took long, deep breath and scratched his forehead. Interviewing murderers was easier.

"I..., Well, I loved your daughter," he said, feeling his face flush, the words sounding strange as he said them, as if he was talking about someone else, about people and events from a very distant past. It was like prom night. Being grilled on how he was going to treat their precious baby. But then he paused and felt lighter; it was a relief to say that, to speak out loud those words that he had only whispered to himself. *Why had they been such a burden?*

Lauren had dropped into his life and before they had even gotten to know one another, they had fallen in love, or something like it. But maybe it was the closeness of their work. They saw each other daily and worked on problems of her job often. He was on the end of the phone line when she ran into trouble or needed a police detail to clean out a house. Or when the crap from the mayor's office got too deep, or when they just wanted to be together, sitting in her office alone, silent, staring.

"Surely, Mr. Nagler, it cannot be as painful as discussing her absence."

"Mrs. Fox, Lauren, well, was different. I remember walking away from our first meeting shaking inside because I knew that I had just met someone who stuck. And each time I saw her after that it became more and more, I don't know, interesting. It had been a very long time since any relationship had been interesting." *Since the third grade.*

"She called me after that meeting," her mother said. "She was as star struck as you were. I had never heard her speak of some with such curiosity. You were special to her as well, Mr. Nagler."

He felt the sadness rising, the quivering in his heart as beautiful Lauren Fox once again filled him with the love that had changed him.

But then he asked, "Did she tell you about my wife, Martha?"

Adrienne Fox smiled softly.

"Of course she did. And I'm sorry she died so young. What a heart-breaking story, I am so sorry. I remember Lauren saying it was hard for her to think about such an event, since she was so close in age to your wife when she died."

Nagler stared at the ground. All those years he had talked to no one about Martha, not even to Dawson, really. But that day Lauren Fox accompanied him to her grave, the words poured out like water from a crack in a rock face, words he hadn't spoken for years.

He ran his hand over Martha's name cut into the red granite slowly, as if touching the cold stone would transmit his touch to his wife's face.

Lauren touched his shoulder.

"Love like that doesn't end, Frank. It grows silently and holds us together. You don't need to be ashamed of it, or afraid to talk about it," she said. "And you need to stop blaming yourself for her death. There was nothing more you could have done. I know that your love meant everything to her. I'm sure it gave her great strength."

Frank Nagler looked up from the ground and at Lauren Fox's mother. "I hadn't realized that was what I was doing. All the anger I had directed outwardly for years was just a way of denying that it was cancer that killed her, not me. But when you're twenty-four and the woman you are supposed to spend the rest of your life with dies, it's pretty easy to blame yourself. I always worried that your daughter thought she was Martha's replacement."

"Was she?"

"No." He glanced around the quiet yard. Sunlight spotted the lawn between the canopy of branches still holding close the turning leaves; new late roses bloomed and added bright red to palette of the faded pinks of those just past and the stiff brown edges of those now dead. This is nothing like the place he and Martha had grown up in, those hard Ironton streets.

"The place Martha and I grew up in was a darker, more troubled place than here," he said. "Martha was my way into the world, even when we were kids. My family wasn't rich, so things were harder. But she just had this ability to get everyone's attention, and then laugh when they looked her way. We were kids. Everything was a big adventure, a big gamble, and then I never knew why, but being with her made everything easier. I was uncomfortable in public and sort of used Martha as my way in. And after she died I just pretended for a while she was there helping me. I loved her and needed her and never thought she'd die. And then she died and I eventually backed away from the world."

He let out a big breath. "I'm sorry. There's a lot of things going on. I haven't talked to anyone about Martha for a long time."

Adrienne Fox's eyes were red and she clutched a tissue to her mouth. "You speak so well of her. Lauren was right. She said there was more to you than anyone knew."

"I don't know," Nagler said, embarrassed he had rambled on so. "By the time Lauren came to Ironton, I had that whole aloof cop thing down pretty well. No one bothered me, so I was able to get away with it. But it was a different behavior when Lauren and I met. I had added years of police work to the layers, so I, like everyone else, had this image of themselves. I had done some good work as a cop, was known to be reliable and effective. But then you start believing that you are something you're not and start believing your press clippings, start thinking that you are better than you are. But Lauren had this way, quietly, that said, 'oh yeah, prove it,' and I realized I had to be better, be sharper if I was going to be with her. I was just trying to keep up with her. She had a way, your daughter did."

Do I continue?

"Then something changed. Maybe it was working so close," he said "Every day, there was some big issue. We rarely talked about anything else, it seemed. There didn't seem to be enough time. She was so filled with her job, the details, the grant applications, the ways to make a banker come up with a hundred grand for a housing project, how to get the county to kick on for a river clean-up, and the dreams." His voice cracked.

"I remember the day they broke ground for a playground. It was big deal, something she had worked on for months, the first big project she had pulled together. The night before we had a disagreement - she said she felt uncomfortable about us being seen together so often - and I hadn't seen her before the ceremony. It's not like it was secret. We were seen everywhere. Anyone could come into her office and find us there. The old town manager always scowled at me when I would run into him in the hallway outside her office.

"But it made something clear. No matter how close we were there always seemed to be a gap between us that never went away. She said she was shy, but I wondered about that because I had seen her back the toughest landlords against a wall without fear and it didn't seem to me that a shy person would have been capable of that. But on that day, there was something else going on. Her face seemed shattered and she was acting nervously, as if she was being watched. I couldn't get close enough to ask her about it. Being completely in the dark, I was sure her state of upset had something to do with me. How's that for ego?"

He paused and glanced at the tree line. What the hell was he doing? Where'd this need to confess everything come from? "What are the words you're supposed to say to break through that, I don't know, wall? Especially when there wasn't one there before? What are you supposed to do? I never figured it out."

"Personal fortitude and lack of shyness are not the same thing, Mr. Nagler," Adrienne Fox said. "Lauren was always brave and forthright. She lived a life filled with friends and adventure, but at the end of the night she would be the one coming back from the high school dance alone because she had turned down every dance. She would want the quarterback to ask her to dance, but then would stand in the shadows while he walked by to ask another. That was the contradiction of my beautiful daughter. She was so much of the world, the center of everything, yet so afraid and lonely. She was a little girl who grew up very much alone. Her brother is ten years older and her father and I worked. So she had a lot of time, perhaps too much time, alone. When she talked of you I prayed that you would be the one that burst through that bubble she surrounded herself in."

Nagler ran his fingers through his hair. *What I knew about her and what I didn't know.*

Later Nagler and Adrienne Fox walked through the neighborhood. A river cut off the back side and stopped the housing development, opening the land to farms that rolled toward Pennsylvania with waving corn.

"Lauren told me she went skinny dipping in the river," Nagler said.

"I would not be surprised," her mother said. "But why are you telling me about it?"

Nagler laughed. "Because she'd want me to."

His head suddenly filled with Lauren's soft voice as she told him of swimming in the river. She and her two best friends went to a pool behind a corn field and after trying to talk one another out of it, stripped and jumped into the water, splashing in a girlish frenzy. He recalled she said she started undressing and was standing in her panties before the other girls, giggling, joined in. They were all sixteen and had been friends since grade school, she said.

"What are you thinking, Mr. Nagler? Of my slim, naked daughter and her young friends?"

Her voice had no edge, but was soft with a newfound concern.

He laughed; the sudden lightness in his heart amazed him...

"She had just come out of the water," he started to explain the vision. "On the other side, on a big rock. She turned and faced the others, shimmering, naked, the water dripping off her shoulders, breasts, and thighs. She tipped her head forward and shook the water from her hair and let out a shriek. Then she jumped back into the pool and the three girls met in the middle and embraced for a long, long moment, arms locked around each other's necks, their breasts and hips touching, locked, kissing each other's necks and shoulders and promising they would be friends forever."

He glanced at Adrienne Fox, expecting her face would be hard, angered by the embarrassing story.

"That is how she told the story to me," Nagler said. "I think she did it specifically, first, yeah, to see how I'd react, to see how embarrassed I'd be, but mostly, because she understood it said something about her that no one in Ironton could guess. A risqué tale from her youth. She told it without blushing or shyness. She told it because she wanted me to see that she was a lot tougher than anyone thought she might be. I wonder now if she told it because she was saying that something was about to happen."

They turned back to the house.

Nagler finally got to ask his cop questions, but other than a few generalities, it was clear that Lauren Fox had told her parents little about her time in Ironton, but that alone was intriguing. It was either so dull or routine that it was not worth speaking about, or it was so strange and dangerous she didn't want them to know for fear they would speak to the wrong people, and more he guessed, so they would not be able to tell anyone about it, providing them a measure of protection should anyone come asking. Like me.

On the front porch before Nagler said his thanks and farewell, Adrienne Fox said, "It's possible, Mr. Nagler that that place Lauren was trying to draw you into was not as you saw it, but instead the only place she felt safe. She was drawing you there not only because she loved you, but because she trusted you. It was the place where she was always alone. She was asking you in to make her feel less lonely."

Maybe that was so, he thought. *It is hard to be lonely in a world that demands your attention.*

He said had one last question.

"When was the last time you saw her?" His voice was firm and his face hard.

Wow. That was harsher than he'd intended.

Adrienne Fox's face went blank and lost color. She covered her mouth with her hands. "Is that why you came, Mr. Nagler? Of what do you suspect her?" The previously soft voice took on harder edge.

He stammered a reply. "Oh, no. Please. I'm sorry. I didn't mean to imply anything. I was just..." he shrugged slightly and waved his hands, "... asking." He looked at the ground and half-smiled. "It's a cop thing. A routine question. I'm... I'm sorry. But I do need you to look at this photo."

He pulled out a five-by-seven blowup of the lion-headed gold ring that had been pulled out of old bog. "Does this ring look familiar?"

Right away, Adrienne Fox said yes. "It looks like a ring Lauren bought as a graduation gift for herself. Sort of a congratulatory splurge after completing her master's degree. Why are you showing me this?"

"The ring was found in Ironton's old bog as part of the search related to another case." Nagler said. He didn't say it was on the finger of a detached hand. "We're trying to find the owner. And, no it doesn't mean that Lauren is - or that she is in any - if it is hers, it simply could have been lost or stolen, or a similar ring that another person owned."

Nagler could not find the words, could not say "missing" or "dead." He'd said them dozens of times, said them to stunned mothers and angry fathers, curious husbands, wives, wailing sisters, but he could not say them to Lauren Fox's mother. He wondered: Can I say them to myself?

The color had not returned to Adrienne Fox's face. "It is all so curious," she whispered. "Then I best give you this," she said, and pulled a small brown envelope from her sweater pocket.

It contained a key.

"It's the key to her apartment in Easton," Adrienne Fox said. "We own some property there and she lived in one unit after leaving Ironton. All her mail was sent here. She was hiding. That's why her car is here. She told me to give this key to you, if you ever appeared here. I debated for days whether or not to call you so to give it to you, and nearly forgot about it until you called to ask to speak with me."

"Do you know what might be in the apartment? How long ago did she live there?" Nagler asked. "Did she say what she was hiding from, or whom?"

Adrienne Fox closed her eyes, forcing tears out. They ran down her face freely as she made no effort to wipe them away. Then she covered her face with her hands. She shook her head. "No, she never said, and she told us, warned us really, never to ask. I fear to ask: How much trouble is she in?"

Nagler offered his handkerchief so Adrienne Fox could wipe away her tears. Hiding or running? It was odd how it looked the same.

"Mrs. Fox. Lauren is okay. I believe this," Nagler said softly, trying to be as assuring as possible after scaring her half to death. "But do you have any idea where she might be?"

Adrienne Fox looked off into the brighter distance, the answer troubling her eyes, which withdrew, growing darker.

"We're not sure," she said. "We got a telephone call from her months ago in which she said she was leaving Easton because she saw a woman from city hall who had caused her trouble. But she didn't say where she was going, just that she would contact us when she was settled. We've had no contact since. She told us not to worry. But how could I not worry?"

"Did she say who that was?"

"Yes. I'll never forget the name because I thought it unusual.

Glance."

Shit, Nagler said to himself. Debbie Glance. Again.

He was going to have to speak with her. But how? He wasn't supposed to be investigating anything, and he knew that if Foley suspected he was poking around at anything, they could pull him off the desk, knock him back to patrolman, or fire him.

This is a strange box I'm in.

****

The road to Easton, a town in Pennsylvania just across the Delaware River from New Jersey, is a winding, old country road that by accident became the main route from the northwest part of Jersey to Pennsylvania. It hugs a river on one side and runs along a steep cliff on the other. It was a perfect road for riders on horseback, slow wooden wagons laden with hay or iron ore, or for tourists, but, filled with traffic, not for anyone in a hurry. The fifteen miles to Easton took more than forty minutes. It was all the subdivisions. He must have passed a dozen. Houses perched on hillsides, lawns spreading right to the riverbank, and with them acres of shopping centers. He passed one shopping center that seemed to be nearly a half-mile long, with three large stores at the either end and in the center, and dozens of smaller ones scattered in between.

Was this what Gabriel Richman had in mind for the iron bog?

Nagler shook his head. Why did Ironton miss out? The monied interests in this state can pretty much do what they want, where they want. But they didn't want Ironton. How strange, when it seems so easy to get. Did someone or something scare them off?

The key. Was he being played by Adrienne Fox, too, he wondered. He felt lighter after all the unburdening, the acknowledgment of the tangled emotions; maybe that would clear his head. What might be in that apartment? Evidence of innocence, or a confession? Then there was Debbie Glance. *She found Lauren Fox, why can't I?* Nagler asked himself. *Because you weren't looking for her, and Debbie Glance clearly was.*

As he drove, he went over and over the stove-works fire and all the confusion, lights, odors and sense of desperation when firefighters realized that three people were still inside the burning hulk; then the commands, men and women scrambling for helmets and flashlights as an arc of flame flashed overhead, the wet battering of the brick by thick, gleaming ropes of water fired from the hoses on trucks that lined the roads and fields.

commands, men and women scrambling for helmets and flashlights as an arc of flame flashed overhead, the wet battering of the brick by thick, gleaming ropes of water fired from the hoses on trucks that lined the roads and fields.

He was interviewing the survivors as they were treated for burns or smoke inhalation, or just offered soup. He had spoken with a dozen and had yet to find Del Williams.

That was the last question he asked, "Did you see Del?"

The answers sounded alike: "Yeah, man. He was standing in the middle of the camp, yelling at us to get out, god dammit, get out. A couple of the guys passed out, and he was pullin' on their clothes and sleeping bags, yellin' at them, you know? There was smoke and fire all over hell. So thick ... couldn't see or breathe... Get out, get out. God dammit, get out."

"Do you know where Del went?" Nagler asked.

"Man, they was just layin' there. And Del, he was pullin' and pushin' at 'em. Man. Just get out. Get your asses outta here."

Four of the buildings were ablaze when Nagler arrived, creating a wall of fire maybe three hundred yards long and a hundred feet high. The fire companies surrounded the buildings and a dozen water streams arced from the black ground to the red and white canopy of flame and smoke, flashing in and out of the yellowed spotlights.

There had been only one other fire of such magnitude in his lifetime, a lumber yard fire when he was a kid. He had been able see the glow of the fire from his house in the hilly streets in the north part of the city. He hunched on the roof of his house and watched the horizon burn. The glow lasted all night, like the sun rising in the wrong piece of the sky.

That was when he learned about Ironton's other great fire. All the papers at the time wrote about it.

It was Ironton's version of the Great Chicago Fire, an uncontrolled blaze that consumed more than half of the downtown. The fire started in a pile of hay in a barn attached to one of the city's old railroad hotels and quickly spread from wooden building to wooden building until it reached the outer wall of the city's first brick building. Firefighters used the wall as a fire break and stopped the advance of the flames, but had to watch as the rest of the buildings collapsed into blackened heaps.

Why'd I remember that? Nagler wondered. When was that? He remembered. It was during George Richman's first term as mayor.

He parked the car in Easton just off the main drag, got out, and looked for the house number of Lauren Fox's apartment.

He remembered recalling the Great Fire and staring out over the burning stove-works. He summoned the snatches of the city's history. George Richman already owned the mines and the ironworks and the railroads before he became mayor, but he was just one of the city's industrialists. As mayor he changed the direction of the city, a change, Nagler recalled, that began after the fire that leveled half the downtown.

The change was hailed as the great revival of Ironton. There were lots of furiously written newspaper stories that made comparisons between Ironton and the mythic Phoenix, the bird that rises from its own ashes. Pages of hot words, grand descriptions and florid quotes from officials. Nagler smiled. Glorious, old-style, over-wrought newspaper prose. Didn't think Dawson was that old.

****

The apartment smelled closed up and stale. It was still furnished in manner that suggested it was used by a family member and not a tenant. The matching couch and chairs were plush, the rugs padded and thick. The refrigerator had an in-door ice maker and the bedroom was dark with thick floor-length drapes. It seemed to have been recently cleaned, as if Lauren's parents expected her to return after a months-long vacation. Yet there was nothing personal in the rooms, no left be-hind bracelet, jacket, magazine, notepad, nearly empty shampoo bottle – not even a sock under the bed – nothing that said Lauren Fox, dark beauty, odd, at times, dresser, dreamer, doer, schemer, was even here. She left Ironton without a trace, and now Easton, leaving, it seemed, even less of a trail. Still, she'd made sure her mother gave him the key.

He pulled back a curtain and glanced at the street below. It seemed quiet and ordinary, just rows of apartments or condos, cars lin-ing the sidewalk, flowers in wooden boxes on windowsills, a settled place.

It was the quietness that got his attention, the lack of substantial foot or vehicle traffic. It was so quiet that a stranger might draw attention, and it made him wonder if this was where Lauren saw Debbie Glance.

The apartment looked swept clean. Did you think it was going to be obvious? He chided himself. So he searched: he opened drawers, closets, looked under the bed, felt beneath framed photos on the wall, under the mattress, looked in the linen closet, but found nothing.

It was in the freezer, under a pile of empty ice cube trays. A manila envelope with his name written in black marker.

All the weight returned, the questions, the churning in his gut; the wall again closed. He flipped the envelope over a time or two, finally staring at his name. The "F" had that flair that Lauren used in the first letters of names, even when she printed. He pulled open the clasp and took out about a dozen sheets of paper.

"Hi, Frank," the top page began. *"If you are reading this, you've already met my mom. I figured you'd get here sooner or later."*

CHAPTER 14

Lauren Fox

Attached to the first page was a yellow sticky note.

"Hi. I wrote most of this while still on the job in Ironton. It started as a way to keep track of what was going on, but later it became a record of other things. Lauren."

In the margin, she'd written, *"I had to do it this way, Frank. Sorry. In the end you'll understand why."*

It was written like a diary...

I arrived in Ironton, New Jersey about four years ago. I was hired by the city with state funds to begin programs that would lead to more jobs and better housing.

I thought I had better start writing down things about the third week I was in the job. There was so much going on, so many details to organize, that I began to lose track of them. After I missed a meeting with the town manager and he scowled at me for about ten minutes, I began to get organized.

At first I despaired over the condition of Ironton. I mean, how could a city with such a history of success, a city with strong leaders and past economic strength fall so far? I saw homes that had not been repaired obviously for years, and when I asked how the city could let the landlords get away with it, I was told that's just the way it is. But children were being exposed to bedbugs and rats and filth. Blocks of houses were like that. Jiminy. Drugs were everywhere. I looked up the Census data and found almost twenty-five percent of the city's population earned less than twenty-five thousand dollars a year. The high school dropout rate was nearly fifty percent. I learned the city was a destination for immigrants and maybe ten percent of the homes had three or more families living there. The newest immigrants were from South America and not one person at city hall spoke Spanish. I know I didn't!

I was overwhelmed. *O-ver-whelmed.* I called my mother and cried on the phone, and she'd listen because that what mothers do. But then my Dad would get on the phone and in that brusque Dad-way would tell me that I had to get past the fears and concentrate on the solutions.

Then he'd say, "Rome wasn't built in a day." He always said that. And it always made me feel better.

So I started to sort through the work, even though it took the city a month to get a computer into my office. I bought a lot of legal pads and kept hand-written notes. The state wanted to see three issues tackled: Job creation, housing, and code violations. I wasn't sure what the city officials wanted. Their attitude seemed to be, the state told you what they want, so give it to them. But it wasn't that easy. Most of the state grants required some city money or labor. Mayor Richman said he would get the city council to set aside some funds and get the county to use inmate labor for some of the projects. But, you know, he didn't really seem to care about the state funds or what could be done with them.

Later I found out it was because he wanted to build a shopping center on the Iron Bog. I had spoken with Maria, my contact at the state, about that project and she made it pretty clear that no one in state government would support it, no department would fund it, and I was going to have to tell the mayor.

I thought I was going to be sick before that meeting.

Mayor Richman had already held his press conference about the shopping center plans and the big billboard had already been unveiled. Talk about being too big for his britches. I thought he would have waited until he had done a study on the site to even see if it could support a shopping center. I mean, it's A SWAMP! It's a big hole in the ground filled with water. Oh, dear. So, yeah, okay, the concerns professionally were the environmental correctness of the thing, and the location and inability to attract financing. But, jeez, it's still a big swamp. What was he going to call it? Swamp City. Home of Discount Pricing?

He didn't want to hear that the state was willing to support a project for the big parking lot along the river. The state would have paid for the studies and the engineering and we could have built a project that would put jobs in the center of the city.

Mayor Richman just muttered about how the state was trying to run Ironton again, that they had tried it in the past and they were the reason there was a big, empty parking lot in the middle of downtown.

He told me to get out. And then he told me he was going to assign Debbie Glance to monitor my office. I had never even met her. I was a little scared. I wanted to quit, but Maria said she would speak with the mayor and calm him down.

So I stayed. Debbie Glance was not assigned directly to my office, but she began to get involved more often.

I learned a lot about Mayor Richman in those days, not the least of which was how mercurial he was. It seemed like no one had told him "no" before because whenever someone did, he grew cross and short; sometimes he left the room or called an end to the meeting. He reminded me of a little kid. I know he was the mayor and was used to leading and directing and generally bossing people around - blah, blah, blah - but walking out of a public council meeting as he did one time because the council asked questions about the bog plan, seemed juvenile to me, not mayoral. Even I knew he needed the council's approval and I'm not political at all. I thought he would have been more polished, more professional, but even in meetings he would talk about how "they" were not going to stop him, that his family had a legacy of leading this city in hard times, that he would bring the city back to its glory days when his grandfather George Richman founded the modern Ironton.

No disrespect Mayor Richman, but what I learned about your grandfather was that he was nothing more than a robber baron. He was a rich industrialist who bought political power and turned the city into his own cash cow. I think what really gets the current Mayor Richman was that he is nowhere near as rich or skilled as his illustrious family member, and all the huffing and puffing is not going to make him so.

Then in the middle of all that, I met Frank Nagler.

Wow. Everything, I mean, everything, changed.

I met him at a community meeting. He was the key speaker, discussing a new program aimed at connecting a new division of community based police officers with neighborhood groups. The response was somewhat predictable. The neighbors didn't want more police in their neighborhood; they wanted the potholes filled, the street lights repaired and the drug gangs evicted. It seemed to get pretty personal at one point but Detective Nagler just calmly answered questions and took suggestions.

What I liked was that he made no promises, you know, like the gangs will be run out of town or some other John Wayne-ism. He just told them straight out that there were problems and with their help, the city could make progress. He had a tremendous sense of calmness, and not just because he was a cop and used to taking over a situation, but he projected an aura that nothing ever was going to upset him. When I learned later that his wife had died when he was a young man, things made sense. Nothing else could ever be that horrible.

I guessed that was why he seemed weighed down. I didn't think it was his job. He seemed so much to enjoy the give-and-take with the neighbors. He laughed at their jokes and smiled at the grandmothers, strongly shook the hands of all the men, and once in a while paused with a puzzled face, then grabbed the man's shoulder and they smiled broadly as the connection was made. More than once I heard him say, "Oh, right. I remember that."

His eyes carried the weight of whatever it was. When he laughed they did not sparkle or share in the happy grin that spread across his face. They did not light up when he recalled a person's name and the history between them flooded in, but remained sunken and still; I wondered what could cause such pain.

The crowd filtered out of the room, and I didn't hear any grumbling. I even saw some smiles and heard a few positive comments, as if they were glad someone finally noticed. I was walking against the crowd like a fish swimming upstream because I didn't want Detective Nagler to leave without introducing myself. I heard a person I came to know later as Jimmy Dawson the reporter asking Detective Nagler why he thought it would work this time, and all I heard him say was, "Because, Jimmy, it has to. We can't give up again."

Finally I got to the front of the room and said, "Detective Nagler, I'm Lauren Fox."

Even before he turned around, he said, "Please, it's Frank..."

How do you describe that moment when it feels like you fell off a cliff and you're just floating in the air? Well, maybe that's how you do it. All I remember is that my heart was beating. I could barely speak. And I remember smiling. Later, when I became more rational, I mean, he was sort of handsome, but pudgy, calm, very helpful but it seemed to me that he was like my father. And I thought, oh boy, you know how that goes.

But as we began to work together, I figured out that Frank was as non-judgmental a person as I'd ever met. He gave everyone a chance to explain. He listened. In a place where everyone was at each other's throats all the time, that was a welcome change. He was assigned to my office and it was through him that I came to understand Ironton. He took me below the surface of the bad houses, drug deals, and empty factories and filled in the blanks with the history of the city.

I learned to see how some residents were working to make their neighborhoods better, to make their lives better. I had been through such places, but where I grew up in the suburbs was so far from Ironton it might as well have been another country.

I had read about poverty, studied the impact of generational welfare, and had worked with poor families as an intern for my college degree. But until that moment, until I had walked with Frank Nagler into the smelly, filthy, smirky-smiley world of the truly needy, the undereducated, drug addled, drunken, the truly sunken, desperate world of the forgotten, I thought I had understood. That was the moment I grew up, and for that moment thought I (mistakenly) understood the pain in Frank's eyes. At the point that I thought I had no friends in the city, Frank arrived and gave me hope.

When did I fall in love with him? The first time he looked at me with those piercing blue eyes. He looked right through me, but in a way that was asking questions, asking me what I wanted, asking me who I was, asking me to look inside myself and find what I truly believed; asking me to stay.

Does love exist is such glances? Does it knit together such insignificant things, take form in messages left on phones, waves from passing cars or just an occasional smile? It must, because we had so little time to work at what there was between us before the trouble landed that it seemed to me that nothing would ever come of it.

Then I saw the note. "Hey, sweet girl." I don't think I ever told him how that made me feel. I smiled. I tingled. I cried. I felt whole. They were words of hope in the silence that surrounded us; a silence I alone knew would be deepened.

Then she stopped writing. The next page had just a few words, the start of a sentence: "Then things changed." But "changed" was crossed out, and "got weird" substituted.

Nagler leaned against the wall and rubbed his forehead. It was a strangely written tale. It had an odd tone as if she was writing to explain the whole situation not to him, but a third person. It almost read like a

161

deposition, he thought. It was stranger yet, he thought as he read about her first observations about him, things she never told him or described to him. He felt embarrassed. He didn't like being that closely observed. And then there was why? Why did she go through this charade, the apartment key with her mother, the envelope in the freezer?

****

There was one more page, scribbled in Lauren's wide handwriting, just a few lines and notes.

****

"Reading this over, I'm not sure it tells you want you need to know. I had to leave, Frank. You will hear things. You may have already. There were things going on in City Hall, things at first I tried not to believe, but later could not ignore. I was always having computer problems, and Debbie Glance was in my office repeatedly claiming to fix it. I would stay at night trying to determine what had been done, but I'm not enough of a computer geek to know what to look for. I wanted to tell you about it, but I wasn't sure what it exactly was. Before I could figure out what to tell you, I got a warning. So I left. I have more information for you. It is in a safe place. You'll know where. There is more than meets the eye... I think of you in the morning, remember sitting across the desk from you as we had coffee, sometimes saying nothing, but then you'd ask, "What?" I think just to start a conversation... and I think about how when we were together at an event or just out somewhere, it seemed like a play, watching everyone watching us... I miss the kindness of your touch, how sometimes you'd run a finger down my cheek and across my mouth and I'd kiss it, how you'd softly kiss each of my eyes, and brush a hair from my forehead, and... God I can't do this..."

Staring out the window into the bright sunlight he placed one hand over his mouth and closed his eyes. *Neither can I, kid. Neither can I.*

CHAPTER 15

Frank Nagler was already in the over-crowded room when Mayor Gabriel Richman entered and then hesitated in the doorway, stunned by the number of people in the council chambers. "Be careful," Nagler advised before moving along the wall about half-way into the room. Every seat and spot along the walls were taken, the crowd crammed the hallway leading to the room and flowed through open doors into the parking lot. Richman had hoped the crowd would be calm, but there was a murmur building, a rising growl that he needed to head off.

The fire at the stove-works destroyed five buildings, four in the vacant complex, and another in a cluster of smaller buildings where two businesses had begun renovations.

On the streets of Ironton the fire sparked an outrage, an astonished hurt as the residents realized how their futures were suddenly clouded by the fire. They had barely emptied their homes of the sodden ruins left by the flood, and now a major fire. Suspicious, they whispered. Arson, they thought.

Some radio preacher had Biblicized the disasters. Nagler could still hear his raging voice, calling down damnation, sowing tales of demons loose on the street of Ironton. The earth had cracked and hell was rising with Ironton at the epicenter. Maybe the people believed the mill would reopen. Maybe they believed Gabe Richman's super mall would be built over the Old Iron Bog. Maybe they believed because they had no choice, because the human heart is always filled with hope. To do otherwise was to accept that they were just pawns in some political game, chess pieces being moved on a board by an invisible hand; chumps, losers, dust.

The city was a simmering cauldron of distrust that exposed itself in comments posted online under Dawson's story about the fire that crystallized in the shattering of glass at City Hall as a few gangs of kids rattled noisily through the empty downtown streets breaking glass, dumping trash cans and throwing rocks at the windows of city buildings and businesses. They were caught trying to push a Toyota onto the train tracks.

Nagler eyed the crowd warily. Who was going to start the fight?

Who would be the first?

All we need is street barricades of trashed cars, fires in metal drums, gangs armed with poles and clubs and guns and we could be Belfast during The Troubles, Detroit in Sixty-seven, Watts, Montgomery, Selma, any place the distressed gathered and rose; any place pain became action.

Richman called for a public meeting in hopes of bringing calm back to the city.

Five firefighters had been injured and three people died. They carried no identification and a search for information and potential family members had begun.

Chris Foley thought they were just three of the homeless who had been living in the factory. That's what he told the press. In Jimmy Dawson's story about the fire, Foley said, "We haven't determined the cause yet, but I would not be surprised if we find it started near one of the camp fires of the homeless bums that lived there. I saw the camp the other day. It was a trash-filled, disgusting mess. How could they live like that?"

Richman reminded himself to make sure had a tone of concern in his voice when he spoke about the dead. He stared at the floor a moment before stepping to the microphone. Why had I never visited them?

"Thank you all for coming," Richman shouted above the din, which calmed. "We've taken another blow. Just as the city was recovering from the floods, and people's lives were getting back to normal, we suffered a devastating fire. I'm able to report that the five firefighters injured putting out the fire are recovering. None, fortunately, were seriously injured. But three of our citizens lost their lives. I ask you to join me in a moment of silence to honor the three people who died in the fire."

The room was filled with a shuffling silence that held everyone in its breath as even the hardest hearts acknowledged the pain of three needless deaths; held their breaths until someone in the hallway yelled, "Why honor the bums? They probably set the fire. Isn't that what the cops said? Why didn't you clean them out of there?"

That single shouted, torn voice sparked the conflagration. One cry. The room began to fill with rising voices, at first unsure of their message, but as others joined the shouting masses, they found the rhythm of rebellion, the syntax of pain, and the voices wrapped in the orchestration of rage, became one. In the hallway, the shouter was punched and grabbed and thrown to the floor where he covered his head until two police officers lifted him up and led him out of the crowd.

Richman yelled out, "Please, please, calm down. Please sit. Calm down, please." But his voice was lost in the howl, his feet rooted where he stood. The room vibrated with the concussive, rising sound of wordless rage, the voices of the stricken given air; shook as faces howled into the night. Voices wept, screamed, cracked with rage as they tapped into the seam of anguish that flowed like a flood below the surface, but now given an outlet, gushed to fill the room, lifting the wicked and innocent alike to face a judgment all were unprepared to meet.

Dawson caught Frank Nagler's eye as the room erupted. Nagler jumped into the crowd moving toward Richman, and Dawson climbed onto a bench to get a better view. Fights broke out and Mayor Richman was at the podium calling for calm and more cops. It went on for twenty minutes. It went on for an hour. Who knew?

Nagler pushed his way through the rolling, falling crowd to get closer to the mayor. Several police officers grabbed the collars of men crawling over bodies to apparently reach Richman.

Finally at Richman's side, Nagler yelled, "You really need to get out of here," but the mayor ignored him. Instead he returned to the podium and grabbed the microphone.

"Please, please, please," Richman yelled out as police tried to push through the doors filled with people unwilling to move.

More police arrived and tried to enter the room through the main door. But it was jammed with bodies and for a very long time it seemed that bodies pushing from the front met the force of bodies pushing from the back; someone screamed they were being crushed. Bodies tumbled over the pew-like benches.

From seemingly nowhere, Bartholomew Harrington was standing on the council dais waving his arms.

"Get down," Nagler yelled.

Harrington just smiled, his eyes blazing with frenzy.

"Rise up! Rise up, brothers," Harrington yelled. "Oh, yes, the time to rise up has come."

A couple of cops tried to grab Harrington's legs and pull him of the table, but they were dragged away by several men in the crowd. "Oh, my brothers," Harrington yelled, as he danced along the dais.

Nagler finally got an arm around Richman's waist and pulled him out of the central crowd to a wall behind the dais. "What the hell is he doing?" Richman yelled.

Nagler was screaming out to Harrington. "Get out of here, Bart." Harrington turned to face the mayor.

"Do you recognize these faces, Gabriel?" Harrington yelled. "Gabriel Rich Man, do you recognize these faces?" Harrington pronounced Richman's name in two syllables. Rich. Man.

"They are the faces of your youth, the hard leather skin, creased and cracked, mouths formed into sneers or angry scowls; faces of the beaten. You saw these faces when as a boy you walked past the gates of the iron mills and saw the men leave the jobs for the last time, passing into the streets as a security guard leaned and pushed hard on his tiptoes as he struggled to shove the massive gates closed, and with a loud metal crack jammed a steel bar into the latch. Those are the faces that should haunt you, Gabriel Rich Man. You've lied to them your whole life, stolen from them, their dreams, their goals, their livelihoods. And I have the proof." He reached into his jacket and pulled out a manila envelope and waved it in the air. "Everything you've ever done to these fine people, the citizens of Ironton. And now it is over."

The fighting shuffled to silence as Harrington spoke. Group by group the combatants dropped their fists, shook away the collar or arm they had grabbed and stood in silence to listen.

Harrington walked atop the long table, arms waving; when he caught Nagler's eye, he winked. No one moved to stop him, stunned by the bravado, mesmerized by the madness of it all. Nagler released the mayor's arm when Richman stopped trying to pull away. Richman stared at the floor, and then at Nagler, eyes pleading, why?

Nagler pursed his lips and raised his eyebrows as he tipped his head. *You have no friends in this room, Mr. Mayor.*

"Those were the faces of your youth, Gabriel. The bloom of the great George Richman's day long faded; the mills, the canal, the trains, all gone; the shops, the great stores, the frantic buzz that filled the downtown streets, silent. The vacant stares replaced smiles, torn pants replaced new slacks. Torn pants, torn shoes, dirty-faced kids; streets with holes, houses with no paint, men huddled hopeless. Those were the faces you stared into when you promised you would make things better, when you promised you could return Ironton's glory days. Faces you had long forgotten."

Richman stepped to the table's edge. "Get down, Bart," Richman shouted. "They'll take you down. I don't know what your beef is, but get down and we'll talk."

Harrington turned to the crowd. A few of the men had turned to face the room and stood before the table with arms crossed, a sudden barrier to anyone trying to reach Harrington. The shift calmed the crowd even more. Nagler just leaned against the wall and shook his head in wonder. This was the Bart Harrington of old: dramatic, larger-than-life, putting on a show for the court.

"The Great Gabriel Rich Man wants me to stop," he yelled. "But I don't want to stop. He thought you were cheering for him. He thought you believed him. Only now does he realize how hollow your cheers had been. But you didn't hear him; didn't want to hear him. You swallowed your voices for years as the city lost jobs, factories closed and parks and streets fell to disrepair.

'When is the park near my house going to be fixed?' you asked. 'My kids need a place to play. The city hasn't fixed my fence that was wrecked by a snow plow last December. How am I going to feed my family?' You demanded to know.

"You had listened as politicians asked you just to recall the glory of the past, when inventive men devised machines that needed workers to operate, when Ironton's workers carried the region on their broad shoulders and prosperity spread out from the red brick mills of the city on the river like green streams of hope. When generations of your fathers and grandfathers wiped their brows of hard-earned sweat and proudly held in their hands the product of their labors, the thing that held their souls; when they understood how their hard work had made someone else happy.

"But at the same time they understood the mathematical equation of their existence that said all their hard work would never erase all the steep steps between themselves and the factory owners, never shorten the path of their children to success, or allow them to measure their happiness on the same scale as the bosses'. 'Hey, Gabe, how's that shopping center coming? Hey, Gabe, when am I going to get a job?' You shouted to him. And he did not listen. Because Gabriel Rich Man could not stifle that roar. All he could do was stand in its path as it rushed by. It flashed by him, stripping away all the little constructs he had made in his mind, all the flimsy dreams he had foisted on you, Ironton's citizens, in hopes you would believe him and give him one more chance to connect the random and poisonous imaginings to reality. That's who Gabriel Rich Man is."

Harrington stopped. A couple officers tried to reach his legs to pull him down, but the phalanx of men stopped them. Nagler motioned for Harrington to come toward him. But Harrington just smiled, his face filled with a holy light that seemed to say, *if this was the last thing I ever do, what a thing it is.*

The room was silent as a church on Easter Sunday. Every face was upturned to watch Bartholomew Harrington, who was sweating and breathing hard.

"But know what," he continued, not shouting anymore, but softly, explaining, "you've seen the 'home for sale' signs grow on your street more numerous than new trees, seen stores boarded up and your taxes rise even as the library closed on Saturdays, police were laid off, and you had to pay extra for your kid to play football or take a school trip to New York City. You've seen the suffering.

"But Gabriel Rich Man never saw that. He never saw that your streets were still filled with fallen trees and trash left by the rising water. He never knew that your work hours were cut, never saw your neighbor stare at the want ads knowing that at her age no one would hire her."

Harrington's voice gained new strength; he stood straight and tall, and eyes blazing again, hushed what had been for a moment a busy murmur. "Gabriel Rich Man didn't dispute the shouting newscasters saying how on one hand unemployment was the biggest political issue the country faced, and on the other hand how much it was costing everyone else to have all of you out of work at the same time; heard them say with big sad eyes how bad they felt that everyone was hurting at the same time, but you jobless masses had better find a way to get a job, even at some convenience store, because everyone else was not going to pay for you to be out of work much longer.

"They told you, 'Stop being lazy. Stop asking for help. Get off your ass and help yourself.'

"And Gabriel Rich Man never told them to stop. Maybe your voices cannot be heard through the thick stone walls and double glass windows where Gabriel Rich Man conducts his business every day like some ruler of a small kingdom, not the mayor of an American city, a city in a democracy."

Harrington leaned into the crowd, his voice filled with anger and despair.

"How long can a beaten man be kicked? How long can a woman work one job, put her children to sleep with a prayer of better times, and then leave them for her second over-night job and still be told she needs to do more? How long can you stare into the face of a worker and tell him he is not doing his best? How is it that hate becomes easier than mercy?"

His voice filled with disgust.

"Why didn't Gabriel Rich Man hear you? Because he is one of them. He is one of those men in dark rooms stealing your future, who stole the future of your fathers, who will steal the future of your children. Why didn't Gabriel Rich Man fight for you? Because he only cares for himself. You are mere pawns in the game that he and his friends are playing. They will walk away rich and you will die in your homes, as poor and befuddled as ever. Bring them down. Bring them down!" His voice thundered through the quiet room; shattered the peace like a banshee's cry.

Then he whispered. "It's either you or them. Be strong, my brothers."

Then Harrington stopped talking. He sat on the table, and then pushed himself off and stood on the floor.

He turned to face the mayor, who was being restrained by Nagler.

"They are coming for you, Gabriel Rich Man," he said with a twisted smile, his voice harsh and guttural. Harrington looked over the room. In a cracked whisper he said, "And they are coming for me."

Then he left. A few hands clapped; then more. A voice shouted out, a cheer arose and the wrestling crowd parted as Harrington walked slowly out of the room and left city hall. A police captain looked over at Richman for a signal to go after Harrington, but Richman shook his

169

head no.

In that instant when the roar awoke, when the formless tortured cry rose from throats in that room that finally had the stops removed, in that moment Gabriel Richman, still huddled in the corner of the room with Nagler, knew that his time had passed. How many times can we walk past the tent cities of blue tarps and look away? All that was left was making sure he survived.

Foley and a dozen officers in riot gear finally cleared the room. When he reached Richman's side, Foley turned on Nagler. "Why didn't you stop him, Frank?"

"Knock it off, Chris," Richman said harshly. "Frank got me out of harm's way, for which I'm grateful." He reached over to grasp Nagler's arm. "Thanks, Frank." Nagler just nodded, "Sure, Mayor."

Foley just said, "We've got to deal with this, Gabe, and quickly. Harrington will pay for this."

Richman leaned against the wall and cradled his head in his hands.

On the dais was the manila envelope Harrington had waved in the air. After Foley escorted Richman out of the room, Nagler picked it up and was going to slip it under arm and spirit it away. Except it was empty. Surprised, he opened the clasp and peeled off the flap that had been glued shut and stared into the empty envelope. There wasn't even a note, a single sheet of paper that said, "Gotcha!" or even "Fuck you." Then Nagler just laughed. Don't need the evidence, just make the threat. No one remembers what was in the envelope, only that there was one. *They'll fill in the blanks.*

Foley returned and leaned in over Nagler's arm and motioned to the manila envelope. "What's that?"

Nagler handed it to him and watched as Foley opened the folder and realized it was empty. Foley waved his hands. "What?"

"It's what's going to bring down Gabriel Richman," Nagler said.

"But it's empty."

Nagler looked over the shattered room and smiled. "Exactly."

Foley glanced at the envelope, at the room and then at Nagler. "Why are you smiling, Frank? You don't want to be on the wrong side of this."

Then Foley walked back to the hallway, where Gabriel Richman

170

stood in the doorway, shoulders slumping, a look of fear in his eyes. No, not fear, Nagler decided, confusion and hurt, a man searching for someone to tell him what to do next.

Foley took the mayor by one arm, lead him away and showed him the envelope. Nagler heard Foley angrily say, "It's empty." Richman, understanding all the implications, said, "Shit."

Nagler leaned on the dais, the tension melting away. Wrong side, Chris? *That's what Bart Harrington told him the day that Richman announced his re-election campaign.* "Don't get caught on the wrong side of this," Harrington said.

Nagler smiled. *I'm already there.*

CHAPTER 16

Nagler shook open the paper, folded the pages in half and chuck-led as he reached for his cup of coffee.

Dawson was on a roll, living in newsman's heaven, Nagler thought. The city had exploded with news and he was at every event.

Richman's town meeting, which was called to calm the city, set off the explosion of activity, and, combined with the last weeks of the heavy campaign season, plucked the lid off the old city. Crowds no one had seen in years turned out at political rallies and debates. Protests appeared seemingly out of nowhere as any group of people with a complaint, grudge, issue or concern drew a crowd. The veterans gathered at the city's War Memorial and slowly read off the names of the returning soldiers whose families had been evicted because they ran out of money. A few hundred vets on motorcycles roared through downtown Ironton and lined the great machines along the sidewalks as they passed hats and helmets among the shoppers and gawkers collecting money to support the families.

Teachers gathered at the city park after the cut in state aid to the school district caused a hundred layoffs. Commuters briefly blocked an eastbound train after the state's transit authority cut service and raised fares after a budget shortfall worth millions was discovered. Groups from opposite political sides alternately occupied the train station or the park as the rallies grew in size and louder in tone. Eventually the police were assigned in numbers large enough to keep the groups separate, when they rallied together.

Residents began to appear at city council meetings, which was a real shock to the council since they had become quite familiar with conducting city business in front of rows of empty seats, except the one that Dawson occupied.

Given a voice, the residents presented grievances that at times appeared to be decades old, yet had a freshness that stung: streets in disrepair, flood waters eating away at their lawns and backyards, trash filled, vacant houses, abandoned cars, drug deals, gang graffiti, police who never come when called; each complaint piled upon the other, each fresher, more raw, each voice more insistent, more dangerous if ignored.

172

And Dawson marveled at it all. The stories reminded Nagler how good a reporter Dawson actually was.

"Where have you all been?" Dawson asked in a newspaper column. "We missed you. Let me catch you up.

"Problem is, you've heard all this before. It's the same bad actors treading on a barren stage reading from a well-worn script. You'll recognize the characters.

"But I'll tell you anyway.

"While you were gone, a few billionaires have been trying to buy Congress, and doing a pretty good job of it. Congress took most of the year off except to vote on naming post offices. It might have been okay they did, but you might have noticed in your travels that the economy is running a little slow. Maybe there was something the President and Congress could have done about that.

"Federal authorities charged a lot of politicians with stealing your money, but that happens so often that you probably didn't even raise your head from the pillow; hardly enough of an activity to rouse you from slumber.

"The big banks got in trouble again, but that's been so constant, it's what we expect. The banking bosses will get hauled before a Congressional committee and on television promise never to do it again. But they will; they always do. Your money is probably safer under a mattress, and the bedbug is paying better interest.

"So if you haven't noticed, the world's gone to hell in a hand basket. And know what? Everyone who can, will blame you. Yeah, it's your fault. I saw you out there. You can't make up your mind. You stand on opposite sides of the street waving signs and yelling at one another. You want to tax the rich, send the Mexicans back across the border, and tell women they can't have sex or babies out of marriage. You want all the homeless off the street, but you don't want the government to buy up houses that became empty when the banks foreclosed, yet you want the banks to pay for being greedy. You didn't like the idea that the government bailed out the auto business, but you want all those unemployed people to find a job. You don't want to pay more taxes, but complained when the school board fired a third of the teachers because they ran out of money.

"Everything we used to think was wrong with someone else is

now wrong with us.

"So what you are going to do is put down the signs, take off the silly hats, stop spouting sections of the Declaration of Independence and the Constitution that you don't get right in the first place, and truly don't understand, and buy each other a beer and talk. You can disagree, but start talking. The longer you delay it, the longer all of this will be wrong.

"And once you've decided the guy you worked with for the past twenty years hasn't really changed, but is just one more person trying to do his best to raise a family, grow some tomatoes, take a week down the Shore and keep his head above water, the better off we'll all be.

"And then you're going to head out to the Forty-Six Motel and talk to Tommy Robinson. You remember Tommy. Seven years ago he played quarterback when the Ironton High football team won the state championship. You were standing on Blackwell Street with more than half the town yelling your crazy head off when the bus got back from Giants Stadium. The police cars and fire trucks led the way and for an hour or so, all the things that you thought bothered you were gone because those forty-five kids did the city proud.

"Then Tommy married Camilla and they had that great baby girl. He went to work for the delivery company but also joined the Army Reserves. And a year later it all changed. He did two tours of duty in the desert war and when he came home you all forgot to welcome him.

"Well, you can welcome him now, because the delivery company didn't hold his job, and Camilla and the baby were thrown out of their house, and if it wasn't for the church and some other folks they might have been living in the stove-works when it burned down, and you really don't want that on your conscience, do you?

"Maybe you saw him at the city council meeting the other day. His head is shaved now, but his eyes have that direct, piercing stare of the truly committed. He looks a little beat up. He came to ask the city council for some help. He needs a job and there is some red tape holding up some of his Army Reserve pay. He wants to get his family out of the Forty-Six Motel and back into a decent apartment. The baby is three now and sometimes plays in the parking lot and there are a lot of cars. The city council thanked him for his service and told him how proud they were of him, but they had no answers for his questions.

"After a moment or two of watching the city's leaders stare at one another, Tommy Robinson said, 'I don't want you to feel sorry for me. I just want a chance to raise my daughter well. I just want the same chance that fathers who came before me had. It's not about the uniform. We serve proudly and willingly. It doesn't make me special. I just need your help right now.'

"Then he turned and walked out of the room. He stopped as his wife helped him settle his crutches under his arms and helped him maneuver through the narrow aisle on the one leg he had left.

"So when you wake up this morning, instead of worrying about whether your neighbor is a socialist, or whether the French or the Spanish or the Greeks are going to ruin the American economy, think about Tommy Robinson.

"He's the reason you get to yell at your neighbor, just like generations of soldiers before him. He's the reason you get to be so disagreeable.

"We are a nation that was born arguing. It is what we do best and it is what separates us from all the other nations. So revel in our raised voices, find joy in the sound of the words we speak. Celebrate our differences and defy all those who tell you to conform, to damn the other side. We live to disagree. The louder the better. Roar on, Ironton. Push back against the silence. Rise up. Rise up. And forward."

In the middle of all the activity, the paper ran Dawson's story that questioned the identity of the woman in the bog. Using a federal source that Nagler had provided, the story said that Foley's exact identity of the girl had been premature. The source said the details were not incorrect, but that the single assumption that Carmela Rivera was the dead girl had not been proven without doubt. Leads were still being developed. Foley, in a written statement, said that new information called into question the identity they had been provided. He said his conclusion had been premature, but he was sure that the new information being investigated would show that Carmela Rivera was indeed the woman in the bog.

Richman stood by Foley's side at the press conference when the police officer made his announcement. When asked a question, the mayor merely restated his support for the police department. Nagler watched the event from outside the meeting room, standing just out of sight of those on the podium. Both Richman and Foley seemed even more uncomfortable than he thought possible. Bob Yearning beat the issue with a stick, raising the question at every candidate's event. "When will Gabriel Rich Man's police department solve this case?" Yearning shouted. "When will they bring this woman and her family some peace?" Foley's communication with Nagler had become a series of electronic messages and hand-written notes in inter-office mail envelopes. At his desk in the silence of the night shift, Nagler examined his notes, the photographs, the search reports and all the material he had collected. It was like adding the same list of numbers again and again and getting the wrong answer. He hoped that Foley was too busy to worry about how Dawson got the Carmela Rivera story.

Nagler was waiting at Barry's when Dawson arrived.

The fire marshal had declared the stove-works fire an arson, which seemed both obvious and anticlimactic, given the fights at city hall a few nights before. But the other big news Dawson reported that morning was that the Gabriel Richman's house, the home of his grandfather, patriarch of the city, had been claimed by the bank in a foreclosure sale.

"Foreclosed, huh?" Nagler said as he took a seat opposite the reporter. "Christ, it was his family's home. Why'd he have a mortgage? I thought that place would have been paid off decades ago."

The paper's headline had one word: "Foreclosed." But the next line told the story: "Mayor Richman's home taken by the bank. Just in time for the election."

Dawson wore an evil little grin. "Yup. Already been accused of shilling for the Yearning campaign. I heard about this weeks ago, but had to wait for court schedule to be published as verification so I could read the paperwork. Gabe said what I expected he'd say. Bad investments, market down, working it out with the bank. Said it was nothing. Asked me to hold the story. Told him I couldn't."

"Think he's working with the bank?"

"Well, he's still living in his own house," Dawson said. "There's something else."

"What?"

"You probably haven't noticed, since you're working the night shift, but Debbie Glance hasn't been in the planning board office much of late. I only know this because I was down there the other day with a question about some land."

"You buying land now, Jimmy?" Nagler asked, laughing.

"No. I wanted to ask her about something Barry told me about a while ago. Someone is buying up foreclosed and empty properties and flipping them for a fast profit. Figured the buyers would need some permits for the repairs. No one knew anything, which in itself is strange. But I have something else."

While Dawson fumbled through his bag, Nagler thought of Chris Foley going house to house with his mysterious city form. Asking quietly, Nagler learned the feds wanted a damage survey completed for all the streets within eight blocks of the river. But no one really knew anything else.

Then Dawson said, "Ah," winked, and pulled out a large folded manila envelope and began to open it. "Instead I found this."

Nagler shoved the coffee cups aside as Dawson unfolded several wide sheets of paper that turned out to be tax maps.

"You remember those numbers you and Yang were looking at, but couldn't decipher? Look here. Here they are. Someone is trying to buy the old stove-works."

Dawson pointed to the tax maps.

"Damn it," Nagler said.

They were there, all of them: 10.2167; 10.2171; 10.2245; 10.2246. 10.2301; 10.2319; and 10.2326. They were the lot and block numbers of the parcels of land that made up the stove-works complex. Starting at the sharp curve at the southern end of the property, the seven lots lined up like puzzle pieces.

Nagler looked up from the map. "And the other night those buildings were torched. But why do you think someone is trying to buying that land?"

"Because while I was looking up the mayor's foreclosure listing, I noticed seven listings under the name of OSC Incorporated. That's the name of the company that owns the stove-works. The one that no one could ever find? They used to be called the Ohio Stove-works Corporation. Well, turns out the company did file for bankruptcy, but in Delaware, because that's where all the big companies register their headquarters as a tax shelter. So all their holdings are in foreclosure. But that's not what is interesting. Most often in a foreclosure the bank ends up being the only bidder, drops a hundred bucks and takes back the property so they can sell it to someone else. But that's not what happened here. All seven parcels were claimed by something called Eye Glass LLC."

"Who are they?"

"Don't know. They have a post office box for an address, another one in Delaware, and Sol Cohen, their local attorney, is conveniently out of town. Whoever they are, they'll need millions, because the judgments against those seven pieces of property are huge."

Dawson folded up the maps and stuffed them in the manila envelope and handed it to Nagler. "That's your copy," he said. Nagler fingered the envelope and looked around the restaurant that was filling up with the lunch crowd.

Dawson ran a hand through his hair.

Nagler looked sore and sat a little sideways in the booth.

"You're too old to get beat up, Frank," Dawson said.

"Tell me about. Got kicked in the ribs and maybe pulled something in my shoulder," Nagler said. "Some scene. Foley wanted to haul in everyone, the chief said just hold the ones who beat up cops. Might be twenty. Been over there yet? City hall's a mess and the council room won't be used for months."

Dawson asked, "What do you think got into Bart Harrington?"

Nagler smiled. He recalled Harrington's face. So filled with light and fervor, righteousness and anger; a man transformed. "Not sure," Nagler said. "Glad it did."

In truth, Nagler knew that had gotten into Harrington. *The one thing Bart understood about public life was that it is drama, with actors and soliloquies and grand thoughts played out on a moving stage, the little subplots connected, the winks, the nods, the hate, the love, wrapped around itself, sometimes so tight it became a bubble that needed to be pricked. So he pricked it; the force of that release was the opportunity for resolution.*

But Nagler didn't say that to Dawson; instead he wondered when Harrington would surface again. "He's out there somewhere."

CHAPTER 17

Too many loose ends, Nagler said to himself. He glanced up at the crazy Christmas tree chart on his wall and at the files on the table in the middle of the room and knew it was time to dot the "I's" and cross the "T's." Time to connect the dots, make one and one equal two, close the loop. Time to bring down the hammer. Close the sale.

He chuckled at the silliness. Time to shut the door, blow the whistle…

Time to get this monkey off my back.

During the weeks since the body had been found in Old Iron Bog, Nagler felt like he was hauling around a large sack and every day someone opened it up and tossed in one more thing. Lauren Fox, Chris Foley, Gabriel Richman, Debbie Glance, the body, the fire, Del Williams, the invoices and stolen money.

Then in the middle of it all, he got a call from Manny Calabrese, who said his cousin who runs a jewelry shop in Morristown thinks he sold that ring to a woman in her mid-twenties, slim, with brown hair. A real looker, Calabrese said. "Maybe three, four years ago, Frankie. My cousin, he's not so good with records, which gives me agita, so he can't find the bill of sale, but he's good with rings, especially really nice pieces, and he's always good with women. He remembers every good looking girl he ever saw."

Four years ago would have been about the time Lauren Fox got her master's degree, her mother said. So if Lauren was in Easton, how does her ring possibly end up on a finger of a hand in the Old Iron Bog?

Nagler looked up again at the chart, then stood and ripped it off the wall. Suddenly it was the symbol of all that was wrong, not because it was complicated, but because it was useless.

Crimes have no logic, he reminded himself. They are passion wrapped in a pattern that appears to be logic. How many times had he listened to some lawyer explain to a jury how it was logical that his client had no reason to commit the crime, when it had little to do with reason, but had everything to do with the emptiness of his soul, the coldness in his eyes or the jitter in his loins.

Nagler shook his head. He had been looking at all the recent events from the wrong angle. They were not about who had the most to gain or lose. It was about survival, about who was going to get thrown off the boat and who was doing the throwing.

When you are burning down buildings, you're way past the point of worrying about profit and loss because in the back of your mind you know no matter how many layers you place between yourself and the act, the smell of gasoline on your hands never really washes away; there's always a matchbook with a phone number that didn't quite fully burn and somehow it will all point back to you. So if you planned it, the best thing you can do is set up the fall guy, put that matchbook in someone else's hand and work damn hard to make sure that someone else will get blamed.

Because the guy who set the fire is the weakest link, has the most desperate need and the least ability to lie. They always talk to someone. The tremor in their voice finally gives way to a confession. Yeah, I was there, passing by. I might have stopped. You found flares in my car? Well, you know, I drive on the highway a lot. The cash? Won it at the casino. Hit a lucky streak. Couple of weeks ago? Won a few grand. Since when is going to the casino a crime? Fire, set what fire? Not me, but I think I know who did; heard someone talking about it in a bar.

Nagler let out a long breath. What did the U.S. Attorney use to trap all those officials? A promise to redevelop some property with the chance to get some skin in the game, hold a little side action, a little something for the family. All wrapped up in ribbons because it was going to be good for the city.

Nagler reached over and began to fold up the big chart, then folded it in half and ripped it. Dawson's going to love that, because it was his story from a couple of years ago that had pointed Nagler in the right direction. Lost in the muck of the failed shopping center in the Old Bog adventure, was an ordinance passed by the city council a year before that created a redevelopment authority. The council appointed itself as the authority directorship, with the mayor as chairman. It gave these nine politicians the ability to create projects, choose developers, find the financing, and pick winners and losers. He had circled several paragraphs of Dawson's story. The council could declare almost any district in the city in need of development if it met some basic criteria: blighted housing, high levels of poverty, and this was the one that caught Nagler's eye: parcels that contained a certain percentage of long-standing vacant buildings and the "reasonable" absence of any effort in recent times by the owner to find suitable tenants or undertake rehabilitation. Being vacant for thirty years or more was probably "reasonable absence."

The law had been broadly worded so the city could apply it to the bog, but what other sizable property fit that bill?

It came to him as he watched the stove-works burn. It would have taken the city decades and thousands of dollars to peel that property away from the owners. Could be really costly to fix up, especially for a company that barely existed, its assets so well hidden that it seemed to be no more than a name on the top of sheaves of papers molding away in some Delaware bank vault.

We could make all that go away. A dark silent night, a few gasoline soaked rags stored in strategic spots, a crew of perfect foils sleeping in the filth of the buildings. A quick investigation, finds nothing conclusive, blame the victims, tear it all down. Make it all look like a civic improvement. Jobs for everyone.

Somewhere that story is encoded in these documents and just waiting to be read. Or stashed someplace where Lauren Fox hid it. Nagler felt he has just been hit with a two-by-four: There's more than meets the eye. That's what she had said. Was she coming clean, or passing along a tip? He looked at the piles of paper. It's in there somewhere. Now to find it.

A few days earlier Nagler spoke to the historian who wrote the flier about the great downtown fire during George Richman's day. He admitted he was forced to clean up the history a little bit.

He showed Nagler some letters written back and forth by some residents who had moved away during the first half of the Twentieth Century. They were mostly friendly remembrances about growing up in Ironton, but one of the correspondents posed this question: "Did they ever prosecute George Richman for that hotel fire?"

"What's that mean?" Nagler asked the historian, Stan Girardi.

He was a former teacher and banker who made it his retired life's work to collect in a museum as much as he could of the city's history.

"There was some talk that George Richman might have had that hotel burned down," Girardi said. "He owned it, and for a decade or more during the period when he also owned iron mines and the mills, it was a thriving business. There's no real evidence to indicate he had anything to do with the fire. I've read hundreds of letters from the time, journals, and newspaper stories. There was a lot of speculation. Everyone had a George Richman story. But that's all they were – stories. For a man who was as prominent during his life as he was, and appeared in many ceremonial photographs, there were actually few stories in newspapers about his life or time in office."

Girardi pointed out a few black-and-white photos of George Richman on the office wall. Portly, smiling, dressed in doubled-breasted suits, with a long watch chain running from pocket to pocket, and a top hat, Richman was the person in each photo who attracted the viewer's eye. Nagler could see the family resemblance. Even in photos of other business leaders, he seemed to be the dominant personality, the driving force of the time. Nagler imagined that few people ever said no to George Richman.

Girardi continued the tale.

"It was a different time, Frank. America on the move, the time of the great industrialists and bankers, working together, or conspiring, as many see it now, to enlarge their enterprises, politicians in their hip pockets, as the county's population flowed both west and into the great cities as waves of immigrants arrived here. There were no laws to stop rampant stock market speculation, weak laws to stop corruption, and since most of the big money men controlled the politicians, the law mattered little. The nation's economy was a toy to these gentlemen. When one of them got in trouble, the others bailed him out. Today what happens pales in comparison. The deals are the same, but were driven into the back rooms, and only get revealed when they finally spill over the top and it is impossible to notice. Interest rate manipulation, uncharted millions being funneled into election campaigns by unknown donors, and who knows what else. What's worse, we view it as entertainment. Enron shuts down the electric power grid in California, and we just marvel at how clever they were. Heaven forbid the government regulates free enterprise to protect the little guy, why, that's, that's socialism. We don't want to be like the French, for God's sake. Then Jack Abramson shows up, a perfect bad guy in a black hat and long trench coat, and he provides the blueprint for how to influence government officials for fun and profit, and we applaud when he goes to jail, but demand no changes to the system send no politicians to jail or even vote them out of office. We elect the government we deserve."

Girardi shook his head and shrugged.

"I'm sorry, Frank, but think of it. In the nation's first 80 years, we fought three significant wars. But from the period after the Civil War to the end of the century, we engaged in no world-wide wars, just the decades-long war against the Western Indians, and those battles were as much about the economic expansion of the nation as they were racial wars of eradication. The J.P. Morgans, John D. Rockefellers, the Carnegies, the Mellons, the Thomas Edisons had a different view of their fates than did the Cabots and Lowells and others who fostered the earlier American Industrial Revolution. The world had grown larger, and these men of vision placed themselves like the Colossus of Rhodes astride the harbor and declared the world was their domain."

"On a smaller scale, the George Richmans of the world claimed their city or county as their domain. While their gains and losses were small by comparison with those of the giants of the day, the local impact was greater. The right gamble, or the wrong one, could swing the fortunes of a city like Ironton from triumph to ruin, often in an amazingly swift ascent or descent. So a man like George Richman could influence the way of life in this city in the blink of an eye. More important, the impact of those ventures was seen here, on Blackwell Street, Berry, North, in the city's alleys and neighborhoods, on the tables of working families, in the classrooms of the city's schools. If George Richman's schemes worked, he improved the lives of hundreds of families, but when they failed, those families crashed first. He could move on and try something else, but the ruined families mostly likely did not have that chance."

Girardi sat behind his desk and rocked back in the chair.

"Richman built a lot of the downtown, and it was thought ironic at the time that the building firefighters used to stop the blaze was his department store, the city's first brick building. But the mines were closing down. The iron era was over. Cheap steel was coming into the market place. The great days of Ironton were over, so many thought. But I think the thing that really set Richman off was the construction of a new, straighter, flatter rail line south of Ironton. He saw the future: All the heavy port freight traffic would bypass Ironton, and he would miss out on the tariff he was charging other railroads to haul freight over the section of the tracks he owned. Some letter writers at the time said Richman was losing his shirt and couldn't sell half his properties to anyone. They suspected that with that big downtown fire he collected the insurance money, so to speak. But then a funny thing happened. We went to war again, and iron products were needed. The furnaces were re lit, and this time the iron mills were supported by textiles and boot making. George Richman turned on a dime, went from being an ironmaker to being a retailer and shirt maker. He made more money supplying Army uniforms than he ever made selling iron nails."

Nagler just smiled.

"How much of that history do you think Gabe Richman knows?" he asked.

"I'm guessing a lot of it," Girardi said. "He speaks about his family legacy all the time."

"But is it the legacy of being the builder, or the back room wheeler-dealer?"

"Good question. But I've known Gabe a long time and he never impressed me as a mastermind."

"You might be right," Nagler said, then laughed. "I'm guessing no one was ever prosecuted for the hotel fire."

Girardi laughed. "They blamed it on a drunken teamster and an old horse, neither of whom were ever seen in Ironton again."

Nagler laughed. "Any evidence the teamster worked for George Richman?"

I didn't set that fire, officer. But I heard someone in a bar talking about it.

****

Nagler sat at the dispatcher's desk underneath the bank of a dozen televisions that received live feeds from the cameras mounted at key spots around Ironton. Captured in a blue-tinted haze, in fifteen-inch blocks, the absence of activity was mesmerizing, even at three in the morning. The camera swapped scenes in rotation, each one showing an empty street with perhaps on the third turn, the faint flickering of a street light, or a delivery truck flashing through an intersection. Nagler was amazed that in the middle of the night drivers waited for the traffic signals to change before they passed through the intersections.

"We've trained them well, haven't we?" He laughed. What did they think, that the dispatcher would see they ran the light, instantly call the one patrol car downtown and while they were being written up for that infraction, the officer would find they murdered their family back in Oklahoma? *We're the ultimate voyeurs,* Nagler thought. *A kid with his hands down the front of his girlfriend's pants at the train station, drunks stumbling home, a homeless guy pawing through a trash can. We see it all. We see it all, record it all, and do nothing but watch; just the endless wash of life in the middle of the night. Passing emotionless, silent.*

To his left on the desk was a list of times and dates and key codes, the recordings of events taken by cameras near the stove-works in the days preceding the fire. He had already seen the daytime visit of Chris Foley and Debbie Glance when they met Del Williams, and it was pretty much as Del had described it, ending with Foley reaching into his pants pocket and peeling off what appeared to be paper money and handing it to the homeless man. But Foley also handed Del a couple of bags.

Nagler leaned forward for a closer look. *What's that about?* The visit took place several days before the fire broke out. He watched the scene again. It made no sense that the pair of them were at the stove-works on city business. Neither the police nor the planning department had anything to do with tax appeals, and the place was already a wreck before the storm so there would not have been much for Foley's emergency management office to inspect, either.

More interesting, but inconclusive, was a visit by Debbie Glance early in the evening before the fire. She walked slowly in the shadows of the tall buildings, holding probably a flashlight, and glanced around the corners of several others before meeting up with a taller person in a hooded sweatshirt. A quick, but indistinct hand transfer took place. Nagler had seen the hand shuffle a hundred times before as a drug dealer and the buyer each palmed the drugs and the cash and in a second made the transfer. Was this the guy who set the fire? Was that a payment, or a drug deal?

Nagler reflected on what he'd seen. Debbie Glance. Criminal

mastermind, or hopeless junkie? It almost didn't matter because the video quality was poor because the lighting was so bad. He could identify Debbie Glance from her clothes, but the man she met with was just a tall, dark blur, on the scene for less than a minute, and his face never was shown. Drug deal, Nagler concluded. He knows where the cameras are. How did she hide it so well? City hall was filled with people who would be willing to sell out a junkie, especially a good friend of the mayor. Nagler shook his head. Imagine if Yearning had gotten ahold of this tape? And then he wondered why he hadn't. *You're in deep if you are sneaking around to buy your drugs at wrecked factories in the middle of the night. So why is this such a secret?*

The fire appeared as a gray flash, then a billow of darker smoke, leaking through the windows of the building to the right of the main factory. Flashes and more smoke soon filled all the lower windows of that building, as a new flash appeared in the next building over. Then a third flash and clouds of churning smoke from another building. Bodies ran through the smoke in all directions, disappearing into the billowing mass and running out again.

As he stared at the monitors Nagler wanted there to see more urgency in the running, more purpose; wanted to see bodies in twos and threes supporting others as they all emerged from the fog-like presence on the screens. Smoke flowed from screen to screen like a swarm of millions of tiny insects, rising, contracting, swerving, billowing, driven not by chance and pressure and wind, but intelligence as each of the six cameras recorded a different view of the scene; bursting toward the screen with such force Nagler expected to hear the sound of tiny collisions from inside the monitors. Slamming with such imagined power that more than once, catching the emerging cloud out of the corner of his eyes, he jumped back.

In the main factory, the fire seemed to flash from all the lower windows at the same time. Nagler knew the homeless camp was about a hundred feet from the center of that wall. Maybe they went out the back. Too much fire all at the same time, he thought. He could understand why the fire marshal declared the fire had been set.

Six cameras recorded the fire and Frank Nagler viewed the footage from all of them. Once the flames took hold, they consumed the debris and trash like dry grass. He had been there. He knew how much trash there'd been: Yards of it, piled twenty feet high in places. The building went up all at once, filling with flames and smoke as if staged. Silently the gray flickering fire flashed through the roofs, poured out windows and left the cameras recording a billowing, floating scene. Nagler watched in silence, trying not to fill the void with shouts, and cries and screams.

He was there that night. He already knew what it sounded like.

Nagler stopped the last video. He never saw Del Williams.

"Some scene, huh?"

Who was that? Nagler jumped from his seat.

"What the fuck? How'd you get in here?"

There he was, Howie Newton. White Panama, dark shades, skin like porcelain; white fog.

"Dispatcher let me in. He's outside having a smoke."

Nagler's head was still spinning.

"What's up, Howie? Pardon me if I think it's not good news."

"Your friend Del is at a nursing home I have an interest in, registered under a phony name." Newton's voice was thin and smoky as dust. "I had him sent there, and I'm paying the bill."

"Jesus, Howie." Nagler was stunned. "Really great of you. But why?"

Newton ignored Nagler's sarcasm.

"Fire chief said Del was the guy who got his buddies out the building. He dragged men and women out and ran back in. He even grabbed some firefighters at one point to help him, and they just ran in behind him. They lost track of him in the smoke. Heard they found him near a burning pile of rubbish, his pants on fire and his shirt burned off.   Also heard Foley thinks Del set the fire. Wants to charge him, if he can find him.

"Why won't he find him?"

Newton sighed. *You're not a simpleton, Frank. Figure it out.*

"Because I own the place and they do what I tell them to do. The doctor owes me a favor."

Nagler could see Newton smiling behind the shades. "Why does Foley want to charge Del?" Newton's silence filled the room. It was all the answer Nagler needed.

"Does it ever stop?" He asked.

187

Newton again ignored the cop's tone. "Give me some paper. I'll give you the doc's name and number. Tell him you spoke with me."

"Why Del?"

Newton stepped from the shadowed corner of the room and up to the counter. He stood erect and placed one hand on the countertop.

"I've been taking care of Del since his father died," Howie Newton said. "Pulled some strings to get him that railroad job, and sometimes he did some work for me."

Nagler stood up and crossed to the counter. "Did you keep him doped up, too, Howie? Make him one of your boys? You tell me Del could do nothing on his own, without your help? He was my friend. Did you ruin him, too, like everything else you touch?"

Newton slipped a finger behind one of the dark lenses and rubbed his eye. He'd heard all this before.

"I got him a job washing dishes," Newton said. "He did the rest on his own. He was so proud of that award the railroad company gave him because he earned it. I wished I could have kept him away from the drugs. But he wouldn't listen. But, yeah, he did a little work for me."

Nagler's heart dropped and watched as Newton wrote the information on a pad. "How come you know more about this than I do?"

"Because they don't want you to know, Frank. They want you on the night shift with a couple of officers who owe Foley. They don't want you hanging around City Hall in the daytime when you would notice things. You had to know."

"I do," Nagler said wryly as he shrugged.

Newton passed over the pad.

"I don't like guys like Chris Foley," Newton said softly. "Too much surface. It hides all the scheming. You never know the rules, how they operate. He's wormed his way into a key position at City Hall. He's the police department's chief investigator now that you're on the night shift. How much information does he control? He's a confidant of the mayor. Don't you think he wants something in return? We all operated with the same rules, quietly, carefully, and when we benefited, some family in town had something good happen to them. Guys like Foley are reptiles, cold-blooded. Predators. As long as they win."

The room fell silent. Behind Nagler the televisions flashed scene after scene of empty streets, groping teens and flashing traffic lights.

Nagler stared at the old man. Howie Newton knew everything. What did he know about this?

"Why are you concerned about Foley?" Nagler asked. "Is he behind all this? And speaking of Foley, and the mayor, I saw you all the other night outside an old warehouse near your club. Did you burn down the stove-works, Howie? Was that what that meeting was about?" *No, of course not. Not his style. He's the back door man.* Newton didn't flinch, didn't even look up as the question was asked, as if it was beneath him. "Also talked to some homeowners down by the river. Seems someone is trying to buy them out using a straw man. Is that you, Howie? Sounds like you." That wasn't exactly right, but Nagler let it hang in the air.

Newton didn't flinch, or smile, or shift his hat away from his eyes. He didn't even move.

"I could help you, Frank," Newton finally said.

Is that what this visit was all about? I've seen how you help. Nagler turned back to wall of monitors rather than say anything else. He didn't want Newton to see the scowl on his face or the darkness that settled in his eyes. *So many layers. How can I get to him?*

He turned back to where Newton was standing. "I'll pass," he whispered coldly.

The room was silent, with just a hiss from some machine in the background. Newton turned to the door, and without saying a word, left the building.

"Son of a bitch," Nagler yelled as he slammed a fist into the countertop.

CHAPTER 18

Nagler found Dawson at Antonio's. It was the bar Ironton's politicians favored for election night celebrations, where they danced to Sinatra under the flickering light of a mirrored ball while with large sweaty hands they felt the sweet asses of their young female campaign workers, spilled drinks on the thick scarlet carpet with huge black squares, and promised everyone in the room better days were coming.

But at three in the afternoon there was no celebration, just a few couples giggling in the dark corner booths while tinny classic rock leaked over the intercom and six televisions were all tuned to different channels. One sports fan at the opposite end of bar from Dawson was watching a repeat of Sunday's Giants games and yelled "YEAH!!!" every now and then.

No one came to Antonio's in the middle of a weekday afternoon to celebrate, Nagler decided.

"Look at those guys," Dawson said as Nagler approached, pointing at the television set above the bar where two commentators were talking over one another. "Self-important, ideologically blind. Two guys who have opinions based on nothing, who think that anything that happens in the world happens to someone else. So secure they don't think anything bad would ever happen to them, so they can say anything they want."

Wow, Nagler thought. *And I haven't even ordered a drink yet.* Nagler pulled out the bar stool next to Dawson and sat down.

"You okay, Jimmy?"

"Long day, Frank. Spent the morning with Gabe Richman, having him explain to me how the fire at the stove-works was a blessing in disguise - You know, how the city might be able to acquire the property cheaply and sell it, or finally force the owners to put it up for sale after all these years. Asked him about the arson investigation and he clammed up after that. Asked him about Debbie Glance, and he said she's on a medical leave. Asked him about the storm clean-up, when the city might get more of the federal money, and he just sort of drifted away. This was one last chance to make his campaign speech, and he didn't seem interested."

Dawson finished his bourbon and ordered another. "Leave the bottle, Denny."

He poured a drink and emptied it. Nagler ordered a beer.

"Then I was talking to Yearning. Did you know he failed to file federal taxes for three years? Claims he's been in dispute with the IRS and..." His voice trailed away and he filled and emptied the glass.

Nagler moved the bottle of bourbon away.

"I heard you got fired, Jimmy."

Dawson tilted his head up to the ceiling, then glanced again at the television, and surveyed the bar. "Yeah. This afternoon. Had it out with Upton."

"Sorry, Jimmy."

Dawson shrugged.

"He was going to get me sooner or later. Said it was corporate, that about fifty others across the company also got fired." He picked the glass, which now held mostly ice and a little tawny colored water from the bit of bourbon still in it. "I'm not worried," he said, but his eyes were sunken and his voice soft, and he stared at the bar a lot.

"Like I said, I'm sorry, Jimmy. Let me know if you need anything."

Dawson smiled weakly and nodded.

"What's going to happen here, now, Frank?" Dawson waved his empty glass around the bar. "They city's staggering around like a drunk on a three-day bender. The mayor seems to be losing touch and if the residents aren't careful they'll elect Yearning as mayor and he's so dumb and full of himself at the same time, he'll just make things worse." He put his hands on his forehead and squeezed. He glanced over at Nagler with his eyes half-closed and smiled, snickering. "Hell, maybe the IRS will get him before Election Day. That would be fun." He glanced up at the television, frowned and shook his head several times, stopped, and repeated the move.

"And the Trenton crowd is making its usual mess of things and the towns and cities are going to get a big bill from the state because the annual budget is a few million short and they think that's just fine. They'll be more layoffs and more people out of work, and the Trenton boys will say, it can't be helped. The governor is auditioning for some federal job and like the other governors is beating up on his state workers and firing teachers and cops while trying to tell the voters that everything is just fine. Don't teachers and cops and secretaries vote, too? Are you really going to vote for the guy who fired you? And then – and I love this - the governor is hanging around with his rich buddies who want to build the world's greatest shopping center on that swamp in the Meadowlands." He slapped the bar. "Jesus, Frank. What is it about politicians, shopping centers and swamps? But you know what, the whole state's a swamp, sucking all that is good down into the mire. We're hip deep in black, slimy water and we applaud the idiots who drove us off the highway ramp at hundred miles an hour and planted us in the muck like they did us a favor. The politicians, the bankers, the industrialists, the investors, the regulators. They all have their hands in our pockets and they could care less if we fail because, Barnum was right, there's a sucker born every minute."

"Hey, Jimmy," Nagler said. "Ease up."

"Sorry, Frank. Yeah. Maybe."

They both stared straight ahead for a long silent moment.

"Think you'll ever see her again?"

"Who?"

"Lauren."

Nagler chuckled and stared at the bar while he swirled the last of the warm beer around in the bottom of his glass. He shook his head slowly back and forth before he said, "No. She's gone." He turned in the bar stool to face Dawson. "I spoke to her mother after I found that package in the apartment in Easton. She said Lauren was out west, down south -" he shrugged, "somewhere. I thought she was lying, but it doesn't matter."

But it did. For all of his wanting it not to be so, she still might be a suspect in the money mess at city hall. For all of his trying, he had not been able to conclusively rule her out. Dan Yang, as he unraveled old computer files, found more and more links of funds that passed through the community development office. What was missing, Nagler knew, was the finger print on the weapon, the signature on letterhead, anything definitive that actually tied Lauren Fox to the funds. Nagler was also having a hard time determining a motive. But then, a few hundred thousand dollars sometimes was a motive in itself. Then there was Debbie Glance and the computer problems. That was one of the issues being on the night desk had complicated, so he asked Dan Yang to look at the paper trail from that angle, so far without result. Nagler had not told Dawson about any of that; as far as Jimmy was concerned, this was about love.

Dawson spilled some more bourbon over the ice in his glass and a little more on the bar. He looked over at Nagler and comically blew out some air from clownish cheeks and dabbed at the bourbon with a tiny napkin.

"Drunk yet, Jimmy?" Nagler smiled. "I'll give you ride, call you a cab."

"Not yet," Dawson replied. He stared at the silent television above the bar, and then turned to look at Nagler with clear eyes.

"You're gonna hate me for this, Frank, but it seems like the day to do it. You and Lauren? In my opinion, you two never really trusted each other, you know that?" Dawson said. "You may have really loved each other, but you never trusted each other."

"What are you talking about?" Nagler asked, irritated. Not again. "And why are you talking about it?"

"I saw you. At those events. You'd talk and hold hands a little. Smile. Man, Frank, you looked like high school sophomore half the time. You really needed the practice. Still, I hadn't seen you look at someone with such affection in years. It was so intense. And man, I've never been in love with anyone, but I saw the way Lauren looked at you. Woulda made me a Catholic just to go to confession if she looked at me that way."

"Hey, Jimmy, you need to go home."

"In a while. This is not the soon-to-be drunk Jimmy talking. This is your friend Jimmy. I'd watch you two, and it always seemed like you were walking around a circle. For all the closeness, you guys were distant, like neither of you wanted to be the first to commit. So you waited."

Nagler ran his fingers through his hair. "If you've never been in a relationship with a woman, how do you know about trusting one?"

"I was in a business that relied on trust, just like you. You and I trust each other, Frank. It's the basis for the business we conducted. We both know what trust is and how to build it. But you and Lauren never figured that out. I saw you guys. You never got to the point where the spoken became the unspoken, where words didn't matter. Instead at times it seemed that each of you did something that each of you knew would cause trouble. I don't doubt you loved her. I could see that. Hell everybody saw that. But when you and Martha looked at each other, it was more than a look of love and devotion; it was a look that answered all the questions. That's trust. When I saw you and Lauren looking at each other, there was a puzzle in both of your eyes like you didn't believe what you saw there. Instead of answering the questions, it seemed that your glances were asking them."

"So what's wrong with that?" Nagler asked. "Maybe we were trying to figure it out."

Dawson started laughing.

"Damn, you're a pain in ass, Dawson." But Nagler was smiling.

"Casablanca," Dawson said. "You know that airport scene where Rick puts Ilsa on the plane? 'The troubles of two little people don't amount to a hill of beans in this crazy world,' or whatever Bogie said."

****

Dawson finished his drink and poured another. He glanced over at Frank Nagler, who had his head in one hand, staring at the bar with unfocused eyes.

"Aw, go home, Frank. Made you miserable enough for the day. Leave all the shit we spilled on the floor right where it is. There will be more out there in the morning."

Nagler paused, half smiled, and then rose from the bar stool slowly and looked over at Dawson, just sitting there half grinning, half asleep. Maybe Dawson was just emptying his tank, getting rid of all the anger, frustration and fear. Maybe he was right. "You gonna be alright, Jimmy?"

Dawson blew out a laugh. "I'm always alright, Frank. You know that."

Nagler reached over and grabbed Dawson's shoulder. "Call me."

Dawson rolled his head around few times and smiled to himself. "Yes, Frank," he said in his best mocking "Yes, mother" tone.

Nagler just shook his head. "Jesus, Jimmy," he said, and turned for the door.

"Hey Frank," Dawson called out.

"What, Jimmy."

"You have the soul of a lonely man, my friend. Find her. She made you more human. You laughed more, told better stories, had a smile on your damn face, for Chrissakes; you were easier to be around, and got rid of your collection of really bad ties. Find her. This city has thrown away too many people, Frank. Don't throw her away. Forget all the pain and doubt. Don't worry about what happened or what might happen. You care about her and she cares about you. In two billion years when the damn sun crashes into the earth and we all are stardust, no one will give a crap. But right now, now when this city is crashing down on itself, the two of you do care. And that's what matters. Find her."

Dawson stopped talking. He hadn't meant to sound so angry, but he had watched his friend drift along for the past months. The old Frank Nagler would have seen Foley and his ilk coming long before they even hatched a plan to get rid of him. The old Frank Nagler would never have let Lauren Fox leave town. *I don't know what's in your heart, old friend, but it has me a little worried. And for me to worry about someone other than myself is something.*

Nagler was near the front door.

"Don't be stupid, Frank," Dawson yelled out. "Find her."

Nagler shook his head, though he wore a slim smile. Dawson.

"Hey Jimmy. It was three little people."

"What?"

"Bogie said the troubles of three little people."

CHAPTER 19

"Hey, Frank, it's Martinez," the voice on the phone said. "You need to get down to the Flats ASAP. Found body parts."

Nagler had taken a call like that from Martinez before when on a case a hunch played out, or his search team found what could be evidence, but his voice had never had the urgency of this call, the holy-shit tone of fear; the sound of a voice leaking from someone who just that moment before confronted the thing they feared most.

"Did you call Foley? It is his case now," Nagler said.

"Yeah. Called his office, his cell, paged him. No luck. It's odd," Martinez said. "Also called the mayor, figured he'd like to know."

Nagler arrived at the end of the rail yard just as the medical examiner and a crime-scene crew arrived. This place and what they might find here had been on his mind since that first rainy night. It had been a single thought in the back of his mind when he first saw the headless, handless body in the Old Iron Bog, the one bit of knowledge that never has never changed or weakened over time; the one name: Charlie Adams, and yet Nagler held it at bay like an unspoken danger; fingering the key, but never sliding it in the lock, never turning it, never opening that door.

That first night Nagler knew that Adams had not committed the crime, but the wet, dark scene triggered memories that Nagler had been pushing to the back of his mind ever since. What had terrified the city before Adams had been caught was that he was not just a killer, but a stalker. His victims had been selected like prizes, examined, chosen, cornered; every dark alley in the city was a potential vantage point, from which haunted eyes peered into their lives. No one, not even Frank Nagler, wanted to revisit that time.

The old canal path was littered with branches torn down by the storm and overgrown with brush and weeds, making it a slow slog. A shiver spidered down his spine and the old Adams-induced tension returned, made worse because he was uncertain what he was about to see. With Adams the tension was accompanied with an institutional anger he developed when he thought his investigative skills were being mocked, and mixed with a general sadness that when they found one more victim, another family was going to learn that a daughter had been butchered.

The river had receded finally, swirling in a slow whirlpool of black water that masked the soft holes of dislodged stones, the pockets of squishy mud and leaves that grabbed the boots of more than one searcher and tumbled them into muck.

Martinez was directing an officer to stretch more yellow tape across sections of the river bank to project objects that had been found. He nodded to Nagler and the medical examiner and silently brought them to a spot to display two black plastic bags and a duffel bag.

"How'd you know?" he asked Nagler.

"Didn't," Nagler said. "Well, wasn't sure… what's in the bags?"

One by one Martinez opened the bags. The first one contained a pair of blue jeans, a women's blouse, sneakers and underwear. The second bag contained wrapped thickly in a series of plastic bags, a woman's hand, and the duffel bag contained a woman's head. It was wrapped in several layers of clear plastic and at first glance did not appear to have been damaged by water or exposure.

"Jesus," Nagler said, pulling back. It spooked him even though he had been expecting it.

The medical examiner leaned in for a closer look. "Anyone touch them?" he asked.

"No." Martinez shook his head "We opened the bags to see what was inside because we've been finding all sorts of other stuff, but once we saw the hand and the head, we left them on the ground where we found them and taped off the area."

Nagler nodded and then leaned over the medical examiner's shoulder.

"What are the chances this is the same woman?" he asked.

"Circumstances indicate that is could be," Mulligan said. "The head and hand were clearly severed. But the search here could reasonably turn up a torso. I'll have a better idea after I run some tests."

Mulligan carefully pulled the head from the duffel bag and did a cursory examination through the plastic wrapping. "Young, Caucasian, possibly a brunette." He placed the head carefully in the bag. "I hope there are no others. Are you alright, Frank? Sorry, I didn't mean to upset you with the examination…"

"I'm fine," Nagler said weakly.

No, I'm not. Just for an instant, when the woman's head was turned sideways, the hair, the shape of her nose, the thin lips; for just an instant, it could have been Lauren Fox.

For the next two hours, while the medical examiner conducted a further examination, Nagler wondered about Lauren Fox. Her mother said it had been months since she left, and the letter he'd found at the apartment had no date. She'd left Ironton at least two years before the storm and the discovery of the body in the bog. But Debbie Glance was following her within the past few months. Why?

He was about to follow that thought down the rabbit hole when the medical examiner called.

"She's our Jane Doe" Mulligan said sourly. "She's Carolyn O'Leary, from Baltimore. I sent you a copy."

Nagler read the report with both relief and anger. Carolyn O'Leary was nineteen, a college student who had been missing for eighteen months. Mulligan said she was strangled with rope before she was beheaded. A Baltimore detective told Nagler she had been part of a small-time drug gang in college. They had busted her twice for selling marijuana, both misdemeanors. She had disappeared during a series of undercover actions that had netted about a dozen arrests. Her family was from Indiana, and they had not seen her in more than two years, he said.

In the photo Baltimore sent to Nagler, Carolyn O'Leary was a blonde. And now she was a brunette, the hair color changed to conceal her identity, Nagler guessed.

So how did you get here? He wondered. *And who put you in my bog?*

He stood up, filled a cup with coffee and walked to the window to stare out onto the city hall parking lot. Sometimes Lauren's Bug was parked there, four rows back, next to a DPW truck that had flat tires. His hand trembled and his eyes filled. It wasn't Lauren.

After a minute he called Foley, and got no answer. The voice message said the mailbox was full and would not take any more messages. He then called the dispatcher and asked if Foley left any special instructions about how to reach him in an emergency, and was told no.

Nagler barely heard the knock on his door, only turning when the door creaked open.

It was Martinez, holding another package with an evidence tag.

"Sorry, Frank. Thought you should see this."

Nagler breathed once and turned away from the window.

"No problem, Ray. What's up?"

"One of the officers found this while we completed the search of the Flats," Martinez said grimly. He held the package open. Inside were a muddy Yankees cap and a brown herringbone tweed jacket. Bartholomew Harrington. Both the cap and jacket were smeared with blood.

Nagler flinched and then softy said, "Damn it."

"Body?"

"No," Martinez said. "On a hunch I sent a crew back to the Old Iron Bog. I'm taking this to Mulligan."

Nagler nodded and said thanks before Martinez left the room. Why didn't you just run, Bart?

CHAPTER 20

Debbie Glance

Nagler had been put back in charge of the investigation into Carolyn O'Leary's death since Chris Foley had apparently gone missing. Not even the mayor knew where he was, or why he'd left. Nagler wanted to take time to find him, but confirming O'Leary's identity had set in motion a large ball that was rolling downhill with Nagler trying to keep up.

More important was the call he got from Dan Yang. Buried deep in all the lines of code and mangled computer files, in all the pages of invoices, submerged in the electronic chatter, they found the proverbial matchbook, the one with the burned edges and half a telephone number, with just the hint of gasoline, and on the edge, at the spot where you hold the cover closed while the match was struck, they found the proverbial fingerprint.

The old lady in the pink house coat watched Nagler step out of his car and squint into the angled sunlight. He glanced at the rows of condos, the artificially square bushes that lined each sidewalk, the single tree that had been planted on the right side of that sidewalk, the same tree again and again, all the same height. He followed the tree line to the buildings made of cement patterned to look like old brick, and then at the same door style but each painted a different color to highlight the individuality of the owner's home, and then at unit 16A where Debbie Glance lived.

The old lady had curlers in her hair, a newspaper stuffed under one arm and she crushed her cigarette out with her left slipper.

"You a cop?"

"Might be."

"Been a lot of cops here lately."

"How come?"

"I tell them she ain't here, but they come back again. Can't be very good cops."

"Well, that hurts."

"Why, you a cop?"

"No, I'm the milk man."

The old lady in the curlers smiled crookedly.

"She still ain't here."

"Where'd she go?"

"Why, you got some heavy cream?"

"Yeah, that's it."

"Midway Motel."

The Midway Motel wasn't midway to anywhere or midway between any two places. Its wrecked sign with purple neon letters just said "Midway." The "Motel" lettering had stopped working years ago. It was two stories of shabby rooms with plastic drapes, bed covers the owner bought for two bucks each at a warehouse sale, brown stains in the toilets and shower faucets that leaked. Picture windows that faced the street had cracks like spiders webs and were held together by long strips of gray tape.

A Chevy Impala had been occupying the same parking space for so long, weeds had grown up through the driver's seat.

Sometimes authorities had to bring welfare families here, which Nagler hated, but they had to get them off the street, and the Midway was on the list of places that would take them in. But it was also a place where they rented rooms by the hour, and he had hauled more than one rolling stoner out of a foul room.

Debbie Glance was in the last room on the second floor on the back side of the motel. Nagler had been in this room too many times, sucked in the stale odor of rotted food, perspiration, unwashed bodies and the sweet hint of drugs boiled over open flames.

A shaft of light stabbed through a crack in the torn drapes enough so Nagler could see the floor was covered with candy wrappers, potato chips bags, fast food containers and pizza boxes, just crap everywhere. Junkie take-out.

"How long's it been?" he asked.

"Three weeks? A month? Shit, I don't know. Guess you figured it all out, huh, Frank? Smart old Frank Nagler."

"What are you on?"

"Heroin, mostly. A little coke, got it from the bartender at Lydia's. A little crack, traded the motel owner an ass fucking. You know,

201

whatever dulls it all."

"Are you trying to kill yourself?"

Debbie Glance opened her mouth to speak, but turned her head instead and shut her eyes. She was hunched in the middle of the bed, wrapped in a sheet and blanket with just her head exposed. The woman with the perfect hair, manicured nails and who had seductively, triumphantly, slipped open the window of Gabe Richman's Escalade had been replaced by someone shriveled inside her skin, which sagged around her eyes. Her hair was the color of dirty bleach water and it hung stringy and greasy from her head and stuck to her neck in the dampness.

She tugged at the sheet, then pulled it open and tugged it closed again. Her shoulders quivered and her fingers twitched.

"Can you help me, Frank?"

Nagler hated that question. Every junkie and drunk he had ever arrested asked it. Can you help me, man? I'm hurtin'. Man, I'm hurtin.' Just need a little. Can you help me out?

And it was just a con, just a dodge, a way to blame someone else for the needle tracks in her arm.

"We got a lot talking to do first, Debbie," Nagler said.

"Then you'll fix me up?" she asked.

Nagler flipped on the light switch and the dim overhead lamp popped on. Debbie Glance cringed into the sheets like Dracula at dawn. She covered her head for a minute or two and only slowly uncovered.

"Don't know," he said. He listened to his own voice grow icy, toneless and hard. "If I like what you tell me I'll make sure the county cops get you over to the rehab unit. Right now, that and a cup of coffee are about the only kindness I'm planning to offer."

She looked up at Nagler and pushed herself back to the head of the bed and leaned her head against the wall and stared at the ceiling. When she looked back at Nagler, the sad junkie face was gone, replaced by a hard, bitter stare. "Want do you want to know?" Her voice scratched out of her throat like the cough of a dry faucet.

Nagler pushed a pile of clothes off a chair and sat.

"The whole deal. But wait," and he pulled out a tape recorder, placed it on the table next to the bed, and turned it on. "Ok, now."

Debbie Glance looked at the recorder and laughed once, staring at the machine, trying to calculate whether she could one more time tell a tale that would get her out of the mess. She had done it before, many times. Every time. She closed her eyes.

"Okay. I'll tell you what you want to hear. Isn't that how this goes?" She laughed bitterly. "The whole deal, Frank. Goes way back."

"Got nothing but time, Debbie." He reached into the paper bag he was carrying, pulled out a paper coffee cup and passed it over to her.

She grabbed the cup and tried once or twice to pry open the little plastic tab on the lid, but her shaking fingers slipped off the side. Finally she pulled off the lid and spilled half the coffee on the bed. "Fuck." With both hands, she steadied the cup to her mouth and sucked in the coffee.

Then she looked at Nagler. "Don't judge me, Frank."

He shrugged.

She sighed, then began.

"First time I shot up I was fifteen. Got it from the assistant wrestling coach. In return, he got me, three days a week. Then his team got me, then a few football players, then anyone who had a twenty dollar bill." She laughed. "I was everybody's whore, Frank."

She laughed again. "Never really told anyone about this, Frank. Been my little secret. Feels weird. I've been lying about it for so long."

Nagler shrugged. "I'm a cop, Debbie, not a shrink. Not sure I care."

She winced, tipped the empty coffee cup to her mouth again, tossed it aside and then twisted the edge of the sheet into a rope, and then began again.

"For graduation, I went with a few athletes and their girlfriends to the Shore. I was the party. While they were downstairs getting drunk and playing kissy-face I went upstairs found the biggest bed, took off my clothes and got high. I had a giant baggie of drugs. Heroin, coke, crack. Some prescription stuff they stole from their parents. Then they came, one at a time, two at a time, I didn't care. They boys were huffing and puffing, with their stale beer breath and their oooh babies, they were just stupid.

"They didn't even know I was just numb, because if I hadn't been numb, I would have been dangerous. They never knew how close I came, after maybe the fourth or fifth time I had some guy's cock in my mouth and another up my ass, how easy it would have been to take that razor I had and slice it off and slice myself. I did it in my mind, but I was so wasted…"

Her voice drifted off to a sing-song whisper.

"Early the next morning one of the cheerleaders, the poor little lamb, came into the room. I became aware she was sitting on the bed and probably had been for some time. I pretended I was still out of it. She reached over and pulled down the sheet and began to finger my nipples. Then I rose up and pulled off the sheet and kneeled on the bed. I kissed her hard, my tongue gouging out her mouth, till she relaxed. I pulled her on the bed and put my hand between her legs and told her that playtime was over. She wouldn't even look at me later. Know who that was? The mayor's wife. Little banker's daughter, copping a feel in the middle of the night. Trying the other side, the little bitch.

"Thick as thieves, they are. They gave me a thousand dollars, Frank. I went down to Union Street and bought as many drugs as I could and took them home, locked the door to my room and took them all. I was either going to die or become fucking holy, or it didn't matter to me which one it was."

"Jesus, Debbie. What a story," he said flatly with a touch of sarcasm, and watched as she relaxed on the bed. "But, you know what? - The junkie-whore gig doesn't cut it. I don't give a shit. Now, you're going to tell me the rest."

"And if I don't?"

"I'll haul you out of here wrapped in your bed sheet, throw you in the local lock-up, where you'll sit strung out for thirty-six hours until Monday when maybe the county guys might finally arrive." He stood up and leaned closely over her on the bed. His voice was loud and harsh. She pushed her head into the wet, filthy pillow to avoid his face. "You'll have hot flashes, then chills, start sweating and you'll throw up, and your head is going to hurt like it's going to explode and your body will turn itself into a pretzel as that old need rises up again. But there won't be anything there to quench that thirst because if any of your cop buddies try, they'll be gone. The game is over, Debbie. I run the night shift, and nothing happens there that I don't know about." The room with bare walls rang with his anger.

There it is, Nagler thought. He was so sick of the whole thing and he'd dumped it on poor, wrecked Debbie Glance. His voice was hard, cold, and uncaring.

She stared at the ceiling and the closed her eyes. "No place to go, is there, Frank?"

Nagler leaned against the door. He spotted a pair of pants and a shirt and tossed them on the bed. "Get up. Take a shower. I'm going to get you sobered up and we're going to talk."

Debbie Glance smiled slightly. He saw she was trying to conjure one more con.

"You really don't have anything, Frank," she said. "The computers -"

"We have your old computer, Debbie," Nagler said. "I know you think they were all replaced, but actually they are all in storage while the city's tech guys wipe the hard drives. We have your hard drive --You know, the one you used to print out all those invoices you mailed to me, the one with all the letters to the Delaware bankruptcy court? We also have all the messages you sent to Foley and Richman, all the questions and answers, all the details, the amounts, the bragging, the self-satisfaction. When did it start to fail, Debbie? When did you decide to send me copies? Where they about to sell you out? I read the comments Foley made. You were the liability."

I didn't set the fire, but I know who did. I heard someone talking about it in a bar.

She went pale and started breathing hard.

"I've also got you and Foley on video walking the stove-works site a couple days before the fire. And a woman who might just be you a few hours before the fire broke out carrying something that looks suspiciously like one of those little propane lighters. Something is flashing on and off in her hand."

Damn it.

"Did you set that fire, Debbie? Did you kill those three people? Did you?"

He stopped talking and turned away. He was yelling at her. His voice and head and heart hurt. Oh, Del. Oh, Lauren.

He turned back. "Why'd you do it, Debbie? Did you get tired of doing it right, making the system work the way it is supposed to? Did you honestly think you could cheat your way to the top?"

Nagler watched as she just rolled her eyes.

"Don't you get it, Frank? Everything is rigged." Her voice was cold and hollow, like the sound leaking from a stove pipe. "Someone is always holding the other end of the rope. I figured that out a lot time ago. I knew the moment I kneeled down in front of that wrestling coach and put his dick in my mouth that was how I would survive. And when some glory-hound quarterback rolled me over and passed me on to his pal, I knew that I would end up on top. They were just like you, Frank. You just don't see it. They weren't using me. I was using them."

And yet here you are, Nagler thought. *A face in a cracked mirror.*

But then the cop kicked in. "Look," Nagler said. "I'll make sure you get clean. But if you jam me up on this, you're on your own. I'll be outside. You've got about fifteen minutes."

She huddled under the covers, and toyed with the sheet. Then she nodded.

"It was Foley, Frank. Most of this was his idea, and he found a perfect foil in Gabe Richman. The mayor wanted to be known as the man who saved his hometown. He lusted after it, schemed to make it happen. He saw his family name on that old department store and swore that the only Richman that this town would remember would be him. Poor Gabe. He was just sixteen year old kid with a hard-on. He knew it felt good to stroke it, but didn't know what to do with it otherwise. But Gabe is as dumb as a post. He couldn't plan, couldn't see what do to do. That was Foley's role. As a cop, he had free rein to get into the city records. As a police officer he could plant a false trail to keep investigators chasing their tails or wading through boxes of paperwork. Besides we wanted to keep Gabe's name out of it. Can't have the mayor involved in stuff like this. It only worked if he was mayor."

"What was your role?" Nagler asked.

"I was the facilitator. Why do you think I worked in all those different city offices? Shifted from office to office when needed. Also, I was good at math," she said. "We used to laugh when old timers at City Hall would talk about the legendary Howard Newton and how he kept two sets of books. We had four, maybe five. We could show you anything financially you wanted to see. Presented in just the right way so you would see just what you were asking about. And then your dear Lauren Fox showed up and she became the perfect foil. I dumped a lot of financial stuff on her computer, so if anyone decided to look, it would appear like it was her idea."

"If you were so good, why you are here in this cheap motel all strung out?"

"The fire didn't turn out the way we planned," she said, her voice fading.

"Meaning no one was supposed to die," Nagler said.

She closed her eyes again, tightly, squeezing out all the pain that would leak out with tears.

"Yeah," she whispered. "Foley saw me after. I was shaking and nervous. Hadn't had a fix in two days. Foley said I had to leave. If the cops questioned me about anything he knew I couldn't handle it. But," she laughed, "He's in charge of the investigation. No one will know anything." Debbie Glance had a twisted smile in her face. "No one will know anything," she repeated weakly.

She threw off the blanket and stood up, naked, and slowly walked to the tiny bathroom.

"Was your wife as beautiful as I am, Frank?" He mocking hardness returned to her voice.

"What? Don't you dare." Nagler stood and clenched his fist. He breathed deeply and turned to the window. "You don't want to do that, Debbie."

"It's always about fucking, Frank," she said. "I could turn anybody's head. With this body, these boobs and this mouth, I got anything I wanted." She laughed and ran a hand across her breasts to her hips. "Oh, I know, it looks a little warn out now, but the American pharmaceutical industry is a wonderful thing, the maker of many products useful to a woman my age."

"Stop, damn it. Stop." Nagler turned back, found a robe on a chair and tossed it to her. It fell to the floor.

"Nervous, Frank? Afraid you might want this? I know about you and Lauren Fox, how you never got it on. Is there trouble in the neighborhood, Frank?"

She leaned against the bathroom door, her legs slightly open and one arm extended above her head.

"Gabriel Richman bought it. Poor Gabe. He never understood he was just my ticket into the circle of power. As long as I spread my legs for him, he would do anything I asked. Even steal from the city he loved." She smiled. "Payback is a bitch, Gabe dear." She spoke in a child's voice. "Pay me a grand to fuck all your friends, and it takes a long time to repay that debt."

Nagler opened the door and slammed it against the inside wall.

"That's it. I'm gone. You can sit her in your fucking junkie fantasy and rot, for all I care. We have the computers, I have this tape. We'll put the two together and all of you will go away for a long time. Looking at you, Debbie, you won't even last until we come back for you. The choice is yours. Cut this crap or cooperate."

She tried to smile, but her face collapsed a little at a time, a small grin, a wrinkle, to blankness.

"I didn't set the fire, Frank," Debbie Glance said, suddenly sober. "That was Foley's deal. We looked at the financials and realized it would take years to steal all the money we needed to own the stove-works site. Foley just said, aren't we just going to knock it all down anyway? I remember he laughed so coldly when he made the decision. We'll just burn it down, he said. Blame it on the homeless guys. Once we owned the land, we'd sell it to the city for redevelopment, and then rig the bids so that companies we controlled got the work to rebuild it. It's is so easy, it's stupid, Frank. And, know what? It's legal."

She ran her hands across her breasts and mouth, the leaned on the door, her legs suddenly weak. "I'm gonna take the fall for this, aren't I, Frank? No one will blame the mayor. He just got led astray by his junkie-whore. And Foley? Foley the cop, squeaky clean. Mr. Integrity. It's so stupid. If you caught me on tape at the stove-works it was probably a night I was buying drugs." She lingered at the door. "It all goes away pretty fast, doesn't it?"

Nagler stood near the front door and glanced at her gray face. "It's over, Debbie. You're all screwed."

Her eyes were hollow, her mouth drawn, and she stumbled slightly as she tried to pull the bathroom door closed. "No one will know anything," she said in a sing-song voice of a child.

"Last question, Debbie," Nagler said. "The girl in the bog. We found the rest of her in Smelly Flats and we know who she is. Is she part of this?"

Debbie Glance's face went blank. Then, as if finally slipping out the drug haze and finding herself naked in front of a cop, she stepped behind the door and shielded her body.

"She...she..." and Debbie Glance began to weep. "We didn't kill her, Frank. She was already dead."

"Did you chop her head off? Were you there?"

"It was Foley," she said. "I don't know how he met her. He had me buy some brown hair dye to make her look like Lauren Fox. He said it would just piss you off and he'd be even with you for some old case, some old murder. He talked about it all the time. He hated you, Frank."

"You know that Foley is gone? Skipped town a few days ago and we can't trace him."

Debbie Glance leaned heavily on the door as the blood ran from her face. "That bastard," she said. "So, I'm screwed, huh, Frank? Is that poetic justice or what?" She stumbled into the bathroom and shut the door. Nagler heard one long painful cry.

For just a second Nagler felt sorry for her, but that second was lost in the wave of revulsion that swept over him as he stepped into the parking lot.

It wasn't enough that the three of them had set up what might be the biggest fraud in Ironton's history, but they used some dead kid as a set up to cover it all up?

He leaned against the side of his car and just shook his head. He had to get her clean, he knew.

There were a hundred ways to tell this tale and she needed to be credible. They'd just go slowly. Take her through the invoices, the mechanics of the transactions, then move on to the bigger things. He shook his head. Parts of it were still hard to figure. They were missing something. Dan Yang said the initial transfers were small, a couple hundred dollars, and it went on for a couple of years before money started moving all over the place. The amounts got bigger, the moves more sophisticated, but without her explanations, there would be no one to tie the scheme together. That was what puzzled him. If she wanted to blow this all up, why save all the altered copies? Maybe she wanted something to trade, he guessed. Yang was still processing her computer's hard drive and figured he'd find all the originals in one of the thousands of files. He slammed his fist against the outside motel wall. Then there was that dead girl in the bog. Nagler shook his head. Damn it. He recalled viewing the taped visit Foley and Debbie Glance took to the stove-works, the one when they met Del. It was suddenly so clear. When they were walking to the meeting, Foley was carrying a duffel bag. After they meet Del and walked away, his hands were empty.

They went after Lauren.

Maybe.

Those three weren't smart enough to form that plan themselves, or rich enough to pull it off. Maybe that's why Richman's house had gone into foreclosure. Even still, so what?

There had to be someone else involved. Someone in the background with the financing and the ability to make it all go away when the shit hit the fan. What are we missing?

Nagler looked at the door and then at his watch. She was going to jail, not a dance. He walked to the door and knocked. "Debbie," he called out. "Come on." When he didn't hear any shuffling, or get a reply, he cracked open the door. The room was hazy with steam from the shower and he could hear the water running. Jesus. "Come on, Debbie," he shouted. Again there was no reply. "Debbie!"

He smelled the faint smoke when he reentered the room. When he opened the bathroom door he saw a lighted votive candle, a half dozen burned wooden matches, a handful of pills scattered on the floor along with a baggie that still held some white powder and Debbie Glance lying dead under the running shower. A shoelace was still tied to her arm and the fingers of her right hand still clutched the syringe. The water swirled with blood from the slash on her neck. A thin doubled-edged razor blade floated on the bloody water.

Nagler called Dan Yang.

When Yang arrived, Nagler handed him the tape recorder. "This will help you make sense of all those invoices," he said.

"What about -" and Yang nodded his head in the direction of the motel room where Debbie Glance died.

"Do what you have to do," Nagler said.

"They'll have questions for you, you know," Yang said.

"Nagler shrugged. "I'm sure they will," he said as he walked away.

CHAPTER 21

Nagler sat like a rock anchored in the hard iron soil. Ironton Park swirled with kids at play, screaming their young lungs out as they jumped from swings and bounced each other off the see-saw; mothers weary from the chase leaned against the new fences and just watched, raising their heads from time to time when a pain-filled scream pierced the excited air.

He had been slowly walking through downtown, just to get out in the air. The streets throbbed again with noise, the buses, trucks; the sidewalks again filled. Repair crews were long gone, replaced by painters and carpenters installing doors, fixing windows, remodeling storefronts. The city had replaced the banners that had hung from light poles and some of the merchants had tables of goods for sale on the sidewalks. Come to life, they seemed to be saying. Come back to life.

Nagler recalled a conversation he and Dawson had the night after the city hall riot.

"People are just walking around like nothing happened, Frank. Look at them. Talking on their phones, reading papers. We can really fool ourselves sometimes, can't we, Frank," Dawson said.

"What do you mean?"

"The city's been in turmoil for weeks. Dead bodies in the bog, the floods, the stove-works fire, riots at city hall. And everyone is just walking around like nothing happened."

Nagler looked out the window at the street scene.

"Maybe just getting back to normal is what we have to do," he said. "The best way to cope. I'll bet a lot of those people had to repair their homes, or had to help family fix theirs. Some of those people lost their jobs because of the floods. Maybe they spend a few nights sleeping in the high school. After experiences like that, normal probably seems pretty good."

He remembered that Dawson just shrugged. "Maybe."

Find her.

The phrase stuck in his mind.

Don't know if I can, Jimmy.

Find her.

211

He wanted it to be true, that he could find her, but at the same time he didn't want it to be true. I could find her, he told himself. I'm a goddamn cop. A couple phone calls, and Internet search or two and I could find her. But he didn't make the phone calls, didn't search the web. Just carried her around.

As he was walking though the downtown he stopped by the train station. A gang of high school kids was on the platform waiting for a train. At first he just watched them. A few leaned against the station's wall tapping on their cell phones, a few hunched in the corner smoking. Some had paired off, clutching one another in an end of the world hug. They held hands, smiled sweetly and sometimes kissed. The girls leaned their heads on the chests of their taller boyfriends and remained still as the boys stroked their hair, softly touched a finger to their girls' lips or tickled their ass and waited as the girls pulled the roving hands away.

At first Nagler watched with amusement as a parent who has kids that age might, but the amusement vanished and he looked away. Then he left. As he passed through the parking lot near the train station, he watched a man and a woman embracing, kissing deeply, and then folding into each other arms. He stared quickly at the ground and walked away.

He didn't want to be watching romantic couples express their affection for one another; didn't want to watch happy loving couples share that love. He pulled back from the world and walked on.

Find her; find yourself. That's what Dawson had meant.

Nagler was sitting in the gazebo in the center of the park. He and Lauren would have lunch here a couple of days a week in the warmer seasons. The shade, the noise of traffic and happy children was like a shield against the troubles that swirled through the town. They'd spread their lunch out on the bench that rimmed the outside of the shell and just take in the sounds, the scenes, sometimes talked, sometimes not.

The old warehouse that formed the park's western border was receiving a colorful mural that told Ironton's history in bright wide swirls of blue and green, yellow and brown paint.

Two students were outlining a wooden canal boat being hauled through town by a mule, and another splashed black and gray paint to bring to life a steam engine resting at the town's Nineteenth Century station against a faint background of reddish factories and tall smoke stacks.

"You'd hate to think what Ironton might have been like if the canal basin was not built here," she said one day. "All those strange foods and fashions the immigrants added to the mix. The city was this wonderful melting pot of the world. New layers of people filtered into the existing layers, the edges of the old neighborhoods blurring as they filled and grew smaller. They left the old troubles behind."

Nagler recalled that he looked at her sharply after she said that. Left the old troubles behind. It didn't seem to him that she was talking about the city.

He started to ask her what she meant, when she stood and said, "Time to go. Lunch is over. Thank you, sir."

Two weeks later when she disappeared, he knew that had been a conversation as scripted and planned as any speech in a play. It had indeed been time to go.

Nagler leaned his head against the post, suddenly light-headed. He had been watching some children ride the whirl-a-gig in the playground. They grabbed the metal handles and pushed the heavy metal circle slowly around until they began to run alongside to keep up. Then one by one they jumped on and held on for dear life as the spinning ride twirled and twirled. When it slowed they'd let go and squealing, fly off on to the grass. Their mothers would yell, and giggling, the kids would do it again.

But it wasn't the twirling, spinning ride that sent his head elsewhere. Instead he saw in his mind the dedication ceremony for the playground. It was more than two years ago and it was the last time he saw Lauren Fox.

It was the biggest event to happen in Ironton in years. Something so positive that even the snarling politicians of the city could not find anything harsh to say. Corporations had donated the funds, and volunteers from a dozen organizations worked under the supervision of Tommy Tavel, the public works director, to clean the site and erect the playground equipment. Schools hung banners along the fences, and the excited students pulled at the locked gates while the speeches were given.

Nagler recalled they had not seen much of each other in a week or more. His assignment had changed, and with the playground and a

213

project at the middle school, Lauren had been out of her office more than she had been in it. But more, there was the silence. The phone calls diminished, the emails were not returned. Was the blush off the romance, or was it all just work?

Lauren was working the crowd as she usually did at these events. There were speakers to line up, and because this was a playground dedication, she had to get a dozen mothers to control their four-year-olds. He watched as she smiled at the children and got them to stand as straight as possible even as they fidgeted and looked over their shoulder at the swings and rides and climbing frames inside the locked fence.

She shook hands with the corporate donors, the city officials and when they were all seated, she stood off to one side and waited. That was when he saw her look at the ground and rub her eyes. She looked away from the scene a moment and out into the street.

Then she turned and found his face at the back of the crowd and he started to smile back. But she wasn't smiling. Her face was filled with a hurt he didn't understand. The ceremony had begun and she intently paid attention to the speakers. But her eyes were dark and while she tried to show a pleasant, interested face to the crowd, Nagler could see it was just an act. The veneer was soft, but it was a face of hurt and anger, and from where he stood, Frank Nagler knew it was aimed at him. He just did not know why.

The sounds of the playground and the street returned. He could still see her on that podium, still see her torn face. Oh, Lauren. Oh, sweet girl. What did I do?

Find her, Jimmy? She was right in front of me and I couldn't find her. Spill me out of this twirling gyre, let my feet find ground. Stop the noise in my head, hide the flashing pictures; let the spinning end.

He leaned forward and covered his eyes with his hands and inhaled deeply and exhaled slowly. That old feeling came back, the one that left a hole inside him, loneliness returned. He sat up and glanced around. The invisible sheen, like a plastic wall, was back. He was on the inside and everyone else was on the outside. Stay there, he thought. Never again.

He saw Lauren stand on the podium and then saw her sitting on the bench inside the gazebo.

"Nothing is simple, Frank," she said as she picked up the food wrappers. "Nothing is at it seems. There's more here than meets the eye." Then she winked.

Nagler smiled, and then shook his head. That's what she had written on that sticky note in the packet she left in her apartment freezer. *There's more than meets the eye. Did she mean us? All those feelings kept to ourselves, how we justify our hurt later with indifference?*

Or had she meant there, in the park? She'd known he'd come back here. *Am I that easy to read? That easy to fool?*

One by one he examined each section and piece of equipment in the park. The bandstand was old, maybe seventy-five years, the war memorial dated back to after World War I.

The playground.

What had she buried under the playground. And why?

****

The metal box was found under the second fence post the backhoe operator dug up.

How did she manage that? Nagler wondered.

The only moment of concern during the dig was when Gabriel Richman and the city council president showed up.

Nagler saw them running across the city park and headed them off.

"Stop," Richman yelled. "What are you doing? Frank!"

Nagler took the mayor by the elbow and led him away from the backhoe that was angling toward the corner of the fence that surrounded the playground. The operator had already dug several shallow holes around the posts so that the cement anchor that held them in the ground could be removed.

Finally near the gazebo, Nagler stopped.

"They found a sinkhole under one corner of the fence," Nagler lied. "City engineer ordered the fence to be inspected and repaired. A kid stepped on some grass near one of the posts and his foot sank into the ground. The digging will be done today, they'll pour new concrete and the playground will be open again in two days."

"Why wasn't I told?" Richman asked.

Nagler shrugged. "Don't know anything about that, Gabe. I was just assigned to make sure no one got near the work site."

Richman looked at Nagler and then at the playground. Nagler couldn't tell by Richman's expression whether he was stunned to see the city's new, expensive playground being dug up, or whether he was still in shock from Debbie Glance's death. *I wonder if he thinks it all died with her.*

Richman had issued a statement about her, but had made no public appearances since the death. Yang had discussed the tape with his contact at the county prosecutor's office who had been working with Nagler and Yang for weeks deciphering the invoices.

Ironton police were told Debbie Glance was found by the motel manager.

Doesn't have a clue, does he? Nagler asked himself. *Or he's hiding it really well.* The county prosecutor's office was working with him and Yang to nail down all the details they had, and until that task was completed, the indictments and arrests would wait. No one wanted this case to collapse.

Meanwhile, the campaign had been rolling into its last week and both Richman and Yearning had appeared at several debates and forums in recent days. *Maybe he's just too busy, or just too arrogant,* Nagler thought. *But if you act like nothing is wrong, then no one suspects. So Richman smiles and waves at campaign events, and shakes hands and purses his lips and furrows his brow when he speaks with a business owner whose shop was flooded out, and snarls and yells when Yearning suggests that he is a corrupt politician. Richman speaks about leadership and dreams, about rebuilding the city, about rising from the floods and the swamps and standing glorious in a new sun. And the crowds cheer, and wave their silly hats and signs; they chant his name. He smiles back, a man in his element. Love me. Adore me. I am yours.*

****

It was so easy.

Nagler was stunned it was so easy. And Debbie Glance had been right - Most of money movement between accounts was legal. It became a crime when they failed to pay it all back to the city.

Account after account. Shift a few dollars here, shift them later to a reserve account, and at the end of year, when the law allows public officials to cover shortages in some accounts with funds from other accounts that have a surplus, shift them again. Pass an ordinance, sign a resolution, promise to build something, fix something, start something new, and then a few years later announce that the matching funds failed to materialize and the project was killed. By then, everyone forgot about it. State audits the books three years later, makes notes about minor accounting errors, the city promises they will be fixed and it all rolls over again.

Nagler stared at the metal box when the backhoe operator pulled it from the ground along with a load of soil. No one knew. What did the backhoe operator three years ago think when she told him to stop digging and let her place the metal box in the hole he had just opened? What did she say, it was a time capsule, maybe? A box of children's letters? But there she had placed it, two feet down, filled with papers and computer discs double wrapped in thick plastic, taped tightly shut.

The scheme was laid out it in exquisite detail. Charts, invoices, budget resolutions, notes, emails. Nagler was amazed that Lauren Fox could compile the record.

It had been going on for ten years, starting with the transfer of several hundred dollars into an account labeled "development." Seems they started small to see if anyone noticed.

Five years into the scheme the funds began to move into "investment" accounts and from what Nagler could see that money never made it back to the city. By that time, the records showed the amounts had grown into the thousands, a sign of growing confidence.

But in the last few pages of the documents, the how became clear, and with that answer, the who. One question remained.

"Why?" Nagler asked.

Howard Newton sat quietly under the white Panama, staring out onto the manicured lawn at the Trenton Street Club through his dark shades. The fingers of his left hand drummed on the chair. In his right hand a fat glowing Cuban cigar emitted a stream of smoke. He flicked some ash onto the floor and took a long draw, the smoke filtering out of his mouth like haze off a cold lake; a screen, it hovered around his face, obscuring what Nagler thought was a thin-lipped smile.

"That's a loaded question, Frank," Newton said. He was remarkably calm for someone who had just been told he could be charged with a list of crimes Ironton would talk about for years. But maybe that is what he wanted. "Why what?" Newton continued. "Why'd we do it? Why use Lauren Fox? Why get caught? Where do you want to start?"

Nagler just shook his head. Newton was enjoying this. "I've known about your deals, Howie, but they were all small-time hustles. A lot of small-time hustles, but still."

"You don't know half of it, Frank. Every hustle leads to another one; every scheme brings new players, new ideas, new money. All of this stuff began years before Richman ran for office the first time. You know his father worked for me? He was an accountant and auditor. Used to audit the city's books. It was his system we used to fool the state. All the house flipping that was going on? That's why I foreclosed on Richman's house. Make it look like it was on the up-and-up. Needed to keep the money in motion. Even with computers, if you create enough layers, the money is hard to find. But then it got sloppy. Debbie Glance had a needle in her arm half the time or was sucking something up her nose, Foley was trying to act like the big-shot cop he thought he should be, and Gabe Richman started talking again about saving the city."

Newton sucked on the cigar again.

"I tried to tell him that no one could save the city; all you could do was keep it afloat and plan to save yourself. I thought he understood that, but then he started talking about the shopping center and the Old Iron Bog. I couldn't head him off. Don't know where he got the idea, but he latched onto it and wouldn't give it up. They had no discipline. Put a few bucks in their pockets and they act like a Rockefeller. When I started, I learned to keep it all low-key. No flashy moves. But these guys," he waved his hand in the air dismissively, "Bah."

Newton paused and sighed. He glanced at the cigar and popped open a gold Zippo.

"When Lauren Fox showed up, she started talking to the state about redeveloping the old stove-works. We'd had our eyes on the stove-works for years, just waiting for the right moment to go to court in Delaware and claim it. We could have used Lauren's plan with the state as a way in. It would have been perfect, and if we got caught, Lauren would have taken the fall. All the paperwork was in her name. But Foley got greedy, impatient. It wasn't like it was going to be one big payoff. He already had thousands in the bank, but the stove-works deal would have paid out for years, set him and his kids and their kids up for life. It was so sweet. But he wanted to burn it all down two, three years ago. I don't know, Frank. But I was right. As soon as he put that poor girl in the bog, I knew it was going to collapse. One thing too many, one act beyond the reasonable, the step into the swamp, pardon the pun, from which we'd never recover. That day you saw us at that old warehouse? Was me telling them it was over, that Debbie Glance needed to shut down the accounts and bury the money. Something in me just snapped and I said enough is enough. They thought I was wrong, thought they could string it along. Richman thought he would use the election to turn all this crap into gold. But they did not know what I knew: That I had been feeding Lauren the documents and told her at some point she was going to have to run and hide. Damn clever of her to bury them in the playground. Sorry I messed up your romance, Frank."

"But why?" Nagler asked again.

Newton adjusted his sunglasses and removed the Panama, flicked something off the rim, stared at it a moment, and placed it back on his head.

"Why Lauren? Because she was an honest kid and I understood that people would believe her. Besides, she was figuring out that something was rotten at City Hall. She came over to talk one day, out of the blue. She didn't know me from Adam, just knew I was a former mayor. Started asking about some old ordinances we had passed to get state funds. She wanted to know how the political process worked. It's funny. What started her asking questions was an application to the state for money to redevelop the park. It got rejected because Debbie Glance messed up the application. She had the wrong amounts and wrong dates, everything. But I recognized that was going to be the end. I'd lost control of it. These things are like a fine symphony, the harmonies, the counterpoints, the themes, they have to mesh. When you do it right, you do it once and no one knows the difference. When you start trying to cover your tracks, it becomes obvious."

Nagler shook his head. "We always think we are electing the best candidates money can buy, but it's a joke," he said. "And then it turns out to be true."

Newton waived his hand in the air, the air leaving a trail of ash floating like dust.

"I'm an old man, Frank," he said. "I've got cancer, emphysema, a bad heart – doctors said any one of them could kill me in six months. Death will make an honest man of you, I guess. You may not agree, but I always thought of myself as a good man. Yeah, we did things, but know what? No one died. We helped many people. We took our time because it wasn't about bragging or attracting attention, but about living. But some time ago it all changed. Foley used to talk about the millions he was going to make. That little shit used to make nickels and dimes running numbers as a kid, and I guess he never got over it. Wanted to be a big shot. And, boy, he was pissed at you over that Charlie Adams thing. That was, what, twenty years ago? Long time to hold a grudge. Same with Gabe Richman. He wanted to be the man who saved Ironton. The people who saved Ironton worked in the mills, plowed the streets and taught our kids in school, and owned the shops on Blackwell, and put up the memorials to the vets. They cleaned the sidewalks, took in the homeless, watched out for their neighbor. Where'd that all go, Frank? I'm glad I got out of politics when I did. Today every handshake has a dollar in it. Every speech is bought and paid for. Our grandparents came here because they believed the streets were paved with gold. Man, did we fool them. It's the pockets, Frank. That's what's lined with gold."

Newton laughed. The sound wheezed out of his body like the last blow of air from a steam engine before the brake was released. That was a sound from Nagler's youth. The steam trains, the rattling of iron beams being hauled from the mills to a job site, the shouts of men, the fearsome voice of men at work, building, cities growing, lives lurching forward. And now it was the sound of life escaping from a sick old man who'd turned all that around into one some self-aggrandizing grab for power.

"Why, Frank? We had to stop them. I had to stop them. Believe it or not, I always took the side of the little guy, took the side of people against the institutions, the governments, the selfish business owners. Did I ask for something in return? Sure. We all did. Isn't that what politicians do when they ask for your vote? Keep me in office and I'll help you out."

"It's not that simple, Howie, and you know it. You put the city up for sale," Nagler said.

"Are you sure?" Newton asked. "This whole thing started out as way to get Richman moving on the projects and ideas that would bring this city back. All he did was talk, and to all the wrong people. So I showed him how to tilt the system to his benefit, so that he would look like the leader he wanted to be while the city healed. But those three have holes in their hearts. There is a coldness that turned the enterprise into one centered on revenge, greed and self-importance. I saw it going bad and acted to stop it. I was the only one who could."

Nagler just stared at the old man, hidden behind his dark glasses, Panama hat, stone-faced expression. "Nice speech, Howie," he said bitterly. "Don't you see? You ruined everything here. This city's been falling apart for years, its people hoping against hope that the lives of their kids would be better. Isn't that we all strive for? And you all sit there so full of yourselves that you can't see the damage you've done. You got your share. And Richman and Foley and Debbie Glance... and what did Ironton get? Empty factories and closed shops. Housing that falls down, streets with holes and a whole generation with a dead man's stare. Yeah, great speech. Not sure you're the one to give it." He put his hands in his pants pockets and turned away, squinting into the sunlight. *No more.*

"Ah, Frank. Who better? Who better than the one who has been there before?" Howard Newton asked. And he filled his cheeks with smoke from the cigar and let it out in a thin, uneven stream. Then he smiled. "Who better?" he said and rolled the cigar between his thumb and forefinger before taking one last drag, filling the gray air with one last breath.

Who better, indeed.

Newton's fingers stopped drumming. He sat still as a statue, pulling back under that white Panama hat, receding behind the dark shades, untouchable.

****

Nagler slipped his car onto a dirt patch off the stove-works road and watched the demolition equipment tear into the charred walls. The company that owned it, a company that had been a ghost for decades, had finally surfaced. They paid the fines and the back taxes and agreed to clean up the site. Everyone said it was a start.

Nagler had tracked down Del Williams at Newton's nursing home. With Newton in jail, the doctor who owed Howie a favor called social services and got Del signed up for the medical help he needed and contacted the railroad company about his pension. Foley had indeed offered him two thousand dollars to burn the place down, but Del refused.

"I know who did it, Frank, but I ain't gonna tell," Del whispered. "That two grand got a brother off the street. Foley will go to jail. Seems fair."

Nagler asked him about the duffel bag, and told him he might have to testify about taking it from Foley.

"I didn't know what was in it, Frank. Didn't ask. Knew better," Del said. "One of them guys who hung out at the camp said he was going to the Flats to scrounge for stuff, you know, metal that was being dumped down there. I gave it to him. Told him not to open it,"

Dawson landed a new job at a Newark paper and his first assignment was to write about Bartholomew Harrington. The paper, folded open to the story, rested on the passenger's seat of Nagler's car. The story opened with a scene of Harrington in a municipal court down the Shore in Ocean County arguing that the city had no right to claim his client's property to widen a road. "He was a man again in his element," Dawson wrote. "The bewildered city attorney had run out of objections as Harrington cited chapter and verse of ancient state law and called down all that was good and right to say to the court, to the city, 'No, not this time'."

Is that what happened here, Nagler wondered as he put the car in gear and drove on. After weeks of delay, more federal and state aid money began to arrive in Ironton. The piles of debris were removed and damaged homes had new roofs, porches and lawns. Shopkeepers, armed with grants and loans, replaced the broken windows and doors and reopened, school kids had new computers and engineers began to study the river to see what could be done to reduce flood damage.

The ruined downtown parking lot and stone wall that had been built to feed the river to power the old Union Ironworks were bulldozed and replaced with a mix of sod and stone to hold the riverbank together until a new, grassy bankside park could be installed. Just like the plan Lauren Fox had laid out years ago. Nagler's heart did a turn when he drove by and saw the workers raking in gravel along the river. The past had been washed away. Watching the men and machines rake and shape the riverbank, he conjured the vision of her standing in that same spot describing a riverside lined with trees and grass and park benches. "This is how we change," she said then. "This how we grow."

He had just come from City Hall where the state police had arrested Chris Foley and Gabe Richman. While the tape he made of Debbie Glance's confession provided a road map of the criminal enterprise, more supportive evidence had been needed. The word of a dead woman was not enough.

But Yang and Nagler had pieced it all together, using the scraps of data Debbie Glance had mailed to Nagler, the full version of the records Newton gave to Lauren Fox, and Newton's confession. The last piece was found in a records box that had been moved to Newark before the storm hit. Three years before it was found on the finger of a detached hand in the Old Iron Bog, the fine gold, lion-headed ring had been reported stolen by Lauren Fox. Chris Foley had filed the initial report, and a subsequent report, indicating the ring had been found and returned to its owner, that was stapled to the initial report. But the ring was never returned. Instead, Nagler learned from Foley's buddies on the night shift, who had become very friendly toward Nagler after Debbie Glance died, Foley gave the ring to some young hooker from Atlantic City he was seeing regularly. All they knew, they said, was that Foley said one night he had to help her out of a jam.

Later, Nagler pulled the car onto the side of the road overlooking the Old Iron Bog.

That's where Martinez's crew had found Harrington's body. It was stuffed into the back seat of Foley's yellow city vehicle. Shot three times. The scene suggested that Foley tried to slip the vehicle into one of the deep holes inside the bog, but he misjudged the buoyancy and the car floated out some distance with its nose under water and the back side sticking up in the air, but not sinking, grabbed by some underwater debris. It was too far out in the bog to pull back, and the water was too deep for a man to walk out to it, so the vehicle just sat there. Did you know then the end had come, Chris, Nagler asked himself. Did you know then with your car resting ass-up in the swamp that you hoped would cover all your sins, that it was over? State Police captured Foley in an old log cabin in the Pinelends, Jersey's other big swamp. *Perfect.*

Just perfect, Nagler thought bitterly.

As he looked out over the bog that morning, watching the sunlight illuminate the oily sheen that drifted over the sections of open water, Nagler tried to shake off the three pieces of the whole mess that lingered: Chris Foley feigning annoyance and puzzlement that the body dumpers had not tried to hide the woman's body when they brought her to the bog and the sound of Debbie Glance's shaky voice saying, "We didn't kill her. She was already dead."

The third piece was the reaction of the teens who initially reported the body to the police. When Nagler interviewed them, he reminded them they told the police that they heard voices in the bog that night. They said they heard a man's voice and a woman's voice. The woman seemed to be crying, the teens said, repeating again and again, "What have we done? What have we done?"

When Nagler later played them a tape that contained the voices of Chris Foley and Debbie Glance, both teens said they were pretty sure those were the voices they head that night in the bog.

A cloud moved to cover the sun, and the bog's surface became dark and smooth as the light disappeared before the cloud's shadow; impenetrable, secrets sealed.

The last call he made was to Lauren Fox's mother. "Tell her she can come home," he told her.

But not to me.

There was one more item in the metal box buried in the playground: An envelope with his name scrawled on it. He almost threw it away. He didn't want to read one more distant attempt by Lauren Fox to make him feel better. No more hints, no more reaching back. Was any of it real? After hearing Howie Newton's tale, it was hard to believe that anything Lauren did was as it seemed. Nagler put the envelope on the table. *I feel a little bit used.* Dawson, it turned out, had been right: *They hadn't trusted each other.*

Nagler grabbed his raincoat and went for a walk. The cold air stung with a driving rain and flecks of snow, a punishing wind. The streets were empty, and the water was pushed along by the wind so it left a smeared, greasy reflection of a swinging traffic light on the blacktop. Rainwater swirled around clogged drains; it leaked into storm drains and into the river, which spilled over lawns and became swamp like. He stopped under the awning that shielded the windows of the old Richman's department store. The owners had painted the windows black to hide the fact that all the stores were empty.

And now we're down to this, he thought. *Secrets, lies, deceit. It's what I'd expect from the likes of Howie Newton and Gabe Richman. They think they can make the world spin just for them.*

I guess I never really knew you at all, did I? The smiles, the soft kisses, the questions in our eyes. Did I need to be in love with you that much that I was unwilling to question anything you did?

He walked again in the brooding rain. He pulled the collar of the heavy coat tighter and retreated inside the shell.

The envelope was still on the table. He picked it up. And he put it down. He walked away. He came back.

What the hell, he sighed.

It was a single photograph of Lauren. Nagler remembered taking it at the park during one of their lunches. She sat facing him, but her eyes were looking off into the distance. A few strands of hair settled on her cheek and her face was serene. He remembered she glanced back at him after he took the photo and smiled, her eyes deep with affection, and he remembered how open, how special, how blessed he felt at that moment.

He placed the photo on the table and with his index fingers squared it up against the envelope. He ran a finger down each side of the photo and then without knowing why, touched her face, trying to make some perfect arrangement as the hollowness inside opened again, the silence drove out the sounds, and inside his empty shell, Detective Frank Nagler placed his left hand across his mouth and began to weep.

****

Later, half-awake in bed, Frank Nagler gave into the feelings that had been bottled up, all the thoughts that had been set aside while the bog case was being investigated.

All the things he should have said.

What is it that cracks the thick stony shell where love hides when bruised? A simple glance, a long, unfocused stare that suddenly snaps to clarity? An unexpected word?

I didn't notice at first, but I was soon filled with you. It was beyond mere knowledge, deeper than sensation; it became part of my breath, a shine in my vision, your name like some unknown foreign taste that clung to my tongue, a nectar that nourished me through the day.

I called you sweet girl.

I stuck notes in reports that I send to you, scrawled it on yellow sticky notes, wrote it in emails, and later when we met, it was a whisper in your ear, sometimes more breath than thought.

Then on days we never met, or did not share some casual greeting, I felt the contraction like the shrinking of a parched fruit, sides sucked in as the moisture drained away, shriveled, weakened, hollow.

Your smile went right through me, and the empty parts of my soul became infused with sound and light; all the hollowness filled with weight.

And all the things that should have been said, will be said.

We'll spend a day sprawled on our backs in a room with a high ceiling, coffee cups, beer cans, food wrappers strewn careless as dreams. I want to know what you were like at three, who your friends were at seven, why you didn't like the girl next door, and fawned over the boy who lived three streets over and sat in the fourth seat on the right side of the school bus and carried a black book bag that had a fire breathing dragon stitched into the back. Was he the dangerous one? The one who walked outside the lines, who shook the very Presbyterian in you to the bottom of your boots?

Did you cheer at football games and just die when the teams lost the championship, or walk in a bubble if they won?

Tell me who was your first love, the first time you and your friends really broke the rules and got grounded, the first time he kissed you and you walked home through leaf-filled streets looking in the windows of your friends' homes.

Tell me what moved you, what music you loved, what books and films, the places that stirred you, the events that made you laugh and cry; what it was that moved your life in the direction it took.

Tell me why you are. Tell me who you are. Tell me what you are.

And I will absorb it, cherish it, revel in its detail and hold it all dear because it is you that I hold. It is you that I love.

And when you are done I will spill all I know at your feet and let you pick the parts you like, laugh at the parts that are strange and fear those things that are harmful. Wash it all away.

And when we are done there will be just the two of us, in that moment, raw, naked, free; just the two of us in that moment with all of time ahead.

AUTHORS NOTES

"The Swamps of Jersey" started as a sketch about a man taking a bus to a local college and killing a woman.

Then it was a novel, a work called "The Game Called Dead," that introduced Detective Frank Nagler, a work that is being revised and is intended to follow "The Swamps of Jersey," as another Frank Nagler story.

While poking around inside that story, in an effort to examine one aspect of it, I discovered a new story.

Then one day, I found myself sitting in a park in Dover, N.J., the real life stand-in for "Ironton, N.J." when I had this thought: "There is more here than meets the eye."

From that thought, the new story, "The Swamps of Jersey," emerged.

A version of that scene appears in the book, and is key to Frank Nagler solving the puzzle before him.

Characters live in their own world. Sometimes they whisper; sometimes they shout. As an author, we just have to listen.

ABOUT THE AUTHOR

Michael Stephen Daigle is a writer and journalist who lives in New Jersey with his family. He was born in Philadelphia, one of five "Navy brats," and has lived in several states in the Northeast United States, where he was an award-winning journalist.

He published an electronic collection of stories, "The Resurrection of Leo," and a single story about baseball and teen-agers, "The Summer of the Home run."

He publishes commentary, fiction samples and poetry at...

www.michaelstephendaigle.com

19852818R00136

Made in the USA
Middletown, DE
06 May 2015